W9-CYE-208

Also by David M. Salkin

Military, Espionage & Action Adventure Thrillers

The Team Series
The Team
Into the Jungle: The Team Book Two
African Dragon: The Team Book Three
Shadow of Death: The Team Book Four
The MOP
Dangerous Ground: The Team Book Five
Crescent Fire
Necessary Extremes

Science Fiction & Horror Collection

Deep Black Sea
Dark Tide Rising (Deep Black Sea II)
Forever Hunger

Crime & Mystery Thrillers

Hard Carbon
Deep Down

DANGEROUS GROUND

THE TEAM BOOK V

DAVID M. SALKIN

A POST HILL PRESS BOOK
ISBN: 978-1-68261-441-9
ISBN (eBook): 978-1-68261-173-9

Dangerous Ground:
The Team Book Five
© 2017 by David M. Salkin
All Rights Reserved

Cover Design by Christian Bentulan

Post Hill Press
posthillpress.com

Published in the United States of America

ACKNOWLEDGMENTS

Writing *The Team* series has given me a tremendous amount of enjoyment. I can only write if you read, and so I give you, my readers, my heartfelt thanks for your continued support. Your reviews and e-mails keep me writing, and I truly appreciate each and every one of you.

As always, this novel contains the names of many of my friends. During the writing of this book, several people made donations to the Veterans Community Alliance—Freehold Township Day Committee in exchange for having their names included in the manuscript. It was fun for them, and also ended up raising money for a worthy group that helps local veterans and their families, a cause dear to my heart.

In no particular order, Jeff Dennis, Vince Norman (who left us all way too soon), George Burdge, Danielle Reynaud, Cheryl "Cookie" Cook, Tina Marie, Layne Gautreau, Kevin Israel, Valeria Jean Kozak, Jessica Coulter, Bill Gallo, Karl White, Steve Burstein, and others . . . thank you all for your generous donations to the VCA. You helped purchase two bikes this year, which two veterans rode from New Jersey to Walter Reed Medical Center. Ooh rah! I hope none of you are offended by your portrayal (or demise!). The characters Chris Cascaes and Apo Yessayan reappear, and are two of my best buds in real life.

Special shout-outs to the Philip A. Reynolds Detachment of the Marine Corps League and ARMS, two other organizations that, like the VCA, serve American veterans. I'm proud to wear the red polo and cover as an associate member of the Marine Corps League.

To the good people at Post Hill Press, thank you for helping me live the dream of being a full-time author. Anthony Ziccardi and Michael L. Wilson, thank you! Also, my thanks to editor Jon Ford for his assistance in making sure we get it right.

For the latest news, follow me on Facebook at David M. Salkin, or on Twitter @DavidMSalkin, or visit DavidMSalkin. com.

DEDICATION

For ALL of my family and friends, who make me laugh and smile every day, I am so blessed to have all this love . . . and in particular, Patty, Rachael, and Alex, my Team!

And for two very special people, both taken way too soon:

Tom Antus, my teacher, my mentor, and most importantly, my friend.

Bruce Buscaglia, friend and classmate since kindergarten. You are both missed, but never forgotten~

And finally, to our veterans and those still in the field, thank you.

CHAPTER 1

USS *John Warner*
South China Sea

Commander Vince Norman sat in his chair behind the two submarine pilots watching the outside world on computer screens that revealed five ships and a small island. The new *Virginia*-class *John Warner* (SSN-785) wasn't equipped with a periscope. Rather, this next-generation submarine boasted a photonic mast that could view the world with high-definition and infrared cameras from below the surface.

Norman's XO, Lieutenant Commander George Burdge, sat at his console typing on his keyboard.

"Logging ship IDs now, Commander," he said quietly.

Commander Norman studied the ships on his screen carefully. The vessels were all Chinese; three military and two that looked to be freighters bringing in more equipment, weapons, and supplies to the newest artificial island in the South China Sea.

LCDR Burdge broke the silence again. "Got 'em, skipper. Two frigates, the *Heng Shui* and *Liu Zhou*, and a destroyer, the *Wuhan*. The other two are supply, but definitely government vessels.

Master Chief Adams, a radar and sonar specialist who had a habit of always speaking in a whisper, turned his head toward the commander.

1

"Lots of active sonar and radar out there," he reported. The newest electronics equipment aboard the *John Warner* could do things that ninety-nine percent of the world's ships couldn't, including reading active radar and sonar, jamming enemy electronics, and cloaking itself to the most sophisticated sonar outside the US Navy arsenal. It was three hundred and seventy-seven feet of Bad-Ass.

"Hold steady and slow, Mr. Talbot," said the commander to his sub pilot. "We need to get a little closer to the pier area. Satellite pictures aren't able to see what they're bringing in so we need to take a peek ourselves."

"Aye, aye, skipper. On course at ten knots," replied the pilot.

"Enemy submarine detected, three miles, bearing two-seven-zero. They don't see us," reported Master Chief Adams.

"Very well. Just keep tabs on it. Can you ID it?"

"Negative, skipper. Best guess is a *Yuan*-class. It's way too noisy to be a nuke."

"I concur. Tag it and stay frosty."

The master chief used the ship's sophisticated computers to "tag" the submarine, and the smart little box kept track of the enemy sub automatically, remembering the ship's name and details, while the crewman continued monitoring the other ships.

"Time to target six minutes, skipper. Going to get crowded," said the pilot.

"This isn't bumper cars, Mr. Talbot," replied the skipper with a small smile.

"Aye, aye, skipper."

Above the sparkling surface, Chinese sonar operators scanned the ocean's surface and depths for foreign vessels. Only a few months prior, the United States guided missile destroyer USS *Lassen* crossed within twelve miles of China's newest artificial island. To the Chinese, it was an encroachment on their territorial waters and a clear violation of international law. For the Americans, it was a political statement reaffirming the United States' position that China has no legitimate claim over the waters surrounding the artificial islands, and the Chinese threat to freedom of navigation posed an international destabilization of the region. In July of 2016, The Hague had sided with the Philippines that China's historic claims to the South China Sea were not legitimate. China ignored the ruling and continued building islands.

As usual, both sides rattled their swords and played a game of chicken. To complicate matters even more, Vietnam, Indonesia, Malaysia, the Philippines, Brunei, and Taiwan all had their own list of disputes. Vietnam, Malaysia, Taiwan, and the Philippines had also built their own artificial islands, complete with airstrips. All of these new islands could prove to be very dangerous ground, indeed.

At almost one and a half million square miles, the South China Sea just wasn't big enough for everyone.

CHAPTER 2

CIA Headquarters
Langley, Virginia

Director Holstrum sat behind his desk drinking yet another large black coffee while he read a classified memo. His intercom snapped him out of his concentration.

"Director, Mr. Yessayan is here to see you."

"Send him in."

Apo walked into the director's office in his usual calm demeanor. Today he was dressed in black slacks and a crisp white shirt with Italian loafers. No socks—it was July. It was Apo's "corporate look." The man, often referred to as "the Chameleon" by his peers in the agency, could show up looking like anyone. A short, thick man with a dark complexion, the bald, middle-aged Apo posed no threat when he entered a room. Anyone seeing him in the hallways of CIA might mistake him for an analyst or accountant. The fact that he spoke fluently in Arabic, Farsi, Pashtun, Kurmanji, Spanish, and French and had a working knowledge of a half dozen other languages wouldn't be evident. Nor would his hand-to-hand combat skills. Apo Yessayan was, very quietly, one the CIA's most lethal and efficient agents. He had been to more countries than he could count, and quite often left multiple enemy dead behind him.

"Morning, Mr. Director," said Apo, crossing the elegant office and sitting in a high-backed black leather chair.

4

"Coffee?"

"That would be quite wonderful, actually."

The director pressed his intercom and spoke to his executive secretary. "Susan, can you please locate a Turkish coffee for Apo?"

"Yes, sir. I'll be back in five."

"*Turkish*, even? Is this a suicide mission?"

Holstrum smiled and shrugged. "Maybe I'm just being courteous."

"This is why *you're* in the office and I'm out in the field. You're a shitty liar, boss."

"How's your Malay?"

Apo made a face. "Malay? Am I going to Malaysia or Thailand?"

"Neither."

Apo sat back and crossed his arms. "That leaves Indonesia and Singapore."

"You left one out."

Apo furrowed his brow and thought for a second. "You got me."

"Brunei."

"*Brunei*?" Apo let that hang in the air for a moment. "As I recall, the same family has run the country for six hundred years. What's got Brunei on your radar?"

"First, your language skills. Any Malay?"

"No. Tough language. I could probably find some Chinese speakers in a jam, but most Bruneians speak a little English anyway. What's up?"

"A very, very old piece of history."

"You have me intrigued."

"A broken arrow."

Apo sat back and crossed his legs, pursing his lips as he scanned his memory for missing nukes in that part of the world. "In Brunei? Closest I can remember was near Japan in the sixties."

"Very good. Yes. In December of '65. A bomber flipped off the *Ticonderoga* and we lost the plane, the pilot, and a one-megaton nuke. The navy declassified it in 1980, although they gave the wrong location on purpose to avoid tensions with Japan."

"So?"

"So it's happened a few more times than we've admitted. There's another one—two, actually—sitting not too far from Brunei very close to a brand new artificial island."

"The Chinese?"

"The Bruneians, actually."

Susan knocked and opened the door with a small tray. There were two demitasse cups with dark coffee that perfumed the air. Apo closed his eyes and inhaled deeply.

"Marry me, Susan."

Holstrum smiled. "He says that to everyone that makes good coffee—ignore him."

She smiled and placed the tray on the small table in front of him, then took one of the cups and gave it to her boss. "I figured you wouldn't be opposed to one yourself."

"You sure you don't want it?" asked Holstrum.

"Oh you can be *sure* there's already one on my desk. In a *real* mug."

Holstrum smiled. "You'll be awake until next week."

She shrugged and closed the door quietly behind her.

"So Brunei is in the island-building business now, too?"

"It would appear so. But we have a few troubling facts that need follow-up. First, the Sultan of Brunei, Sir Hassanal Alam, has made some interesting changes of late. He instituted Sharia law last year. Since then, stoning to death, public whipping, sometimes to death, and the hacking off of limbs has come back into fashion. That said, none of the Sharia laws apply to him or his brother. They each have dozens of sex slaves, as well as multiple wives and children. They throw huge parties, with plenty of drinking and sex and other activities that would get anyone else in the country hanged in the town square."

"How nice. Maybe I'll book a vacation."

"Drinking alcohol gets you forty lashes for the first offense. Double for the second."

"Well *that* crosses it off my bucket list."

"Sultan Alam is one of the richest men in the world. Twenty billion in the bank. As he's gotten older, he's become more devout. Might be to save face because of his brother's embarrassing shenanigans, but whatever the reason, we've picked up some chatter."

"Ah. The plot thickens," said Apo softly. He sipped his coffee and closed his eyes, enjoying the taste.

"We believe that ISIS has been making overtures to the sultan. Malaysian police arrested a group last May who were planning an attack. You remember Jakarta was attacked."

"Right."

"Word on the street is, the sultan keeps pushing his country deeper into Sharia. Might make a nice training ground for ISIS."

"We have any intel?"

"Nothing confirmed. Just rumors. But they make sense. Which brings us to our problem."

"A couple American nukes sitting by an artificial island controlled by Brunei, which might have Islamic fundamentalist leanings . . ."

"Correct."

"I love this job. Never a dull moment."

"What if a Canadian petrochemical company was to go to the sultan and offer to lease some offshore oil platforms? If they go along with it, you'd have a base of operations from which to start looking at the bottom of the ocean."

"Why bother? Can't we just get a sub over there and look without asking?"

"The sub already found the wreck site—the USS *John Warner*. It can't recover the bombs, though. We'll need a surface vessel for that. Problem is, there are so many Chinese subs and navy warships in the water over there, we're likely to bump into one and start World War III. China, Vietnam, Malaysia, Taiwan, and the Philippines also have surface fleets all over the South China Sea. Yesterday, an Arleigh Burke-class destroyer, the USS William P. Lawrence, was buzzed by two Chinese J-11 fighters, scrambled out of Fiery Cross Reef, where they built a ten-thousand-foot runway. We didn't even know they had fighters there."

"Seriously? Satellites didn't pick them up?"

"No. We have subs there now doing reconnaissance while the destroyers continue to cruise up and down the shipping lanes to make it clear to China that they don't own the whole damn ocean. It's a mess, Apo."

"Yeah, well maybe the president should have taken an actual stance five years ago. That horse is out of the barn, boss."

Director Holstrum wiggled his eyebrows a few times uncomfortably. He wasn't a fan of the commander in chief, but the boss was the boss and the CIA didn't always get its way. "I made it known a while back that the island could pose a problem. We'll leave it at that."

"Okay, so now what? I go to the sultan and offer him some dough to build an oil platform—then what?"

"Then your oil exploration team pretends it's mapping the ocean floor. Mapping the bottom would be logical. You set up the rig at the wreck site, recover the nukes, and then we have a team pick it up by ship. The second the nukes are secured, you leave."

Apo nodded. "Okay. But why would the sultan make a deal with the Canadians? He's a multibillionaire. He's got his own oil platforms and specialists, doesn't he?"

"He does, but it's not uncommon for larger companies to partner with these nations. It's a good deal for the sultan.

They control the mineral rights, and the company shares in the output. If they miss on a drill, it doesn't cost the sultan anything. If they hit oil, the sultan keeps sixty percent. Big Oil usually has the best geologists and equipment for mapping the ocean floor and searching for deposits. We cannot have those nukes fall into the hands of terrorists."

"You think they still work? After sitting on the ocean floor for—how many years?"

"Plane went down in '72. And yes. The cores are still intact and with a simple new arming device, they'd have all they need."

Apo made a face. "If we knew where the plane was all this time, why didn't we clean this up years ago?"

"Because we never had a plane carrying nuclear bombs in that part of world, so how could we lose one? This is top secret. We can't do a search and recovery operation for something that never existed. It was only discovered by accident when all this reef building started. We've had a lot of submarines patrolling in the last two years. Our newest sub, the *John Warner*, has equipment like we've never had before. It detected the radiation, and that was cross-checked with old records of the plane's projected location when it went down. They're our nukes. No doubt about it."

"How deep?"

"Not deep at all. The ocean floor around the Spratlys and Fiery Cross Reef is like a mountain range. The mountaintops make hundreds of tiny atolls and islands. The plane is sitting in maybe six hundred feet of water. Had it landed another forty yards south, it would have fallen another thousand feet. At six hundred feet, we can get to it. In fact, the SEALs from your last mission are being trained for deep-water recovery."

Apo smiled. "So you've already started working on this. They were a good bunch."

"Agreed. Some of the best. I'll make spooks out of them yet."

"So when do I start?"

"If you take the assignment, you start tomorrow. I have a new teammate for you to meet. He speaks Malay and Chinese."

"Okay. What's his name?"

Holstrum smiled. "We call him Batman."

"Batman."

"His name is Wang Wei. He uses the American name Bruce, which replaces his given name, Wei. So it's now Bruce Wang."

"Bruce Wang. Bruce Wayne. Batman," mumbled Apo.

Holstrum shrugged. "Easier to remember, right?"

"He skip the mask and cape?"

"No. And you'll have to dress up like Robin."

"I don't remember you usually being so funny. This is a suicide mission, isn't it . . ."

"Most likely."

CHAPTER 3

Special Operations Command Pacific—SOCPAC
Camp H. M. Smith, USMC
Aiea, Oahu, Hawaii

After almost two months of downtime, the team had been reassembled and flown to SOCPAC in Hawaii without much information. Director Holstrum had told the team's commander, Master Chief Al "Moose" Carlogio, that they'd be getting advanced underwater training in Hawaii. That suited Moose just fine—all of his remaining special operations team were SEALs, except for one Marine sharpshooter. The original team had included CIA officers and US Army Rangers as well, but there had been casualties and retirements along the way.

When they arrived at Camp Smith on Oahu, the SEALs were ecstatic to get back underwater. The sniper, an Oklahoma boy named Eric Hodges who could hit an ant at a thousand meters, was just happy to be on a base that had "USMC" painted on the sign.

They were situated and given quarters by a chief warrant officer who ran "special projects"—a polite name for top secret operations. The same chief warrant officer, Layne Gautreau, escorted them to a meeting room for their first briefing. A Louisiana boy, Layne's accent was somewhere between southern and Cajun, and the SEALs had to listen closely when he spoke. To Hodges, an Oklahoma boy, he sounded closer to "home" than anyone else on his team.

11

The team took seats in a classroom setting with a large screen at the front of the room. They expected someone else to come in and speak to them, but CWO Gautreau was not only their greeting committee but also their briefing officer and future instructor. When the men had taken their seats, CWO Gautreau walked to the front of the room and typed into a laptop on the front table. On the screen, an image of what resembled a space suit filled the screen. It was orange with a round helmet, the front of which was a thick clear acrylic. Although the joints were flexible, the suit itself was rigid enough to remain standing while empty. Standing there on the screen, it looked a lot like an orange Michelin Man.

Layne smiled and spoke in his slow Cajun style. "Welcome to SOCPAC, gentlemen. I've spoken with a couple of you, but for the rest of you, I'm Chief Warrant Officer Layne Gautreau. I'm one of six special operations deep-water salvage instructors here at SOCPAC, and I've been charged with preparing you for your next mission. My instructions did not come to me via the normal chain of command. I've been in the navy for eighteen years, and I've only spoken to the Director of Central Intelligence one time—which was two weeks ago when he personally explained to me what I was preparing you for. This will be interesting, to say the least."

Gautreau turned his attention to the screen. "What you see here is the latest and greatest in deep-water diving."

Eric Hodges smiled and said, "Thank God. I thought you were sending us to Mars in that thing."

"Negative. Gunny Sergeant Hodges, have you done any diving at all? You're my only land animal."

"Negative, Chief. I just shoot bad guys." He smiled and added dramatically, "From a place you will not see, comes a sound you will not hear . . ."

"Very well. You will be mostly observing your teammates' training for diving, and use some of your downtime to hone your skills from a rolling deck. The rest of you SEALs will enjoy your time here. That Newtsuit is an ADS 2000. This Atmospheric Diving System can bring you to two thousand feet while keeping you comfortably at one atmosphere inside the suit."

That got everyone's attention.

Master Chief Vinny "Ripper" Colgan, the second in command after Moose, let out a low whistle. "Sweet ride."

"Yes, sir. The ADS can keep you down working for almost eighty hours, and bring you straight up with zero decompression time." CWO Gautreau looked at the lone Marine. "Normally, Gunny, divers can't go to two thousand feet outside of a submarine. And even at a couple hundred feet, they'd need to decompress to avoid the bends—nitrogen bubbling out of their blood. You follow?"

"Yes, sir. I don't dive like these fish, but I've been around these guys long enough to have the basics."

"Good." He changed the slide, and a US Navy single-seat turbojet appeared on the screen. "This, gentlemen, is a Douglas A4-E Skyhawk—a Vietnam-era attack aircraft capable of delivering as much conventional ordnance as a B-17 bomber. It was designed to be able to deliver two nuclear bombs to the Soviet Union or anyplace else on the globe the president decided to turn into a lunar surface."

He changed slides again, this time showing a very grainy, somewhat blurry, black-and-white image of what looked like a wrecked Skyhawk, lying upside down. "This, gentlemen, is the remains of a Skyhawk that was lost while flying over the South China Sea in 1972. She disappeared three hours into a planned nine-hour flight. The picture was taken by our newest *Virginia*-class submarine, which has advanced imaging capabilities. That sub, the *John Warner*, detected the radiation and investigated, taking these images."

He changed the slide to a map of the area, showing Vietnam, Brunei, Malaysia, Indonesia, and the Philippines. There were many small islands notated in the open ocean between Brunei and Vietnam.

"This is the southern edge of the South China Sea, currently a very busy place. Brunei has decided to build an island here," he said, pointing with a laser pen. "There's two twenty-megaton bombs sitting in that plane right next to where they plan to do it."

"How big is a twenty-megaton bomb?" asked Jon Cohen, one of the original SEALs from the team.

"One megaton can power your house for about a hundred thousand years. Nagasaki and Hiroshima were about *three* megatons *combined*," said CWO Gautreau.

Moose interjected. "It's a metric fuck-ton of explosives."

"Thank you, Master Chief, for putting it into layman's terms. Yes—an unintentional forty-megaton yield is a bit of a problem. Or worse yet, intentional, by a terrorist organization. Which brings us to why you gentlemen are here. I am going to train you to use the ADS 2000, and you are going to get those bombs."

Moose made a face. "Don't you have specially trained deep-water salvage guys that do this stuff?"

"Yes, we do. And that was my conversation with Director Holstrum. The problem is, our divers are just divers. Apparently, you all have other special skills, and you won't be conducting this operation in the traditional manner. After I get done training you on the ADS, I have to give you a crash course in offshore oil rigs. That is, as soon as I get finished Googling that shit myself."

"I'm not sure I follow," said Moose.

"Yeah, well, this is going to be complicated. Welcome to SOCPAC . . ."

CHAPTER 4

Istana Nurul Iman

The sultan was in one of his studies. With 1,788 rooms, including 257 bathrooms, Sultan Alam had lots of options. The Istana Nural Iman, or "Light of Faith Palace," was the largest single-family residence ever built. On this particular day, the sultan had an unusual meeting.

The massive double doors of his study opened slowly, as the hydraulic hinges silently swung open the twenty-foot-high bronze and ivory doors. One of his senior staff bowed and then announced their honored guests.

"Your Excellency, Sir Hassanal Alam, Sultan of Brunei, I present to you Mohammed bin Awad and his associate, Hamdi Fazil." The sultan's aid bowed again and backed out of the room in a bow, closing the massive doors behind him.

The two guests walked into the study and approached the giant desk, behind which sat the Sultan of Brunei. The ornately carved gold-and-black desk was almost twenty feet long.

"Your Excellency. *As-salaam alaykum*," said Mohammed with a bow. Hamdi bowed as well.

"*Wa'alaykumu s-salam*. Come in." The men spoke in a combination of English and common Arabic greetings. The Arabs didn't speak Malay, and the sultan spoke only limited Arabic, but they all spoke English in varying amounts.

The two men sat down in chairs fit for royalty, which they were not. In fact, the two of them had grown up poor, and

15

hadn't done any traveling at all until after they had decided that international terrorism would be their careers.

Mohammed bin Awad was Syrian. He had spent his teen years back and forth between Syria and Iraq selling guns and ammunition with a few cousins. The Americans eventually caught up to his cousins and killed them all by drone strike on a trip he had missed due to illness. The food poisoning from some bad lamb had saved his life. Now, at thirty-eight years old, he was a rising star in ISIS. Mohammed looked much older than his thirty-eight years. Poor nutrition had led to dental issues, and years of living under the hot sun had weather-beaten his face. With his beard already pushing out some gray hairs, the man could pass for his late fifties.

While his "career" had started out more for financial reasons than ideological fervor, the death of his cousins created a strong hatred of the Americans who were responsible. When he realized he could combine his hatred with an opportunity to obtain power and even wealth, he joined with ISIS and quickly became a mid-level commander because of his connections for weapons and ammunition, something the jihad was always in need of obtaining. He impressed the top-tier commanders, who decided he was a rising star who could help them spread influence all over the world.

Hamdi Fazil was a Sunni Pakistani who had spent a little time in Afghanistan trying to kill infidels before ending up in Syria by way of Iraq. He had also managed to kill a few impure Muslims in Iraq along the way. For Hamdi, violence was not only a part of his Sharia view of the world, but it also satisfied his sociopathic brain, which had been perverted in the Pakistani madrasas since he was a very young boy.

The repeated rapes and beatings he suffered at the hands of the "Islamic scholars" had changed a normal young boy into quite a violent killer—a requirement for his current employer. His traumatic formative years led him to abusing anyone smaller than himself, and as he aged and grew into a large brute of a man, it meant that almost anyone became fair game. He left a trail of raped boys and girls and beaten or dead bodies wherever he went. At six foot four, 260 pounds, with a pockmarked face and black, unkempt beard, Hamdi was the stuff nightmares were made of.

The two of them glanced around the room nervously. They had never been inside a palace before, and the grandeur was overwhelming. They tried to be calm, but the room did what it was supposed to do to visitors—it awed and intimidated them.

Mohammed took a deep breath and spoke. "Your Excellency, thank you for inviting us to your beautiful country. I hope this visit will be the beginning of a new and powerful relationship. With the assistance of Brunei, our faithful servants can spread our influence to this part of the world and help bring Brunei and the region on to the path of the righteous. We are greatly expanding across the Middle East, and it is time to grow our legions here, as well."

The sultan smiled. He had instituted Sharia law the previous year, and had never felt more powerful and at ease in his position as ruler of his small nation. By granting ISIS training facilities hidden in the jungles of his country, they could continue their attacks in the Philippines, Malaysia, and Indonesia while guaranteeing him peace inside his own borders. A deal with the devil wasn't a bad thing if the devil's agenda matched your own.

"Brunei has been set on the right course already, my brothers. What I want from you is assurances that Brunei's sovereignty will never be challenged, and our small country will remain untouched by violence. While I cannot publicly condone training facilities or bases, there are areas in our remote regions where you'll be safe."

"Understood, Your Excellency," said Mohammed. "I've been given authority to guarantee you that Brunei will be under the protection of the Islamic State. With our mutual cooperation, we can spread our influence, and gather needed resources and areas where we can train and grow our legions. Leadership understands that discretion will be needed, and Brunei will never attract the attention of foreign powers."

The sultan nodded. "We have a multitude of problems. The Chinese continue to expand into our territorial waters. And while the Americans announce to the world that they oppose Chinese aggression, they do nothing. Malaysia, Indonesia, Vietnam, and the Philippines now encroach into our territorial waters as well. Perhaps if China were to change its leadership, they would be less likely to build islands in our waters. Has the Islamic State had any success in China yet?"

"Small steps, so far. In the Xinxiang Uighur region, we are pushing for brothers to join the fight. We're attempting operations in Hotan and Kashgar, but it's taking some time."

"Hotan and Kashgar—the ancient Silk Road? How appropriate. Increasing operations in the Chinese mainland will be vital to refocusing Chinese aggression internally, and away from the South China Sea."

"There are over twenty million Muslims in China, Your Excellency. Given some time, we can build our presence there. The northwest region is fairly remote and easier to work in than other parts of China. We are confident that in another year, we will have enough followers to begin operations throughout the mainland."

The sultan smiled. Brunei could never stand toe-to-toe with China. Even the Americans and Russians worried about the Chinese. But with a few million brothers in arms creating chaos in the mainland, the great Dragon would be weakened from within.

"You will deal with my minister of the interior. Abdul Ali is waiting for you in his office. This is the only time we will meet face-to-face. In the future, your dealings will be with Minister Ali only. This meeting never occurred, of course, and if there are ever attacks traced to Brunei, I will publicly condemn them. In the meantime, you'll have whatever you need."

"Thank you, Your Excellency. Blessings upon you . . ."

The sultan called one of his secretaries in, who led the two men away to find the minister, who was the only one who knew the sultan's plan. Fiercely loyal to the sultan, Abdul Ali was more than happy to assist foreign fighters who would weaken their enemies at no cost to Brunei.

"The enemy of my enemy is my friend . . ."

CHAPTER 5

Office of the Secretary of State

"Madam Secretary, I have Mr. Sawaad on line two," said Robert Clemmons, the secretary of state's executive secretary. He stared at her and waited.

"Thanks, Bob." She dismissed him with a flick of her hand and picked up the phone. Clemmons walked out without comment, straightening his tie in absent-minded aggravation. He *hated* when she called him Bob. He was Robert or Rob, and had told her that several times when she first hired him. She could give a crap.

He sat back at his desk and half listened to her whispers inside her adjoining office.

"What have you got for me?" she asked.

Pause.

"How much?"

Pause.

"Ali, you're getting greedy."

Pause.

"Yes, yes, I know. It's dangerous for me, too, you idiot. Fine. Fine. Send it. Yes. The money will be transferred now."

"Bob!"

He took a deep breath and walked back in. "Yes, Madam Secretary?"

"I need you to send another wire transfer to my contact in Beirut. Ali Sawaad. Two hundred thousand."

"From the Foreign Office intelligence fund?"

"Of course. Jesus Christ, Bob. Do I need to do it myself? I need it done now."

His face flushed. "Yes, Madam Secretary." He walked back out. The woman insisted on being called Madam Secretary. "Ma'am" was somehow an insult. He had never met anyone with a bigger ego. Her plans for the White House were the only reason he stayed on. Robert Clemmons had his owns plans for his future, and hooking on to her coat tails would get him there, but damn she was getting more impossible to be around each day. The fact that he had sent over three million dollars to an unknown contact in Lebanon worried him, of course. But this was above his pay grade. If she had a confidential informant or was working some classified mission he wasn't privy to, so be it, but this sure seemed different than any of her other calls or procedures for sending money. He returned to his desk and began the arduous process of wiring the money.

Back in her office, Secretary of State Danielle Reynaud walked around her desk and shouted out to the adjoining room, which was full of staffers. "I'm not to be disturbed until I tell you otherwise." She closed her door and pulled her private cell phone, hitting the contact for Jeff Dennis, her senior political advisor and one of her most trusted allies. When she was president, he would have a cabinet post.

"What have you got?" she asked, skipping the "hello, how are you" time-wasters.

"Your biggest problem has been taken care of," he said quietly.

"Do I get to know how?"

"I'm sure you'll be reading about it in the paper in another few days. Those damn Chinese are most likely behind it, but one never knows. Perhaps Holstrum really *is* the monster the public will read about."

She paused. She wanted to ask more, but knew better. "Anything else?" she asked.

"Working on some support from a few overseas friends. Some sizable donations."

"Carefully, Jeff."

"Of course, Madam Secretary. I'll let you know if anything else comes up."

She hung up and sat at her desk with her arms folded across her chest. She and Jeff had pulled a number out of thin air the year before. A billion dollars. That's what she would need to win the White House. It was an intimidating number to raise without ending up on the front page for the wrong reasons. If anyone could do it, though, it was Jeff Dennis. She decided she needed a distraction and began looking through more pictures of antiquities and artwork from the Middle East that had been stolen from national museums and galleries, as well as historic landmarks. The treasures would be lost or destroyed if not purchased by *someone*, so it might as well be by someone who had an actual appreciation for such things. In another ten years or so, the sale of those same artifacts on the black market would fund a few homes around the world.

The piece she had just purchased for a cool two hundred thousand was a sculpture that would go in her home in Virginia. It was Greek, and one of the loveliest statues she'd ever seen. The face seemed to glow in its soft white marble, with delicate features that seemed perfect in their anatomy. While two hundred thousand dollars was a lot of money, it was fair for something like this. Besides, it wasn't like the money was coming out of her personal checking account, anyway. Ali Sawaad was listed as one of her confidential informants that provided great assistance to her office on Middle East affairs. His only real assistance had been in turning her homes into magnificent art galleries, with the cash ultimately ending up in the hands of ISIS, who purchased weapons and ammunition with the funds to continue their massacre. In a sea of never-ending violence in that region, the secretary merely waved it off in much the same fashion as she waved off the folks that worked for her.

⊕

Back in Langley, CIA officer Cheryl Cook got an automatic e-mail. Her sophisticated computer system alerted her whenever money hit the account she'd been watching for the last five months. Ali Sawaad just got another two hundred thousand dollars US. She ran the routing numbers and shook her head. What *balls*.

CHAPTER 6

Langley

Director Wallace Holstrum sat behind his desk with seven different files all open in front of him. It was nine in the morning. This was usually the part of the day when he was at his best. Not today. Seven different high-priority situations came in almost simultaneously—all unrelated, all equally sensitive and distressing.

The director had been scanning the files and trying to prioritize his day, which was obviously going to be a long one that included some briefings at the White House. His phone buzzing in from his secretary made him jump.

"Mr. Director, I have FBI Director Gallo for you . . ."

"Tell him I'll call him later, Susan."

"No, sir. I mean he's here in the office. Now."

Holstrum's face showed his surprise. Bill wasn't one to just pop in unannounced.

"Okay, send him in."

The door opened and Director Gallo walked in, looking ashen. The normally outgoing man looked so grim that Holstrum immediately asked, "What's wrong, Bill?"

Gallo walked in and sat in the chair across from Wallace. He crossed his legs and smoothed his slacks as he tried to find the correct words.

"How long have we known each other, Wally?"

The CIA director sat back in his chair, still puzzled. Bill was one of a handful of people on the planet other than his mother who could call him Wally. "A long time, Bill. What's up?"

"I don't know how to say this other than to just say it . . ."

His secretary buzzed again. "Sorry, sir. Your wife in on line three, says it's urgent."

Bill nodded. "Yes, it is. Call her back in two."

Wallace folded his arms and told Susan to have her hold on. "Bill? You want to clue me in?"

"At this moment, there are FBI agents in your home, removing your personal computer."

"*What?*"

"I'm really hoping that it's the Chinese or some other source, Wally."

"What are you talking about, Bill?"

"Over a thousand images of kiddie porn have been downloaded into your hard drive over the past few weeks. Agents were doing a regional sweep. Your name came up in the net."

Wally's face turned red and he leaned forward, seething. "Bill, you know damn well I didn't download any kiddie porn!"

"I would very much like to believe that. It's why I'm here personally, and not some agent you don't know."

"Bill! I'm the goddamned director of the CIA! You think I'd be downloading kiddie porn? Hell! *Any* porn? This is ridiculous!"

"Wally, I want to believe you. I *do*, actually. But I'm required to follow this up and investigate. You understand."

"I do *not* understand! This could be a matter of national security. Someone wants me taken off my post, even temporarily! If it's the Chinese, then they're up to something bigger." He held up two files from his desk, now closed. "You see this? This is the goddamned Chinese trying to start World War III! I don't have time for this bullshit!"

"Wally, my team is going to have to search your work computer . . ."

"And you know damn well that won't happen! I have top secret files on here that even *you* aren't allowed access to!"

"I know it's going to get complicated. The director of homeland security will decide how to proceed."

"Bill! Are you hearing anything I'm saying? I'm in the middle of a shit-storm over here! I don't have time for an FBI investigation into some crap someone put on my hard drive! Hell, I barely even use that computer. I spend so much time on this one, I don't even want to see a computer when I get home."

"We have all the log-in times. Most downloads occurred at night or weekends. We can cross-reference that against your log-ins here at work. You can't be two places at once. It could help clear you."

"Bill! *No* one is getting into my work computer. No one."

Director Gallo shrugged. "I'm sorry, Wally. That's going to be up to Homeland Security. I'll have to tell the White House, too, you understand."

Susan buzzed in again. "Sir, I'm very sorry, but your wife is still on hold and she sounds upset."

Wallace shook his head angrily and picked up the phone. "Hey, I know what's going on. It's not a problem. Just let them take whatever they need, okay?"

Director Gallo stared at his shoes, feeling uncomfortable. He tried not to listen to Holstrum's wife yelling from her side of the phone. Wally hung up and stared at Bill.

"So now what?" he asked, angrily.

"Now my team runs their computer checks and tries to see where all this came from. The Chinese are good, Wally. It won't be easy, if it's them."

"Well it sure as hell wasn't me! And you know that!" He was pointing his finger at Gallo, wishing he was poking him with it.

"It's not my call, but I'm guessing DHS may want you to step aside until this is cleared up."

"And that's exactly what whoever put that crap on my hard drive *wants*, Bill! I've got the Chinese air force buzzing ships in the South China Sea, the Iranians playing bumper boats out in the Strait of Hormuz, Mexican drug cartels, ISIS, a half dozen new terrorist threats, and you want me to take a week off?"

"I'm not sure we can wrap this up in a week . . ."

"Bill! This is ridiculous! I'll call DHS myself!"

"I've already called. Sorry. The director is on his way over now."

CHAPTER 7

Interglobe Oil Exploration
Vancouver, British Columbia, Canada

Apo and Bruce "Batman" Wang were sitting in a small office that had been set up for them by the staff at Langley. It looked like a Hollywood set dresser had staged the office, right down to the office plants. A lot of time had been spent creating a fake background on the company, and then backdating it so it looked to the world that Interglobe Oil had been finding oil all over the world for the last fifteen years. Hacking and cracking into Facebook and LinkedIn had been complicated, but anyone who researched the company would find years' worth of news, connections, and commentary from all over the globe.

Bruce sat reading one of the many dossiers on the company that the two of them had to learn. He looked up and smiled at Apo. "Hey, man, congratulations on that find near Australia. Looks like a few hundred million in reserves. I didn't really have you pegged for an oil man. Figured you'd have a silver belt buckle or something. Maybe a cowboy hat."

"I look taller in cowboy boots," said Apo.

"You and me both," replied the small Asian. "I think combined we're maybe ten feet tall and three hundred pounds."

"Then you're skinnier than you look," said Apo, rubbing his belly. "I keep wondering what we'll say if anyone walks into our office and actually wants to hire us."

"Pay's better than the current company, you can be sure."

28

"True. Probably less risk on an offshore oil platform in a tsunami than our current line of work as well." He paused. "You spend a lot of time in the field?"

Bruce leaned back in his chair and laughed. "Ohhhh," he exclaimed with a sinister smile. "I get it. The little Asian dude should be a computer geek or a number cruncher, right? You profiling me, man?"

"Absolutely. I bet you make great fried rice, too."

"Okay, *that* is actually true. Best fried rice you ever had. But yeah, I've been in the field for six years. You?"

"I'm older than dirt. Was probably in the field when you were still in grade school. Just got back from Mexico. You?"

"Singapore, by way of Kowloon and Laos last year."

"See? The boss profiled you, too."

"Yeah, well, it's easier to blend when you're Asian and speak the languages."

Apo surprised him by speaking in Chinese. It wasn't perfect, but was still pretty impressive for a Westerner.

"Hey, that's pretty good," said Bruce, surprised.

"Farsi, Arabic, Pashtun, Spanish, French, and a little Chinese, here and there. Oh, and Kurmanji. Also fluent with profanity and sarcasm."

Bruce smiled. "Profanity and sarcasm are required for basic training at the Farm."

Bruce, like Apo, couldn't discuss specific operations, but he was a busy man. Being of Chinese descent, Bruce was in high demand in the American intelligence community. Finding Americans who could speak fluent Mandarin or Cantonese, and were willing to risk their lives for America, wasn't always easy for the CIA. Bruce had been recruited out of nearby American University in DC and excelled in every task he was given. As his spy-craft improved, so did the complexity and danger of his missions.

Only two months prior, Bruce had spent a few weeks in Hong Kong, meeting with Chinese intelligence officers who believed he was ready to spy on the United States for China. Bruce had credentials that placed him at the Pentagon, where they wanted him to send secret documents related to the latest American weapons, aircraft, and radar systems in exchange for large amounts of cash—not an unusual trade. When he returned home, he *did* send them files that included both fake weapons systems as well as a computer bug that would allow access into their computers. Before it was discovered by the Chinese, the CIA successfully hacked over ten thousand top secret Chinese military files. The file was also designed to wipe the drive when any attempt was made to remove it, thus causing additional damage to the Chinese military community.

Bruce, at thirty-five, still found the adventurous lifestyle of a spy exciting and rewarding and, as a result, was an excellent agent with almost no social life. Like most of the men on the team, the job consumed him, leaving very little time for the niceties in life such as a companion or family. His parents thought he was a successful computer programmer in DC, and his occasional visits or surprise checks in the mail kept them satisfied that he was doing very well for himself, although they constantly told him he needed to find a nice Chinese girl and settle down.

A quiet *ding* on the only computer in the office made them jump up. They had sent out only one e-mail in the last two weeks, and the only e-mail they would be getting back would be from the Brunei National Petroleum Company. Brunei Petroleum had holdings in a shale-to-gas facility in British Columbia, which is why the CIA had set up the office there. The e-mail invited Interglobe to come and meet with the its head of operations in BC and, if all went well, potentially attend a second meeting back in Brunei.

"That's it," said Apo with a smile. "Foot in the door. We make them an offer they can't refuse, sell them on the offshore oil platform where we want to work, and go find our nukes."

"It's always fun to seal a billion dollar deal when it's not your money," said Bruce.

"Now you sound like a Washington politician," said Apo.

Bruce smiled. "The director warned me about your outspoken political commentary. I guess you aren't looking for a leadership role in the Company anytime soon, huh?"

"Hell no. I like being out in the field where I make my own rules. Running a company of employees who all act like me would be a punishment assignment. No, thank you."

Bruce typed out a formal reply and set up their meeting. "Dust off your best suit. We go tomorrow."

Apo threw his arms up in victory. "Excellent. You're lead for the meeting. I'll just sit back and try to look like a tycoon. Stress the importance of immediate action. These deals typically take months. We need to be out there in *days*. Let them think the Chinese and Malaysians are pressing us hard, but our geologists want to work the area right next to their new artificial island."

"Right. And because we've been dealing with the Chinese, we have equipment ready to roll if they give us the green light. We can start mapping immediately, and have the platform moved out within a month. Just one thing . . ."

"What's that?" asked Apo.

"What if they say no?"

Apo scowled. "Kill everyone in the room?"

Batman smiled. "I knew I'd like working with you."

CHAPTER 8

Near Ka'ula Atoll, 50 Nautical Miles West of Kauai, Hawaii

The Naval Special Warfare support ship *Tornado* was used to transporting SEALs for covert ops. With a crew of thirty, the 179-foot aluminum-hulled ship had sped from the base in Hawaii to an area northwest of Kauai at a little over thirty knots. Once they arrived at their location, the ship cut its engines and dropped anchor in five hundred feet of water. The heavy chain links crashed through the surface, where they collected at the bottom and their combined weight held the ship in the calm sea.

The team was out on the rear deck watching CWO Gautreau supervise the set up of the ADS 2000. The heavy suit was standing in its metal frame, attached to cables that would hoist it up and over the side, where some lucky sailor would begin a very deep voyage.

Moose made a sad face as he watched. "Sucks," he mumbled to Ripper. He and Ripper had both wanted to try out the suit and be the ones to retrieve the nukes; however, they were both too big to fit inside the apparatus. As large as it looked from the outside, it wasn't designed to be used by men the size of Moose or Ripper. Instead, Jon Cohen was selected from the team. An avid fish geek, Jon was ecstatic to be given the chance to deep-water dive in the most beautiful blue water he'd ever seen. Forget the nukes—he just wanted to see the sea life.

Jon emerged from the ship wearing something similar to a dry suit, which he would wear inside the ADS 2000. It would get very cold at six hundred feet below sea level. Although the air temperature was almost ninety degrees in the strong sun, and the surface water temperature was eighty degrees, at six hundred feet, the water would hover around forty degrees. Even with the heavy insulation of the suit, the thermal layer was a requirement.

"Nice jammies," said Ryan O'Conner.

Pete McCoy, who was oftentimes Jon's dive buddy on operations, also chimed in. "Even has the little feeties on them."

Jon held up a gloved middle finger. Moose smiled and said, "I believe the young sailor has saluted you."

CWO Gautreau walked over to Jon and led him to the ADS. The winch had lifted the top half of the silver suit off the bottom, and Layne helped Jon climb into the legs of the behemoth. Jon's teammates walked over to watch and offer encouragement and insults.

Hodges, the Marine sniper, watched with trepidation. "Have a fun ride in that quarter-million-dollar suit. Just remember, I can ruin it with a ten-dollar fifty-cal round."

"You will do no such thing," replied Layne dryly as he helped Jon get set up. "I find any bullet holes in my suit, I'll know where to look, and I'll send *you* down there."

Jon ignored the comments and remained focused on his preparations. When he was ready for the top to be lowered, he forced a nervous smile and gave a thumbs-up to Moose, who snapped him a salute. The top was lowered slowly, and Jon raised his arms and started maneuvering them into the suit. Once the suit was lowered to its bottom half, Jon's face could be seen inside the helmet, which had a large viewing pane of thick acrylic. The crew turned on the air supply and sealed the halves together.

"Test one, two, three," said Jon.

"We hear you loud and clear," said Layne with a smile. The other men on his ADS support team all gave thumbs up to Jon and smiled with excitement. Two of the four had gone down themselves in the suit, and loved the experience more than words could ever express.

"I hope you took a crap before you got into that thing," said Ray Jensen. CWO Gautreau flipped him off without even looking at him.

"Okay team, commence launch sequence," said the chief.

The support team began checking and double-checking all of the seals in the suit, as well as the oxygen scrubbing tank and thruster package.

"Check your graspers," said the chief. Jon began manipulating the three-fingered "hand" on the suit with his fingers inside. The chief placed an empty mug on the palm of his hand, and Jon picked it up, turned it over, and gently placed it back on his hand.

"Outstanding," he said. "You'll walk the grid we planned, use the thrusters to explore a little, and then tell us when you're ready to return to the surface. Time to surface from six hundred feet is about seven minutes. We'll be in constant contact and can see you, observe what you see, and monitor all systems as well as your vitals. Video is rolling, so go make us a cool movie. Any questions? You good to go?"

"Ready to go, Chief. I'd give you a thumbs-up, but I don't think my thumb looks quite right."

The team walked in front of him so Jon could see them, and they all waved at him. The support team began the winching process and picked him up off the deck in his aluminum suit. They could see Jon's smile as he went aloft. When the winch moved him out over the water, CWO Gautreau asked him for one last confirmation, and then began lowering him into the foamy sea.

Jon disappeared slowly into beautiful clear blue water and continued his decent to thirty-five feet. The winch stopped and the support team monitored the computer systems for any leaks. Once satisfied, they began the final decent to the ocean floor six hundred feet below. Mounted cameras showed Jon's view, as well as his face. He was grinning ear to ear as he watched countless fish glide past him. The water began to get a deeper, darker blue as he descended, and the sea life became less bountiful in number, but larger in size. Giant sea turtles, sharks, and larger fish slowed down to observe this new bright orange creature in their midst, but generally ignored him after a few seconds of inspection.

Jon's voice came over the computer monitor, most likely to himself. "My God, it's gorgeous."

"Okay, sonny, enjoy the ride, but when you hit the bottom, I want to see your game face," said the chief.

"Aye, aye, chief. But the view—it's amazing."

A twelve-foot tiger shark glided past him, its dark eyeball staring through the glass faceplate of the helmet for a moment before deciding he probably didn't taste good. Jon's smile never changed as he whispered a quiet, "*Daaaamn . . .*"

When Jon's heavy boots hit the bottom, he went to work. His training task required him to walk a one-hundred-foot perfect square pattern, following the compass built into the arm of his suit. His helmet lights provided illumination in the darkness of the six-hundred-foot ocean. Although he could feel the cold inside the suit, he was comfortable. More than anything, he was just excited to be down at si hundred feet, alone with nature while breathing normal air at surface pressure. It was nothing short of amazing. When he finished his square walk, he was back where he started, to the satisfaction of CWO Gautreau who was watching from above.

"Excellent. Now take a flight. Fifty feet and back, see how it maneuvers," said the chief's voice inside his helmet.

The thrusters on his jet pack made him feel like an astronaut as he flew through the water column as graceful as a fish. Although tethered to the ship via light wire cables on his helmet, he felt total freedom in the ocean depths. "Skipper, this suit is amazing. Let's go find a couple of nukes!"

"Slow down, Mr. Cousteau," replied the chief. "Time for you to practice picking up objects. Go find some large rocks to pick up and move around. Let's see how easy it's going to be for you to open up a rusty airplane and connect a few large nuclear weapons to cables for removal."

The team watched in silence as their friend amazed them from six hundred feet.

"He makes it look easy," said Ripper quietly to Moose.

"We ever had an easy mission?" replied Moose.

Ripper just looked at him blankly.

Moose nodded. "Exactly."

CHAPTER 9

Kampong Aht
Brunei

Mohammed Awad and Hamdi Fazil, having made all of the arrangements through Abdul Ali, the minister of the interior, arrived at Tarap with thirty of their most dependable men. Once in Tarap, the group got into several small riverboats and followed the meandering brown river south.

The region was extremely remote, with only the river to guide them. Kampongs, small hamlets or villages, would appear for a brief moment as their tiny armada passed by, and then they would see no sign of human life for another thirty or forty minutes. The air was thick with humidity and insects, and rainstorms could be seen in the distance. Giant birds floated in silence over the canopy of the jungle. It was breathtakingly beautiful as well as terrifying.

Hazrol, their Bruneian guide, drove the lead boat. Seven boats followed him, two crammed with weapons, ammunition, supplies, lumber, and construction tools. When they reached a small kampong called Aht, located within the Labi Forest Reserve, they pulled their boats to the muddy bank and began unloading. The Labi Reserve was a large national park of sorts, although very few people ever visited the remote location. Aht had existed for a few hundred years and was allowed to remain after the area had been deemed "protected" by the government. The villagers still wore tribal loincloths and not much else.

They lived in small huts up on stilts above the river and lived on fish and whatever they could hunt and forage, the same way their ancestors had done for generations. Their entire society was an extended family that married outside their own village once a year, the only time they ever wandered more than a kilometer from where they were born.

Hazrol walked through the muddy water and waved up at the locals with a big smile, which was returned. The village was built on stilts over the water and jungle, with the small thatched huts connected to each other by a series of plank bridges. The children stood behind the legs of their parents as they watched the strangers get off of their boats and climb up to their village. The small wooden planks that acted as pedestrian bridges across the brown water below were narrow, and it suddenly became very crowded. Behind the village, the land slowly rose toward small hills and drier terrain that would make a good place to train future warriors of Islam.

Hazrol was eventually taken to the village chief, a man wearing a loincloth and headband of leather and feathers. A long necklace hung from his bony shoulders. He smiled, showing missing teeth among the brown remaining ones. Whatever leaf the villagers liked to chew, it didn't bode well for their teeth.

Hazrol and the man spoke for quite a while, as Mohammed and Hamdi supervised the unloading of the boats. All of the men were soaked with sweat. The group wore over-the-knee shorts and light tunics, sandals, and head coverings called *songkoks*, and carried AK-47s. Their ethnicities were mixed, having been brought in from Malaysia, the Philippines, and even Syria and Iraq. They had all come for one purpose—to spread their vision of Islam.

The men, a devout group, watched the topless female villagers with wild eyes. As hot as they were, they wouldn't even take off their own shirts. To have women parading around naked was outrageous, but quite exciting.

Hazrol and the chief stood up after their chat, and the chief began shouting to his people. From every hut came the villagers to the voice of their chief. They were a quiet group, smiling and holding hands with their older children as they walked along the path of plank bridges. When the entire village was assembled along the planks in front of the chief's hut, the crowd numbered about forty people of every age. They were all slender and brown, with long black hair. A beautiful woman combed her young son's hair with her fingers, getting his long black hair out of his big brown eyes. It was like a peaceful scene from a *National Geographic* photo.

Hazrol bowed to the chief and walked to Mohammed. "This is everyone."

"You're sure? No one off hunting? This is all of them?"

Hazrol spoke briefly to the chief and nodded to Mohammed. "They're all back from the morning hunting and fishing. It's time to prepare the afternoon meal."

Mohammed gave an order to his men, who jogged up to the group along the wooden planks and raised their weapons. The villagers had never seen an AK-47 before and none of them even attempted to run. They smiled at the visitors, most of them holding hands with their families. As the roar of machine gun fire sent birds into the air, the villagers dropped like stones into the brown water below, where they would become part of the food chain. Blood and human tissue showered the sun-bleached planks as the water turned red.

When the assault rifles stopped firing, Hamdi stepped forward and pulled his Makarov pistol. He checked each body, and shot any survivors he found in the head before kicking them into the river below. A baby began crying from beneath its mother, and Hamdi pulled it from her dead body. He pointed his Makarov at the infant and realized his magazine was spent. Rather than reload, he simply threw the baby into the brown river below, where it quickly disappeared beneath the current.

Mohammed shook hands with Hazrol. "You've done well. This will make an ideal location, and we can build training facilities in the higher ground."

Hazrol bowed. "The village is yours."

CHAPTER 10

Langley

CIA desk chief Darren Davis thought for a long time before he made the call. Cascaes said he was out. He and Julia had retired from the Company and disappeared. Darren had respected their privacy and left them alone, but this was different. In a world where the popular motto was "trust no one," an old friend like Cascaes was invaluable. Chris Cascaes had been the original leader of the team going back a few years and several missions. After a career with the SEALs and then with CIA, Chris had been lucky enough to fall in love. He was burnt out, and Julia had been his salvation. The two of them had quit together and taken off for parts unknown months ago. Darren stared at the phone for another moment, then picked it up and dialed.

It rang several times and Darren closed his eyes and got ready to hang up when Chris answered his phone and said hello.

"Hey. I was trying to decide if I'd leave voice mail or not."

"I was trying to decide if I'd pick up or not."

There was only a split second of silence, but it was palpable and awkward. Darren said, "I wouldn't bother unless I thought you'd want to know."

Chris held his breath on his end of the phone, wondering which one of his old friends was dead. "Everyone okay?" he asked cautiously.

41

"Health-wise, yeah. The team's off training and everyone is good. Different kind of problem."

"You know I'm out. Like, *out*-out. I'm done, Darren."

"I know. Like I said, different kind of problem."

There was another pause.

"I have a civilian phone these days," said Chris.

"Yeah, I know. Where are you?"

"Key West. Just got back from St. Lucia. I have to tell you, retired life has been pretty damn fantastic. Thanks for the combat pay. If we keep having this much fun, I may have to actually get a real job."

"Key West is a small place. I can find you easy enough. SOCOM has an airstrip there at their base. I'll be down in a few hours and walk to a little bar I know and give you a call. You free for a drink?"

"Of course. A drink. Can I bring Julia?"

"Sure. See you in a few."

⊕

Four hours later, Chris got a text from Darren Davis. *See you at the Half Shell for a beer and an oyster. Outside table.*

Chris and Julia walked hand in hand to the busy restaurant, a favorite of tourists and locals alike. It was easy to spot Darren—he was the only guy in slacks and a dress shirt, although the tie had been unknotted and was hanging from his now-open collar. Darren stood when Chris and Julia walked in, and the smiles were genuine. They exchanged hugs and back slaps, and sat at the outdoor table under the large yellow awning. It was over eighty degrees, and the sun was beating down on the Keys like it did most days.

Julia slid her sunglasses up into her long dark hair. Her big brown eyes twinkled in the sunlight. Chris pulled his sunglasses off and hung them from his polo shirt. They were both wearing shorts and looked a lot more relaxed than their former CIA boss. The waitress came by, grabbed their order, and left.

"So what was so important that you took your private jet to come visit us in Key West?" asked Chris.

Darren glanced around and leaned forward, speaking in a quiet voice. "Wallace Holstrum's been set up. I'm a hundred percent sure of it."

Chris glanced at Julia and looked puzzled. "By whom? How?"

"Not sure of the 'who' yet, but the FBI has him under house arrest for downloading kiddie porn. They raided his house in a large-scale bust."

"*What*?" Chris said it so loud it was almost a shout. "What the fuck, man?"

They all went silent as the waitress returned with their drinks. They gave her polite smiles and waited for her to leave.

"Yeah, that about sums it up," said Darren, taking a long drink from his cold beer and wiping his sweaty face with the back of his hand.

"I don't know Darren as well as you two do, but doesn't everyone inside think it's a setup?" asked Julia.

"Everyone I know agrees it isn't legit, but the FBI won't back off. DHS came in and made him take a leave of absence while they do a full investigation. Back channels say it may have been a Chinese hack, but we don't know yet. In the meantime, it gets Wallace out of his office and disrupts everything inside the Company, which helps everyone except us."

"Wow," was all Chris could muster.

"Yeah. Wow," replied Darren.

Julia took Chris's hand and held it tightly. "So what does this have to do with Chris or me?" she asked.

Darren stared at the table, took another long drink, and then exhaled slowly. "There are very few people in the world I trust completely. You two make the short list, and you're outside the Company, which may be a good thing in this case."

Chris sat back and looked at Julia, then Darren. "We're out, Darren. I told you that on the phone."

"I'm going to share something that's so highly classified, I may have to arrest myself," said Darren quietly.

Chris and Julia both leaned in closer just as the waitress came back with their oysters. They all leaned back and smiled, and the second she was gone, leaned back in.

"We've been following a case closely that didn't lead where we thought it would. It would normally go to the FBI at this point, but in this case, it can't. In fact, I'm not sure where it *can* go. We have a huge problem, Chris. A political nightmare. The problem is, while it should be the FBI's case, they wouldn't do anything other than tip off the perpetrator and make it go away."

"I'm not following you," said Chris quietly.

"There's a chance, and I'm hoping I'm wrong, that it wasn't the Chinese that fucked Wallace. What if it's our own people? The FBI director and the White House are very tight, not like Holstrum. The president keeps Wallace because he's great at his job, not because he likes him. The secretary of state and Director Gallo are also very tight. Hell, they dine together and Gallo plays golf with the secretary's husband."

"I still don't follow you, Darren."

"Yeah," said Julia. "You need to start at the beginning. Director Holstrum gets arrested for allegedly downloading kiddie porn because someone wants him out of the way. I understand that. But what other investigation are you talking about?"

"Top secret," whispered Darren.

"Understood," said Chris quietly.

Darren looked at Julia, and she nodded.

"We've been following stolen art from the Middle East. ISIS has been destroying everything they see, but occasionally, when they come across something that's special but small enough to move, they try and sell it on the black market. We're talking tens of millions of dollars."

"Okay," said Julia.

"So we found an Arab who's been selling in the US. The person who's been buying the art presents a huge problem. I think you may be in a position to help, Darren. Privately. Outside the agency."

They all took a break and drank their beers.

"Who's the customer?" asked Julia.

Darren glanced around and spoke so softly they could barely hear him. "Danielle Reynaud."

Julia and Chris looked at each other, then back at Darren. "As in, the secretary of state?" asked Chris.

"Holy shit," said Julia.

"Yes. And yes. Holy shit," said Darren.

"So you won't tell Gallo because you think he'd cover it up? Seriously? That's a big leap," said Chris.

"Not at all. Reynaud thinks she's our next president. Gallo wants to stay on her good side. And they're more than just friends."

"No way, he's banging that old hag?" asked Chris.

Darren laughed for the first time. "No, not like that. Good God. Even Gallo wouldn't hit that. No—they have some mutual business ventures."

"Is that even legal?" asked Julia.

"It's a gray area. One that the FBI won't be looking at any time soon."

They each ate a few oysters for a minute and tried to digest what had just been said.

Chris stared at his empty oyster shell. "So you think Reynaud knows that Wallace was on to her and set him up?"

Darren shrugged. "I don't know. I don't think she knew we were on to her. As far as setting up Wallace, it would be tough to do. And I don't think Gallo would help her with that—that's way too risky. Hell, for all we know it can be China or Iran.

But I do know that Reynaud is spending big bucks from a State Department account to buy stolen artwork from ISIS. That's a *fact*."

"So why not just run with that?" asked Chris.

"I don't trust Gallo not to bury it or tip her off. "

"And what would you want us to do?"

"Break into her houses and photograph her art collections. Get some hard evidence that she possesses stolen art."

"I thought you said you had that already?"

"We have wire transfers to a guy we know is selling stolen art, but she's a crafty snake. She'll say the guy is doing State Department work or some bullshit. We need proof. And I can't open a case file on her and have agents breaking into her house."

"Great, so you want me to get arrested," said Chris.

"Us. Not 'me.' Us. If you go I go," said Julia.

"Darren . . ." Chris started to shake his head.

"I wouldn't ask you if I didn't need you. I'll help you get it done. I'll have blueprints of her houses and I can get the alarm codes via computer hack before you break in so you won't trip any. We can take care of outside cameras from our end. We'll hit the houses when she's out of town. I have one agent who knows about this, and she'll help you, too. I just need you to get inside, take pictures, maybe steal something small enough to carry, and that's it."

"And then what?"

"And then, when I have proof, I can go to the president or the DHS director."

Julia looked at Chris. "It's Wallace. We can't say no."

"This is going to cost you another dozen oysters," said Chris, looking sullen.

CHAPTER 11

Bandar Seri Begawan
Brunei

Apo and Bruce were met at the airport by one of Brunei Petroleum's drivers and taken to their office in Bandar Seri Begawan, not too far from the Sultan's palace. They passed a few billboards with the sultan on them, wearing his full military dress uniform. He had presented himself with dozens of medals and ribbons and looked quite impressive. The Malay slogans under the picture saluted the sultan's greatness.

The Mercedes sped along new highways that had very little traffic. They arrived at a modern-looking steel and glass building, complete with a large picture of the sultan in the front window. The driver opened their door and brought them to another man who escorted them up an escalator to a lobby where yet another man greeted them. A woman in a hijab brought them a tray of tea, which they thanked her for, and then they followed the other man down a hallway to a conference room.

They entered the room, which was empty, and took seats at a very large table with enough chairs for twenty more people. They were alone in the room, but assumed they were being observed with unseen cameras, so they sat in silence and waited. Eventually, the door opened and three men entered. After bows, handshakes, and greetings, they sat down and began their discussions.

47

Bruce began the presentation with maps and geologic surveys, all fictitious, but believable enough based on the existing oil fields in the area. He showed an area shaded in red that covered a large expanse near Brunei's newest artificial island.

"If we hit the pocket we believe is located in this location, you'll be pumping natural gas and crude for five hundred years. The production, once in full operation, will dwarf anything in the Middle East. It can make Brunei a world oil powerhouse. I can't emphasize enough just how excited we are." Bruce took a dramatic pause to read the smiling faces. "Now, I'm not saying it's going to be easy. These are going to be very deep drills that will require our most sophisticated drilling techniques and our best people. If it was easy to find, the Chinese would already be pumping the area."

The Bruneians took the bait and one of them snapped at Bruce. "The Chinese have no jurisdiction in this area, no matter what they claim! International law is on our side on this."

Bruce bowed slightly. "Of course. And this is why we are approaching *you* with this deal. The Chinese have been very, very aggressive in trying to acquire our specialized drilling platforms and special skills to begin exploration in this area of the South China Sea. We believe, as backed by The Hague's findings, that this oil clearly belongs to Brunei. By striking oil quickly, you can reaffirm your rights to the area. I envision dozens of platforms flying the flag of Brunei within eighteen months. That said, we would like to begin exploratory drilling immediately. The Chinese continue to expand their claims, pushing south. If you are already drilling and producing, they'd have a much harder time trying to say they found it first."

Several of the men nodded. Their chairman spoke up. "And what do you see as a fair contract?"

Bruce waited before answering, allowing the drama to build. "We anticipate such large production, we're willing to take thirty-five percent, but only if we can start immediately, before any entanglements with China could occur."

The Bruneians tried to hide their total elation. Interglobe has just given away the farm in the worst business move in history. The chairman stood and extended his hand. "Gentlemen, we have deal."

Over the next hour, they began the process of drawing up contracts to begin oil exploration off the coast. While Apo and Bruce had to agree to employ locals to boost the local economy and create jobs, the initial offshore rig setup and geologic mapping would be done by Interglobe Oil staff only. By the time the locals would be brought in to run the daily operations, the nukes would be recovered, the rig would be abandoned, and Interglobe would be a ghost.

When Apo and Bruce left, the gentlemen in the room laughed and exchanged congratulations with each other on sealing the best deal in the history of their company. Evidently, the expression "if it sounds too good to be true, it probably is" didn't translate into Malay. They spent the next hour running numbers and estimates, and privately deciding on how to spend their huge bonuses.

Apo and Bruce left Brunei later that day on the pretext they had other business in the region and flew to Japan, where they took another flight to Okinawa. Okinawa provided a secure area at the American Marine base at Camp Hansen, home to six thousand US Marines. Using a "clean room" in a secure communications building as their temporary residence, they were able to speak freely to Langley without worrying about being bugged, or being obvious that they knew they were being observed, back in Brunei.

After the third time Director Holstrum's direct phone went to voice mail, Apo called Darren Davis. He informed Darren they were in a clean room in Okinawa and caught him up on their travels and the great news about the oil drilling deal.

When Apo was finished with the briefing, it was Darren's turn. "I hope you're sitting down," said Darren. And then he told Apo everything about the FBI investigation. He also told Apo that he was doing what he could to assist their boss behind the scenes. "In the meantime, you'll be dealing with me directly."

They spoke for a while about the possibilities of Holstrum's situation, neither of them entertaining for a second the idea that Holstrum was a pedophile. That left the Chinese, Iranians, Russians, or possibly someone on the inside as the most likely culprits. Even if Reynaud was aware she was under investigation, that was still a long shot. Another "situation that's being looked at carefully."

When they hung up, Apo and Bruce voiced their frustrations and began planning the next parts of their operation, which would now involve lots of moving parts.

Very large moving parts.

That floated.

And drilled for oil offshore.

CHAPTER 12

USS *John Warner*
6° 20' 25" North 113° 17' 47" East

"Steady as she goes, Mr. Talbot," said Commander Norman.

"Aye, aye, skipper," replied the pilot.

Commander Vince Norman was watching the Chinese surface fleet on a flat-screen monitor. Yesterday, the same Chinese ships had harassed another US guided missile cruiser as it traveled a patrol route south from Japan through the South China Sea.

"Change course to Lima November," ordered the skipper. *Lima November*, "Location of Nukes," was the designated call sign of the location of the downed aircraft and its nuclear payload. "Mr. Burdge, you have the chair."

The XO took over the bridge, and Vince headed back to his small wardroom to read the encrypted e-mails he had received through the photonic mast's electronics. The sub could only send and receive communications when the mast was breaking the surface, and each extension of the mast meant lots of new e-mails and possibly new orders via the Submarine Satellite Information Exchange Subsystem. The SSIXS used ultra-high frequency waves bounced off satellites to avoid enemy detection.

It took almost an hour to catch up on all of the messages and intelligence reports. The last one took the longest to read, and gave him a smile. Finally. A real mission. Babysit the crash site and help recover two nuclear weapons in complete secrecy.

51

CHAPTER 13

Special Operations Command Pacific—SOCPAC

An oil platform had been borrowed by the CIA from who-knows-where and for lord-knows-how-much-money and towed in by ship to the waters west of Honolulu. Once there, the team was flown in by helicopter. As they hopped off on to the massive floating structure, the men gazed at their steel surroundings with a sense of awe.

"Damn," whispered Moose, half to himself. "This thing is huge . . ."

"Yeah, no shit," replied Ripper.

"Pretty good view, though," said Hodges, the sniper. He was always looking for a high perch and just couldn't help himself. "I think I could hit a Taliban target in Afghanistan from here."

"You must have some new kind of gun we ain't heard of yet," mumbled McCoy.

"Welcome home, gentlemen," barked CWO Gautreau. "For the next few weeks, you will be living here learning how to fake operating an offshore drilling rig while training for the underwater recovery of two nuclear bombs."

"Offshore drilling and two nukes, what could possibly go wrong?" asked Jon Cohen sarcastically.

"You will *not* be drilling! You will be *faking* it!" snapped the chief. "All you need to do is be able to turn the appropriate dials and operate computers that aren't attached to anything underwater. If all goes well, no one will even visit the rig, and

52

you can just focus on the recovery operation. This training is simply to make sure you can look like a bunch of professional oil rig workers if the Bruneians send anyone out to take a peek, you follow?"

Several "aye, ayes" sang out in response.

"Follow me below deck and stow your gear, then I'll give you a tour of your new home."

For the next three hours, the team learned their way around the massive steel structure. Being seamen, the vessel reminded them of being aboard a ship, albeit a very cumbersome design that wouldn't sail well. It would, however, float in almost any sea conditions, including tsunamis and hurricanes. They each had a small room, slightly larger than what they were used to on US Navy vessels. The furniture was new and everything looked fresh and clean.

"Ah, the private sector," said Moose with a smile as he patted his mattress.

Ripper had thrown his gear into his own room across the narrow hallway. "Hey, I got a TV in my room!"

"Don't get used to it," shouted Moose. "Besides, where we're going, ain't gonna be nothing on TV worth watching."

"Okay, ladies! Topside!" ordered the chief.

The seven members of the team hustled back up to the deck near the helipad, then followed Gautreau into the office, which was the heart of the controls. From the office, they looked down on the platform and could see the drilling machinery.

"Tomorrow, an actual oil worker is coming aboard to instruct you on the basics of running this platform. Today, I'm merely giving you the tour of the rig and some basic vocabulary terms to learn. I have books for each of you to start reading tonight so you have some clue what the man will be talking about tomorrow. You don't need to know how to actually drill and run that part of the rig, but you *do* have to know how to anchor the cables, which is complicated. This platform floats, but gets anchored to the seabed with long steel cables. You're going to get towed into position near the artificial island where the plane is, and then it'll be up to you to anchor this monstrosity into position."

"This thing is getting towed to Brunei?" asked Eric.

Gautreau shook his head. "Fucking Marines. I'm glad you're good at shooting. No. You are *not* getting towed halfway around the world in this thing. It would take a year. You're flying to the Philippines and then being taken to the rig you're going to use. *That* rig will be towed into position, and then you'll anchor up near the crash site."

Eric shrugged. Jon pushed him and laughed.

Ray Jensen looked around with a strange expression on his face. Ryan O'Connor stared at him. "What is it?"

Ray continued looking around. "It's kind of cool. This rig I mean. I could see myself working on one of these when I retired. Out on the water. Quiet. It's pretty cool."

Ryan made a face. "Dude, when we get out of the navy, I'm finding a job surrounded by chicks. You want to spend another decade surrounded by smelly dudes?"

Ray cocked his head. "Good point. But I bet these guys make bank! Collect a fat check and fly someplace with lots of chicks and a pocket full of cash."

"Now you're talking!" said Ryan with a smile.

They followed Gautreau and their teammates down a long set of stairs, deeper into the bowels of their strange new home.

CHAPTER 14

Washington, DC

Chris and Julia had flown back to DC three days after Darren left. He had set them up with a company-owned apartment in a nice, tree-lined neighborhood in Dupont Circle. It was a neighborhood that they could never have afforded on their own, not far from the Argentinian embassy.

"He must really love you," Julia said as she walked into the apartment, gazing around at the furniture and layout of their new temporary home.

"Don't kid yourself. He picked this spot because it's close to one of Reynaud's apartments."

"One of?" asked Julia.

"Yeah. Madam Secretary has two places in DC, one in San Francisco, one in Boston, and one in New York City."

"Why two here?"

"No idea. I'm guessing she lives in one and uses the other one for off-the-grid meetings."

"You don't like her much, do you?"

"Not particularly. I've met a few guys that worked her security detail. They can't stand her. She's about the nastiest, most degrading human being on the planet from what I've heard. The fact that she's corrupt as hell and gets away with it every day is pretty infuriating, too."

"She might be your next president," said Julia with a smirk.

"Yeah, well, maybe not if she's in jail."

Julia stopped walking and stared at Chris. "Hey. Let me ask you something. Do you think there's even the slightest chance that we're being used?"

Chris folded his arms. "What do you mean?"

"I mean, what if we're being manipulated for some political reason to try and discredit her. You trust Darren one hundred percent?"

"Absolutely. He ran every mission I've been on since joining the team."

"This whole thing is just very disturbing," she said. "It's one thing to work a mission overseas against a nation state or terror organization. This is way different. And illegal."

"You don't have to be a part of this. I told you—I'd prefer that you weren't."

"And I told you," she replied, walking to him, "that if you go, I go." She embraced him and gave him a soft kiss. "I'm just a little paranoid. DC scares me."

"*That*, I understand. I feel safer in the jungle, myself."

"So what happens next?"

Chris looked around at the beautiful apartment. "We unpack, clean up, christen this place, and then call in." He smiled and gave her a longer kiss.

Two hours later, they called Darren on his cell and caught him coming out of a meeting. Darren gave Chris a new e-mail address and password set up just for him for this mission, and told him to check it. Chris and Julia read their e-mails, which included the security code for the alarm panel at the secretary's home in DC.

"The alarm code?" said Julia, suitably impressed.

"It's the CIA. If they can't get a residential alarm code, we have a problem."

"No guards?"

"Secret Service is only there when she's there. They routinely sweep the place for bugs and bombs, but they aren't there twenty-four/seven. Darren says he left night-vision equipment for us in the bedroom closet. We're going tonight to snoop around. The secretary's schedule shows her out of town at a function for another two days. Davis will have the cameras turned off at 0300. We'll key in the codes, get inside with the night viz, and take a look. Anything that looks like imported art gets photographed."

Julia smiled. "You know, when we were running around in the jungle getting shot at, I was out of my element. I'm not a combat soldier. But spying and sneaking around? It's my specialty."

CHAPTER 15

Kampong Aht

Mohammed and Hamdi sat in the chief's lodge, now theirs, looking at a map on their laptop. Hazrol had their men clearing an area in the jungle where they would be training. It was heavy jungle, and in four days there had barely been any progress. One of the men had suggested burning an area to clear it, but Mohammed was worried about the smoke being spotted by a Labi forest ranger. It would have to be done by hand, but that was okay—it made them stronger.

Them. Not him. He and Hamdi stayed in the hut watching and planning future attacks.

"We can make this the largest training camp in the world," said Mohammed. "With the sultan's promised cooperation, and this heavy jungle to hide us from satellites, we could have ten thousand fighters and no one would even know."

Hamdi nodded. "Have we been given a target yet?"

"We had a target before we left Syria."

Hamdi waited, slightly annoyed that he hadn't been told earlier. He understood the need for secrecy and his role as second in command, but it bothered him nonetheless. He sat and waited for Mohammed to share the information. After making Hamdi wait for far too long, an expression of his power, Mohammed finally spoke.

"We shall kill the lion."

Hamdi waited, not understanding.

"Singapore, the Lion City, is a commercial and banking world center. Disruption of such a regional powerhouse will impact the entire globe. The Chinese, the Americans, even the house of Saud. A large-scale event in that city can be as devastating as attacking New York or Paris or Brussels."

"Singapore . . ." repeated Hamdi, lost in thought.

"Did you know it was the Jews that developed their armed forces?"

Hamdi's face fell. "How can that be correct?"

"It's true. When the British left and Singapore became a sovereign nation, the new government was worried that Malaysia would invade. Israel supplied and trained the new city-state. Singapore has one of the most sophisticated militaries in Southeast Asia because of the Jews. They even fly American jets."

"The Jews don't have good weapons," said Hamdi.

Mohammed looked at Hamdi, realizing the man was simply uneducated. He leaned forward and spoke in a quiet, serious tone. "Don't let your allegiance to the Prophet blind you to the truth. Israel survives only because it has excellent weapons and soldiers."

Hamdi grew angry. "Those murdering Jews will all be killed!"

"Yes, in time, they will be exterminated. But don't underestimate them. In any event, their planes and ships can't save them. Our forces will enter the country quietly and detonate weapons all over their city. Their financial system will collapse, as will their entire government."

Hamdi was still sulking over the notion that Israel had decent weapons. "When?"

Mohammed smiled. "Patience, brother. We need to train these soldiers of Islam first, and add another hundred or so to our numbers. For this attack to be effective, we'll need a lot of men. One or two bombs won't be enough. We need to cripple the city for months. This takes planning and lots of explosives."

"When do we get the weapons?" asked Hamdi.

"We're working on that now. The sultan's minister, Abdul Ali, has promised us we will have everything that we need, God willing."

Hamdi still couldn't get past the thought of the Israelis having decent arms or soldiers. He randomly blurted, "We should have kept a few of those villagers."

Mohammed shook his head and pointed at Hamdi sternly. "We need the men focused! This isn't Syria, Hamdi. No distractions!"

Hamdi thought about the sex slaves he had enjoyed in Syria and sighed. Once Sharia law was instituted all over the globe, and he was a ruling member of the new order, he would have whatever he wanted.

"Very well, Mohammed. I'll be patient . . ."

CHAPTER 16

Oil Rig off Honolulu

Eric Hodges was lying on his belly, with his new sniper rifle set up on bipod legs. Moose had watched the current and then dropped an empty plastic bottle into the water from two stories up. He watched the small bottle float away quickly. In only a few minutes, it was almost a mile away. Even with his binoculars, Moose could barely see it. Eric had loaded a Lapua .338 round into the new Mk 21 Precision Sniper Rifle, or PSR.

"Five bucks says he hits it," said Jon.

No one would take the bet.

"C'mon. Nobody? Book says 1,500 meters. He's over 1,600!" They all shook their heads.

"It *is* pretty small," said Eric in his Oklahoma drawl.

Ripper sat next to Eric with a spotter scope. "Wind five knots from the west. Target sixteen hundred fifty meters and moving away."

Everyone shoved fingers in their ears.

Eric focused on the tiny bottle and felt the slow rhythm of the oil rig moving in the ocean. It was a slow, steady rhythm, like his heartbeat and breathing. Within a few seconds, everyone around him disappeared, and it was just him and a tiny speck bobbing on the water.

Eric squeezed slowly and the barrel jumped with recoil. They were so far away it actually took a second for the bullet to pass through the bottle, blowing it to tiny pieces.

61

Ripper watched through the spotter scope. "Outstanding. You still got it, kid."

Eric smiled only slightly. "Kinda hard with the deck moving."

"That's what my buddies said when they hit those Somali pirates. But none of them missed, either. Good shootin'," said Ripper.

Moose nodded. "Okay, show's over. Everyone cough up their hundred bucks they bet me." He smiled, but no one thought he was funny.

They watched the helicopter come in a little while later and land on their helipad. A tall, lanky fellow got out of the bird wearing a jumpsuit and hard hat and looking like a guy that would actually work on an oil platform.

He was introduced and brought to the office, where he would spend the next week trying to teach six SEALs and a Force Recon Marine how to operate the basics on a multimillion-dollar oil platform. Fortunately, they didn't have to learn the most dangerous and complicated part, which was the actual extraction of pressurized gas and oil. For their purposes, they just needed to learn how to deploy the anchor cables and, later on, to operate a special winch which would be on their actual rig for lifting two nuclear bombs. Anything else would be a matter of faking it with computers that would "look busy" should anyone inspect their rig.

By the time the man left, the team was ready to fly west and begin their real mission.

The team left the rig by helicopter and flew back to Honolulu. From Hawaii, they said goodbye to CWO Gautreau and traveled to the Philippines on a commercial jet in plain clothes, under false names with Canadian passports. They were all employees of Interglobe Oil Exploration, out of British Columbia. Once in Manila, they checked into a high-end business hotel, where they showered and slept a few hours, and then assembled in the lobby bar where they were met by their friend Apo Yessayan and a new man named Bruce Wang.

It was a busy bar-restaurant, and everyone stayed in character. Apo walked over to Moose and extended his hand. "Nice to meet you in person, Al. This is your supervisory crew, eh?"

"Hey Frank, nice to meet you, too. Yeah, these are my supervisors. We'll pick up the rest of the crew in Brunei once we're set up with the rig." Apo introduced Bruce to Moose, ordered drinks at the bar, and then the team took a large table for an epic meal. Bruce and Apo sat at opposite ends of the table, where they could quietly chat with the men. The loud conversations were about oil, hockey, beer, and women. The quieter conversations were about nuclear warheads, terrorist activity around the globe, submarines, and ships. The men enjoyed a fun night of eating and drinking in between serious briefing information. Tomorrow they would fly to Brunei, a country that didn't allow alcohol unless you were the sultan or attending one of his large parties.

CHAPTER 17

Langley

Darren Davis and his assistant, Dex Murphy, sat in Darren's office. Darren was in his usual state of grumpy and exhausted. He rubbed his face and started catching Dex up on the latest aggravation. "DHS has one of their highest level IT people looking at Wallace's computer. This woman has top secret clearance, but still, this is *insane!*"

"Unfuckingbelievable. The director of the Central Intelligence Agency's secure computer, being examined for kiddie porn? It's beyond ridiculous. Does anyone on the whole fucking planet believe that Holstrum would download that shit into his secure computer?" Dex threw his empty coffee cup into the trash can with extra velocity.

"No one I know. But then again, I don't get to hang out in the same circles as the secretary of state," mumbled Darren.

"Look, chief, I don't like that woman either, but you really think she'd start something *this* big just to screw the director? And how would she even get it done? What are our people saying about all this?"

"That was a lot of questions. First, if she knew what we were looking at, then yes, she might go after us any way she could . . ."

"What does that mean?"

64

"It was a very compartmentalized operation, Dex. I'm looping you in now in case they find shit on my computer next."

Dex sat back and folded his arms.

"Top secret," said Darren.

"Understood," replied Dex quietly.

"We've had the secretary of state under surveillance for months."

"*What?*" Dex turned red.

"Yup. It would be illegal if we had opened an investigation on her. But we didn't. We opened it on a man named Ali Sawaad. It just *led* us to her."

"Holy shit, Darren." He leaned forward and absorbed every word.

"Ali Sawaad is a mid-level piece of garbage that sells art for ISIS. ISIS uses the money for ammo and guns, of course. It just so happens that one of the world's largest art collectors happens to be the secretary of state."

"I don't even know what to say," replied Dex. His face showed his shock.

"Yeah. A real can of worms. Anyway, the case officer is Cheryl Cook. Cookie. You know her?"

"No, sir."

"She's thorough and competent. When the bank routing numbers came back as a US government account . . ."

"A *government* account?" blurted Dex.

"You don't think she'd use her *own* money for this, do you?"

"Holy shit, this keeps getting better and better," said Dex, incredulous.

"Yeah. The secretary uses a little slush fund that covers confidential informants et cetera in the Middle East. Pretty impossible to prove that this weasel Sawaad isn't one of her CIs, except for the fact that we've been following his art smuggling for months trying to use it to find ISIS top-tier targets. We never guessed it would lead to Reynaud. But here it is, and now we have a problem."

"And you think she knows you found out, and this was to bury the boss? That won't make the case against her go away. I don't get it."

Darren shrugged. "You don't get it because you think like an honest guy too much. In her mind, she's the next president. Once she's in the big office, she makes the rules. It's not that far away. If she drags this thing out, it keeps Wally under wraps and maybe she has leverage to keep his mouth shut in exchange for his reputation, who knows?"

"Who else knows about this?" asked Dex

"Wally, Cookie, and us. That's it. As far as I know. I haven't been able to have a private conversation with the director since this happened. He's unofficially under house arrest and on unpaid leave until they finish searching his computer."

"The case files on the investigation into the secretary are on that computer?"

"No. Even their IT people can't access this. They can look all they want. It isn't on his computer. This was run out of my office, and they don't have access to my computer."

Dex stood up and walked around the office for a minute, thinking in frustration. "It still leaves the question of 'how'? If it was her, how the hell would she get that crap on his computer?"

"I don't know. I told DHS that this was our issue to deal with, but they wanted an outside agency."

"We'd do the same thing."

"Yeah, I know. But we need to see what they're seeing. Damn it. I want to know where the IP addresses are located," snapped Darren.

"No way in?" asked Dex, cautiously.

"They separated his computer immediately. He's totally off-line."

"No logs or cloud storage?"

"No. The director's computer can download from the cloud, but there's zero backup that route. It's all on his personal server backup, which DHS has as well. Believe me, I've thought about this nonstop. We're stuck waiting for them."

Dex was still in shock. He stood there shaking his head in disbelief. "The director of the CIA's computer is being scoured by another agency. The Russians and Chinese are going to laugh until they piss themselves. Only in America."

"You know, it could turn out to *be* the Chinese or Russians."

"And if it is?"

"Then we start World War III via the World Wide Web."

"Interesting. We'll call it WWW dot three."

"Very funny. Except it won't be. If you think Stuxnet was big, this would open up a whole new level of cyber warfare."

Dex shook his head again. "Hard to believe that the secretary of state planting porn on the director's computer could be the *good* news."

CHAPTER 18

Kampong Aht

Mohammed smiled as he watched the boats unloading at the muddy shoreline. Dozens of men carried crates and boxes as they off-loaded the boats that had ferried them and their supplies fifty kilometers down the brown river to the small village. For almost three weeks, Mohammed's men had been clearing the jungle enough to make firing pits for target practice and create a small obstacle course to get the men into shape. The men had been living mostly on boiled rice with whatever animals they could shoot in the forest or pull from the fish traps. The now-extinct villagers had created a system of fish traps across the river that supplied a steady diet of carp and catfish. Mohammed hoped that there might be some more food in the new supplies.

He watched for almost an hour as the men unloaded the boats under Hamdi's supervision. The new men were assigned to huts around the village. These weren't just deliverymen; they were reinforcements. Hamdi walked up the rickety plank and found Mohammed.

"We're now a real army," he said proudly. "One hundred and seven faithful servants of Islam. They brought enough explosives and supplies to makes vests for everyone. They also have assault rifles and ammunition."

"Excellent. You're in charge of having the vests assembled."

Hamdi bowed. He had spent much of his career teaching others how to make exploding vests as well as IEDs. "It is my honor. When do we leave for Singapore?"

"We have enough men now. Once you have the vests made and the men trained proficiently on the assault rifles, we will coordinate the boat to Singapore. The sultan has promised we'll have whatever we need. It's over 1,200 kilometers to Singapore and will require a large ship that can enter the port."

"And how will we get past the security?" asked Hamdi.

"We'll pay the right people and enter at night. The sultan's men may also be able to help. The next morning, Singapore will begin burning, God willing."

Hamdi hesitated. "Will everyone detonate a vest?"

Mohammed hesitated. He had no intention of blowing himself up. "The leadership must survive to run the next missions."

Hamdi waited.

"I will need you for the future," he said.

Hamdi tried not to show his relief. He would martyr himself if necessary, but preferred the option of enjoying the conquered foes and serving as a new ruler.

"Have you selected targets?" asked Hamdi.

"Many targets," replied Mohammed with a smile. "You will set the timers on the vests for the same time of day, and we will send our martyrs out to their largest businesses, their stock exchange, their casinos, their tourist hotels, and their hospitals. We will shut down their entire economy and leave them in chaos.

"A reserve force will remain here to train the next group of soldiers. You and I will also remain here. From this location, with the sultan's help, we can run any missions in the future. No one will know where we are, and we will unleash God's will all over the world from this humble post."

Hamdi smiled at the vision of cities burning and infidels torn to pieces. "God willing."

Mohammed continued thoughtfully. "Hazrol will lead the men to the ship. Each man will have been given his specific target, and at the correct moment, your vests will detonate. My only regret is that we won't be able to watch it as it happens."

Hamdi nodded. "The blood of the infidels will turn the streets red."

CHAPTER 19

Washington, DC

Chris and Julia were dressed for a night out. In her little black dress and high heels, she was stunning. Her dark hair was pulled back in a bun, showing off her sculpted face and glowing complexion. Chris wore dress jeans and a dark shirt under a dressy vest.

They were ready for a night on the town.

Or, to *look* like they were ready for a night on the town.

They waited until after two in the morning to start walking to the apartment building where the secretary of state kept one of her residences. This apartment was almost twenty-five hundred square feet on the top floor of a ten-story building, and worth a few million because of its location. Dozens of embassies from all over the globe made the area their home, which is why the secretary kept her "work apartment" there. It wasn't her official office, just where she could meet with foreign ambassadors, heads of state, and occasional international art smugglers.

The doorman left at eleven each night and locked the front doors behind him. Only residents with a key could get in after that. Or people who had friends in the CIA. Chris and Julia walked slowly, arm in arm, like a couple who had enjoyed a night out on the town. The August weather was hot and humid, and without the excuse of coats, Julia had to carry a very large but fashionable bag. Chris had texted Darren Davis before turning on to their target street, and security cameras and alarms miraculously turned off. Chris slid his key, compliments of Darren, into the lock and opened the door.

The building was quiet, and only dim lighting remained on in the vestibule. They got into the elevator, used their key once again to gain access to the tenth floor, and headed up to the secretary's apartment. When the doors slid open, they were relieved to see the hallway empty. There were two large apartments that took up the entire tenth floor, and both were vacant at the moment. They quickly keyed into the target apartment and closed the door behind them.

Julia opened her bag and handed Chris his night-vision glasses. She then put her own night-vision glasses on and changed out of her heels into flat-bottomed rubber-soled shoes. The two of them walked quietly room by room and confirmed they were alone, then began photographing every piece of art they saw with their infrared cameras. They finished their search in silence and returned to the front door, where they removed and packed the night viz, and Julia changed back into her heels.

The elevator ride down seemed to take forever, and they held hands and prayed no one would be downstairs waiting for them when the doors slid open. They left without incident and walked quickly back to where they'd come from. The next part of their operation would be a little trickier.

CHAPTER 20

South China Sea

The team stood at the rail of the large trawler, eyes closed and faces to the sun, enjoying the warm rays and ocean spray, as she chugged through calm seas. The men always felt much more at home on the water, other than Hodges, the lone Marine.

Apo and Bruce would be flying out to join them at the oil platform once they were all set up. The semi-submersible was in position, having arrived from Palawan the day before, and floated next to its tender waiting for the crew to arrive and drop the long anchor cables in the exact location.

As the hulking steel tower came into view, the team watched in silence. They were used to being the best at everything they did. Trying to anchor the semi-submersible oil platform into the correct position and act like they knew what they were doing would be stressful, to say the least. While most of the systems were set up to be fully automated by computer, there was still work that needed to be done manually, and learning how to run a multimillion-dollar oil rig typically took more than a one-week crash course.

Ripper leaned over to Moose on the ship's bow rail. "So, skipper—you think we're actually going to be able to anchor this thing, or are we about to sink a few hundred million dollars' worth of gear into the ocean?"

Moose wasn't smiling. "I'd rather be dropped out of an airplane behind enemy lines than do what we have to do next."

"Yeah, but do we *know* what we have to do next?"

"You better hope so. I'll go down with the ship. You'll have to answer to Darren Davis."

Ripper smiled. "I'd rather go down with the ship."

"Exactly."

The ship's whistle went off so loudly that everyone jumped. Moose looked at Ripper. "They're playing our song."

Moose walked up to the bridge of the rusty old trawler and conferred with the captain. They would get close to the rig, and then a small skiff would transport them over. Once there, they would communicate by radio with the rig tender's captain until they were in the exact position they needed to be in, at which time they'd drop the cables into six hundred feet of water.

The trawler slowed until it came to a stop, about a hundred yards away from the other ship. The two ships were dwarfed by the massive steel structure that floated behind the tender. The team loaded their gear onto the skiff below and headed over to their new home, chugging through the gentle swells. The skiff stopped at the waterline platform of the rig and tied off, and the boat's three-man crew helped the team quickly unload their gear and supplies. The group worked quickly and efficiently, the way they always did, and in fifteen minutes, their ride cast off and returned to the trawler.

"There goes our taxi," said Hodges.

The team began the task of bringing the gear up to their rooms via the rig's freight elevator, a mostly open metal cage that made the trip up and down the platform relatively quickly, if not loudly. Moose, Ripper, and Pete McCoy headed to the command center of the rig and powered up the computer system while the other four finished carrying and stowing gear and supplies. McCoy had trained on the computer system that controlled navigation and GPS, and it would be up to him to make sure they were in the right spot. The computer's GPS had been put together by Langley's operational and support personnel and was pre-programmed to the exact coordinates of their nuclear target. These same support personnel had also stashed weapons all over the platform. McCoy sat at the large console looking at their location on a map that was similar to Google Earth and showed their location in real time. Moose and Ripper stood behind him, watching the screens.

McCoy turned on the sound for his headset and mic. "Tender *Pissarro*, this is Oil Platform *Sunrise*, come in, over."

An Australian-sounding voice returned the radio call. "*Sunrise*, this is Captain Emerson of the *Pissarro*. You can call me M. I'm ready for your instructions. Over."

"Thank you, M. Alex here," he replied, referring to the name on his Canadian passport. "My GPS coordinates have our location very close to the target. Good job. Over."

"We aim to please, Mr. Alex. Just tell me where we need to bring you. Over."

"The exact location is almost half a kilometer east by northeast. Location is six degrees, eighteen minutes, and thirty-one point thirty-one degrees north, by one-hundred thirteen degrees, sixteen minutes, and forty-six point fifty-nine degrees east. That will put us in six hundred feet of water. You'll see barges nearby. Over."

"Another island popping up here in the South China Sea? Over."

"Affirmative. Seems to be the fashion these days. Over."

"Right-o, mate. I'll have you parked on that location down to the square millimeter in about twenty minutes. These things take a little finesse, though. I'll be off the radio unless you have an emergency. *Pissarro*, out."

McCoy looked over at Moose and Ripper and shrugged. "That's it, skipper. He'll tow us to the spot, and then we drop the cables."

Moose patted McCoy on the shoulder. "Good job. You stay on the console. Ripper, you're with me. Let's get these sailors in position for the cable drop."

The semi-submersible platform was designed to float in place, slightly submerged once the cables were dropped. By allowing some water into the ballast tanks once on location, the floating platform remained stable even in foul weather. The process of dropping the giant cables served to anchor the platform. The massive cables were extremely heavy, and once horizontally seated on the ocean floor, they would fix the platform's position.

Normally, a platform the size of the *Sunrise* would have a crew of about 120 men, but since this operation had nothing to do with drilling for oil, the skeleton crew present was all they needed to get anchored. The men moved about the platform, releasing safeties and unlocking the mechanisms that would drop the massive cables once Pete McCoy hit the buttons up in the control room.

After a few minutes, the platform stopped moving and the Aussie skipper's voice came back over the radio. "All right, mate. Welcome to your new home. Good luck. I hope you hit plenty of that black gold. Over."

"Excellent. Thank you, skipper. Appreciate the ride. We're preparing to drop our cables, over."

"Right. As soon as you drop your first cable, I'll release our towlines and you're on your own. Cheers, mate. Out."

Pete pressed the button that sounded the blast horn, and smiled ear to ear. He had always wanted to do that aboard a ship. Once the blast was finished, his walkie-talkie crackled.

"Ready on the deck," said Moose's voice.

"Ready here. Dropping the first cable, stand by." McCoy pressed the console button and a few hundred tons of steel cable began running off the giant spool. The metal roared and echoed as it spun off the spool. It hit the ocean surface with a giant splash and then just cut through the water on the way to the bottom. The massive structure rocked only a little as its weight shifted.

McCoy spoke into his radio, "*Sunrise* to *Pissarro*, cable one deployed. Over."

"Right. Good luck. This is the *Pissarro*, cutting you free and heading off. Out."

The tender began releasing its cables thus freeing the platform, as its massive diesel engines chugged back to life. As it slowly moved away from the semi-submersible, McCoy began releasing the other anchoring cables. The platform rocked and swayed gently in the water as hundreds of tons of steel dropped six hundred feet. Within ten minutes, the *Sunrise* was firmly anchored on the seabed floor.

From the top of the platform, the team could see the booms and massive cranes flying Bruneian flags off in the distance, busy at work making a new island in the South China Sea.

CHAPTER 21

Jungle, One Kilometer West of Kampong Aht

Zyy moved silently through the jungle with his youngest son, a ten-year-old now on his first real hunt. Although Yin had practiced with his bow and arrow on birds for several years, he had never gone with his father on a *real* hunt. It was an exciting day, and only the two of them had gone out, by design. Zyy was teaching his son the same way he had taught his two older sons, and the same way his own father had taught him. They were descendants of the Penan people, and were wiry and brown, wearing only loincloths, with bowl-cut black hair.

Yin followed his father's footsteps, each of his small footprints inside his father's. The jungle was steamy and hot, and a mist hung in the foliage. A large pangolin moved on a tree branch, and Yin tapped his father's leg, excited to have spotted it before his father. Zyy patted the boy's head and smiled, but shook his head no. The large anteater was not their quarry.

They continued in silence for another thirty minutes, until Zyy stopped and squatted. He pointed to the large hoofprint in the mud and smiled broadly. A large Bornean bearded pig had been here recently. The plants had been torn up as the animal had rooted around looking for food. Zyy removed the bow from across his back and nocked an arrow. Yin mimicked his father, so excited he could barely contain himself.

Zyy moved along slowly and quietly, until he found what he knew he would—lots of other hoofprints. The animals traveled in family groups, and he hoped they would be able to hunt down two of the juveniles. The parents could produce more, thus not ending the source of their food, and the two smaller animals would be easier to carry than a giant wild hog.

The two of them followed the hoofprints along the trail, speeding up their pace as they grew more anxious. They were extremely focused on the hunt.

The sudden sound of automatic weapon fire scared them so badly they dropped to the ground.

Yin looked at his father, terrified. He had never heard a gun before. Zyy shushed him and waited for it to stop, then took his son's hand and ran quickly through the jungle toward the river. Yin knew better to ask what they were doing; he simply ran along with his father, anxious to know what was making the terrifying noise. It sounded like the stormy sky, but the sun was out. Zyy slowed down as they approached the river, scanning the jungle in every direction as they moved.

Yin saw it first.

A small child had been torn apart by the wild pigs. As destroyed as the body was, it was still discernable as a human child. Yin cried out, then put his hand over his mouth. Zyy grabbed his son to protect him, then spotted the body. He led his son past the corpse, toward the river. It was there that Zyy saw the remnants of multiple half-eaten corpses. Birds picked at them, exposing the bones to the hot sun. Zyy was horrified. There were so many. This was no hunting accident.

He whispered to his son to be invisible and silent, and the two of them worked their way along the river until the gunfire erupted again. Zyy and Yin moved toward the sound like ghosts among the ferns. Finally, they found the source of the noise. Dozens of men were firing guns at targets they had set up in the jungle. Zyy and Yin moved around them, giving them a wide berth, until they could see the kampong called Aht. There were many men there, but they weren't the villagers. Zyy's face fell. These men had come and killed everyone and taken a village that wasn't theirs. He whispered to Yin, and the two of them began racing through the jungle back to their own kampong located half a day away.

CHAPTER 22

USS *John Warner*

Commander Vince Norman sat in his command chair looking at the flat-screen that showed the surface world. The first time he saw the bridge of the new submarine he would be commanding, for a split second he was a bit disappointed. He had always assumed he'd be standing at the periscope, looking out through a small window that only he could view. His disappointment vanished when he saw what the new photonic mast could do. Instead of a scene from some black-and-white World War II movie, he was now in the command chair of a *Star Trek* episode.

With his finger, he used the joystick to scan 360 degrees around the surface world. It was 0200, and completely dark outside, but his monitor made the surface look like daytime, owing to its infrared cameras. When he saw the lights, he zoomed in and smiled.

"Thar she blows," he said with a grin.

The new oil platform stood over 450 feet high at the top of the drill tower. It had safety lights on it that glowed bright yellow on his infrared screen. Because they were at periscope depth, they could send and receive e-mail. The captain could have just called the team on the rig by radio, but for security reasons he used the encrypted e-mail. He typed his message to the e-mail address that had been supplied to him on his last surfacing.

JW to team. Welcome to the South China Sea. We're fully briefed on your mission and position and are prepared to assist in all ways possible. We will provide security and intelligence as you operate. We will also provide escort to the trawler that will be transporting your cargo. Communications will be limited, and only at night. Should you need to alert us for comms, use infrared strobe lights on the rig, and we will contact you as soon as possible. This vessel is capable of transporting all of you in the event of an emergency. Will be able to receive reply until 0215. Good luck, JW, CO

The computer on board the oil platform dinged as the message came in, and Moose, who happened to be on watch, entered the password and opened the e-mail. He typed his brief reply.

Team CO to JW. Nice to have you on our six. Will commence recovery efforts tomorrow and advise. CO, Moose. Out.

Moose leaned back in the heavy leather chair and let himself relax as he looked at the closed-circuit TV monitors and sonar and radar screen. Any ship approaching their oil platform would be spotted almost a half-mile out. Hodges was up top with his sniper rifle on "fire watch" while Moose manned the console. Everyone was trying to sleep. Jon Cohen was lying on his bunk, staring at the darkness and smiling in nervous anticipation. All the prepping in the world couldn't prepare him for handling fifty-year-old nukes, and he knew it. He made himself breathe in and out slowly and tried his best to sleep, but visions of deep-sea creatures kept creeping into his brain.

CHAPTER 23

Oil Platform *Sunrise*

The team was up at 0600. Jon Cohen's ADS 2000 had been crated and installed on the bottom deck of the rig so that it was ready to be deployed. A few fake walls had been built around the housing unit, should anyone inspect the rig before the team got there, but the precautions had been unnecessary. The Newtsuit was attached to its support frame by the cable that would remain attached to the helmet when Jon submerged. Once he was in the suit, his team would use the support frame's small winch to move him out over the water and begin lowering him.

The USS *John Warner* had provided the location of the downed aircraft when it discovered the wreckage and detected the radiation, which is why the rig was placed at its current location. If all went well, Jon would find the jet directly beneath their platform. The mission for day one was to locate the wreck, see how easy or difficult it would be to get to the bombs, measure the radioactivity to make sure it was safe to handle, and then come up with a plan to retrieve them. Jon had trained with special tools that included underwater saws and a B3 oxygen-hydrogen torch capable of cutting through very heavy steel. Without knowing the actual condition of the wreck, it was hard to guess how he would best remove the two large bombs, assuming they were still affixed to the bottom of the wings.

83

Ripper woke Moose, who had grabbed three hours of sleep when his watch ended. They let Hodges sleep since he had been up all night while they prepped Jon for his dive, but the rest of the team had assembled. Jon had put on his dry suit, including the hood, booties, and gloves, and climbed into the giant legs of the Newtsuit. Once he was standing in the legs, Ray Jensen and Ryan O'Conner lowered the top half of the suit, which was attached to the winch.

Ray forced a nervous smile at Jon as he lowered the top half of the suit. "I'm pretty sure I know how to seal this up, so don't you even worry."

"I'm pretty sure if I live, I'll kick your ass when I get back to the surface."

Ray and Ryan joined the top and bottom halves of the suit as Pete monitored the air flow and communications. He checked all of the cameras and watched the pressure gauges as the suit was sealed and filled with air. Ryan and Ray checked and double-checked the seals and connections all over the suit—at six hundred feet, the margin of error was zero.

"Comm check 1, 2, 3," said Pete.

"Got you loud and clear, Mr. McCoy," said Jon. "Nice and cozy and ready to dive."

"Comm check good. Air flow good. Pressure steady. Ready to deploy," said Pete. He was all business, partly out of professionalism, partly out of his own nerves and trying to reassure Jon.

Ray and Ryan cranked the winch manually until Jon's feet cleared the deck by a few inches. He hung by his helmet as the two men maneuvered him over the side of the deck, hanging by the arm of the winch. Once he was hanging over the water, they used the automatic controls to begin lowering him very slowly toward the clear blue ocean.

Jon spun slowly in circles as he descended, until he touched the water. Then he slowly slipped beneath the surface.

"How ya doing, Jon?" asked McCoy.

"A-OK, Pete. Water's clear and skin is dry."

Moose shook his head. "His skin better be dry. Jeez. Six hundred feet."

"You're at one bar of pressure," said Pete calmly.

"Suit feels good," said Jon, now moving his arms around a bit and testing his hand controls.

"Two bars external. Internal pressure looks good at one bar."

"Check. Ears didn't even pop. Internal pressure is perfect," said Jon. He smiled as a school of snapper blew past him with amazing speed. The water changed color from bright Caribbean blue to deeper sapphire, and finally to sunless black. Like driving from the mountains to the desert, everything changed as he descended.

It took almost four minutes to reach the black world at the bottom, where he was now operating by the light from his helmet and cameras. "Six hundred and six feet. I'm at the bottom."

"Roger. You'll have slack on the wire to move around. If you get too much extra cable, let us know. Can't have you getting snagged on the wreck. Do you have visual yet?"

"Negative. Walking north. Cameras working?"

"Affirmative. We can see you, too. Geiger counter readings slowly increasing. Stay on your heading."

"Am I gonna start cooking?" asked Jon, only half joking.

"You're less than point-one millisieverts and slowly rising. Maintain heading."

Jon kept walking. He knew the radiation detected by the submarine was extremely low, and was only detected at all because of the pristine environment and sheer luck of traveling right over the wreck. The submarine used its underwater cameras to locate and photograph the wreckage after it had stumbled upon it.

"Hey. I have something," said Jon as he walked along the sandy bottom.

The bomber was upside down and lightly encrusted with mineral deposits, but there was no mistaking it—it was an A4-E Skyhawk, complete with two very large hydrogen bombs still attached to its underwing bomb racks. Because of the depth and lack of sunlight, the metal wasn't heavily encrusted with barnacles, shellfish, or coral—it was mainly just mineral deposits and some deep-water-dwelling animal activity.

"Wow," whispered Jon, without even realizing it.

"You okay?"

"Yeah, yeah. Fine. Just walked into a time warp, though, you know? No one has laid eyes on this in decades. Geiger readings?"

"Holding steady. They aren't leaking. Get closer and record them visually."

"Roger. Moving closer."

Jon walked across the sand bottom until he was standing next to the wing tip. He thought about the pilot of the aircraft, perhaps still strapped in, upside down for decades in his dark, watery, unmarked grave. He pondered recovering the dog tags, at the very least.

Jon tried to bend over and look under the wing, but the suit wasn't flexible enough to allow him to bend that far. He wanted to see the cockpit.

"You okay? Cameras went sideways."

"Yeah, I'm fine. Was trying to look under the wings for the pilot."

"Negative," snapped Moose's voice. "You are not to take any unnecessary risks. Do *not* get under that wreckage. You're there to survey, come up with a plan, and surface. You get stuck under a wing, no one can get to you, you copy?"

"I copy, skipper."

Jon took a breath and gave a salute, as best he could, to the pilot of the plane. Maybe there wasn't anyone in there anyway. Moving slowly in his awkward suit, Jon got as close to the jet as he could. The two giant bombs looked like elongated eggs.

He moved so that his floodlights were brightest at the bomb rack connections.

"There's room to run straps under the bombs and cut at the connection with the torch. Then we just hoist it straight up to the ship," said Jon.

"How much space between the bomb and where you have to make the cut?" asked Moose, standing over McCoy.

"Maybe five inches."

"You comfortable with that?" he asked.

"I'm not particularly comfortable even standing next to these things, but yeah. I can cut the connection without toasting the nuke."

"Okay. Take as long as you need to be ready for your next dive, then we'll bring you back up," said Moose.

CHAPTER 24

Beirut, Lebanon

Carl Stone had been part of a secret MOP team that answered only to Wallace Holstrum. The MOP was used for "cleaning up messes" and didn't bother with minor details like following the law. When Holstrum's special operations team had needed help in Mexico on their last mission, Wallace had called the MOP in as reinforcements. Since that joint operation, the MOP unit and the team had remained loosely connected as part of the CIA's special black-ops group.

After the death of Carl's partner Duane in Panama, Carl had taken some time off. He considered retiring, or at least taking an extended vacation, until he got the call from Darren Davis explaining that Director Holstrum had been set up. Although Carl was no choirboy, he was extremely loyal to his boss. He put off his vacation and took a flight to Beirut at Darren's request.

Carl was a wet-work mercenary, who spoke several languages and had no problem murdering targets deemed dangerous to the United States. Although he was unassuming looking, with thinning blond hair and pale blue eyes, he could kill a person with his bare hands and then go eat a sandwich. The man was stone cold. This mission wasn't a "hit," however. This was going to require some finesse.

For this mission, Carl dressed in Western attire, but wore a labbade and kaffiyeh on his head. He had dyed his hair dark brown and did some tanning as well as using bronzer to make himself several shades darker than usual. He hadn't shaved since getting the call from Darren, and dyed his beard as well. With his new olive skin and excellent Arabic language skills, he could easily pass for an Arab.

Setting up the meeting with Ali Sawaad had been a little difficult. The man was paranoid, which made sense for an international art smuggler, but also created problems when trying to set up a face-to-face. It was only Carl's insistence that he had something worth millions that eventually appealed to Sawaad's greed.

The CIA had been busy in Syria as of late. They had been trying to identify the "good guys" in an area of the world where there were multiple fighting forces with varying interests. The enemy of your enemy was still your enemy in much of this part of the world. Eventually, the CIA had chosen a group of fighters that were both anti-Assad and anti-ISIS. That didn't make them pro-American, but at least they were killing the same people we wanted dead. The CIA had provided arms, technical and operational support, and first aid. They had also taken a few statues from national landmarks, one of which was now in the back of Carl's rented truck.

Carl parked his truck outside of a small factory in an area that didn't look like it had been repaired or repaved since the last war in Lebanon. Abandoned buildings and piles of garbage were outward signs of a country in decay. Eventually, a small car pulled up next to his truck, and a tall, thin Arab got out. Carl's first thought was that the man's knees must have been in his face when he drove that tiny car.

The man greeted Carl by his assumed name, Hakim They exchanged brief pleasantries and quickly got down to business.

"Not here," said Ali. "We'll go inside."

Ali unlocked the metal fence and opened the gate, and then walked into the factory parking lot with Carl following in the truck very slowly. Ali opened a garage door and threw on some floodlights, and Carl drove inside the large building. When Ali closed the garage, Carl cut the engine and got out of the truck. A quick glance revealed lots of statues, furniture, and pottery. Ali had been a busy boy.

Carl walked to the rear of the truck and opened it. Inside was a Greek statue that had been stolen from Syria, the quality better than anything Ali had ever seen. It was a female god, holding a spear and shield, and she was magnificent.

Ali's face showed his excitement, but then he quickly tried to look disinterested. "It's nice, but I have lots of statues," he said.

Carl began to close the rear doors of the truck.

"What are you doing?" exclaimed Ali.

"If you aren't interested, I have several other players in this market. I was told you're a serious man, but if you don't know what you're looking at, I've wasted my time."

Ali walked toward Carl with waving hands. "No, no! I'm interested. Very interested. Did you have an asking price?"

"Half a million, US dollars."

Ali's face fell. "Half a million US?"

Carl made a show of starting to close the door again.

"Wait! I didn't say no. I just need to speak with a buyer I may have. That's a large sum of money. I may need a few days."

Carl feigned being annoyed. "I can give you forty-eight hours. After that, I'll have to go elsewhere."

"May I photograph it? For my buyer?" asked Ali.

"That will require a bit of trust on my part," said Carl, rubbing his chin. "But okay. You can take pictures for your buyer."

Ali grinned broadly and pulled his phone from his belt. He spent the next few minutes taking photos and even a video as he moved around the goddess. A powerful female figure in perfect white marble. He knew just the woman who would want this.

Carl watched him taking pictures and tried not to smile. The statue had been drilled at the base and a tiny transponder installed before the hole was then refilled with cement. They'd be tracking the statue from Langley every step of the way.

CHAPTER 25

Kampong Pak Bin

Zyy and Yin had run through the thick jungle all the way from Kampong Aht back to their own Kampong, Pak Bin. Pak Bin was a tiny hamlet at the edge of the brown river, upstream from Aht. Zyy spent a long time explaining everything they had seen to their ancient chief. The chief had seen guns before, and knew that these men weren't people of the jungle.

It was decided that Zyy and two men from the village would make the long trip west to the Labi Park Ranger Station and tell the Bruneian officials about the murders at Kampong Aht. The chief would take a small group back toward Aht to secretly keep an eye on its new inhabitants from the jungle.

Yin begged his father to take him, but it was a long journey through harsh jungle, and he was made to stay home. Zyy and two adult villagers hugged their families, and then began their run through the thick green jungle. It would take two days to get to the ranger station

⊕

Mohammed and Hamdi sat inside the chief's hut they now claimed as their own. While the other soldiers had to live eight or ten to a hut, Mohammed and Hamdi had needed privacy for command discussions. They also needed more food than the others to stay sharp.

92

They opened their laptop and deployed their satellite antennae. Once they had a connection, they collected their e-mail. The laptop was only used once a week for both security reasons as well as battery life. It would be a long time before they could recharge the computer, and every minute of battery life counted.

"Abu wants us to move up our timetables. The Americans have struck again in Afghanistan and Syria with their drones. They murdered four of our commanders. Abu wants revenge."

Hamdi smiled. "When?"

"Within a week, he wants us operational. I'll have to send a message to the sultan's minister Abdul Ali and tell him we'll need a ship. If we're going to be ready in a week, we need to get upriver to the coast. That will take two days. Are the vests ready?"

"Yes. The men have all been trained and are prepared for martyrdom and Paradise."

Mohammed nodded thoughtfully, and then sent a quick e-mail to the sultan's minister. There were now logistics that needed to be handled quickly, sometimes easier said than done. Hazrol, their Bruneian guide, could take them up the river, northwest toward the port city of Kuala Belait. The river could get them within twenty kilometers of where they needed to go, but then they'd need a caravan of trucks to get them to the port. They'd also need some sort of escort to prevent anyone from questioning why a hundred foreign men with weapons were moving through Brunei. Once at the port, they needed a freighter that could get them to Singapore.

Mohammed closed the laptop and patted Hamdi on the shoulder. "Tomorrow, God willing, we will find the good news from the minister, and begin our mission."

CHAPTER 26

Oil Platform *Sunrise*

The team was up early again, preparing for Jon's second dive. Hodges looked at the team and smiled. He leaned over to McCoy and whispered, "We're kinda like the Magnificent Seven."

McCoy made a face. "I think only three of them lived."

"Guess you're fucked," said Hodges. He smacked McCoy on the shoulder and went to get some breakfast.

After the seven of them had eaten breakfast, Jon was fitted in his Newtsuit and once again lowered into the water. This time he carried the B3 torch cutter that he would use to free the nukes from the jet. The hand-piece for the torch was strapped to his wrist and wired to one finger of his suit's claw. In this fashion, he could pull one finger inside his suit to ignite the high-powered flame. He smiled, thinking that he looked a bit like Spiderman shooting webs in much the same way.

A set of nylon straps were also lowered with him, attached to long cables on the oil platform that would secure the nukes until they could be hoisted the six hundred feet to the surface.

"How you feeling?" asked Moose.

"I'm good to go," said Jon.

"You're going to be down for hours. You hydrated?"

"Yeah. And it's not like peeing in a wetsuit," said Jon, only half-kidding.

"Don't pee in a quarter-million-dollar diving suit."

"Bullshit. The first time I light that torch next to one of those nukes, I'm definitely going to pee myself."

Moose nodded. "Good point. You're excused. Shit, I may pee myself up here watching you."

"The good news is, if I set one off, we won't know it."

"Super. Good luck, brother. You got this."

Jon forced a smile. "Piece of cake. Yellow cake. That's a nuke joke."

Moose shook his head.

Jon shrugged. "Whatever. See you in a few hours."

Jon climbed into the bottom legs of the suit and went through his checklist. A few minutes later, weighted down with his torch and tanks, he began the journey down to the dark world below. The straps were bundled together with Velcro and attached to his upper arm so he didn't have to hold on to them.

When he reached the bottom, Jon began his slow walk back to the jet. A large fish swam by, reminding Jon that he was indeed in the ocean and not outer space, which is what it felt like. When his floodlights hit the jet, Jon's skin got goose bumps. He was about to light a torch next to two nuclear bombs that could vaporize everything in the area.

The first task was pulling the straps apart from the Velcro, which would be easy with two hands, but was complicated when operating two three-clawed robotic hands. It took him a few tries and a few minutes, with his teammates silently watching from their cameras topside. Once he had the straps freed, he then had to loop them under the bombs in three locations and snap them together using oversized carabiners. The carabiners would lock the straps in place, and when he was ready, the crew topside would turn on mechanical winches and slowly start to bring the bombs up. It was painfully slow work that required total focus and patience. Multiple tries for each strap had been required, as they would slip from his claws, or the hooks would miss when trying to snap everything together.

Finally, after the two bombs were secured with the straps, it was time for Jon to turn on his cutting torch.

"Here goes nothing," he said out loud.

"You got this," said Moose quietly from the deck six hundred feet above his head. "Nice and slow, baby. You need a break, we'll bring you up and finish tomorrow."

"I'm good."

Jon turned on the torch, and the flame lit the dark world in a purple-blue glow. He moved the torch toward the first bomb rack, careful not to aim it at the bomb, and began slowly cutting throw the aluminum, which melted easily.

"Like a hot knife through butter," said Jon as he worked.

"Twenty megaton butter," said Moose. "Nice and slow."

It took Jon forty minutes to cut through the bomb racks on each wing, after which time he let out a long, slow sigh of relief. He killed the torch and reported back to his team.

"Bombs are clear, skipper."

"Outstanding," said Moose. "We'll bring them up and hold them beneath the rig until we get a ship here with EOD to take care of them. Stand by."

Ray Jensen pulled the handle on the winch, and the cables tightened, the straps stretched, and with a dull, underwater *pop*, the metal broke free and the bombs began to ascend, free of the wreck. Jon stood at the wing tip and watched nervously, then smiled and said, "Okay, skipper. Bombs are free."

The words had just left his lips when the jet shifted with the sudden weight change and slid hard, knocking Jon to his back as the jet wing slid over him, pinning him to the ocean floor and knocking out two of his lights.

"Skipper!"

His mic went dead.

CHAPTER 27

Washington, DC

Secretary of State Danielle Reynaud was clicking through the series of photographs that had arrived in her e-mail. She was still in bed, checking e-mail on her home laptop computer. Ali Sawaad had written that he had for sale the finest statue he'd ever seen, and he wasn't kidding. The secretary smiled as she looked at the warrior goddess. Of course, she saw herself in the beauty of the statue—its strength, beauty, and courage shined through the marble as if it was lit from within. She simply had to have it.

Danielle clicked on the video link and got goose bumps as Ali walked around the statue filming it from every angle. She was *perfect*.

The secretary called Ali on his cell phone, and he answered quickly. It was afternoon in Lebanon, and Ali was still in his warehouse of stolen art. He knew it was the secretary when he saw the number on his phone, and didn't even bother with a "hello."

"She's amazing, isn't she?"

"Yes. I want her. How much?"

Ali hesitated and cleared his throat. Danielle heard it in his voice and grew irritated. "Okay, Sawaad, don't waste my time. Bottom line."

"There are several others interested in this piece. And it's large, which makes transportation dangerous and difficult . . ."

97

"How much?"

"Eight hundred thousand US. Firm."

The secretary was fuming. "Eight hundred thousand? Are you fucking kidding me, you little weasel? I should just have you arrested by the Lebanese police!"

Sawaad was not afraid of the secretary. As powerful and connected as she was in the United States, she was just some second-rate middle manager to him—and a woman, to boot. "If you do that, I'll be happy to share my customer list with them and cut a deal. Perhaps CNN will be interested as well."

Her face was turning red. "Half a million."

"She's costing me more than that," he lied. "The price is firm. I have Saudis prepared to pay. I only offered to you first because I know your taste and thought you'd like her."

"Damn you, Ali. Okay. I'll have the deposit wired later today. How long before you can get it here?"

"A month. I'll have it shipped to Port Elizabeth in New Jersey. I have people that will drive it down by truck wherever you want it. But it needs to be paid in full."

"In *full*? Ali, if you fuck me on this . . ."

"You are a great customer! I won't disappoint you. But I have to pay for this now myself, and it's very expensive. I need the money right away."

"Fine. This one goes to my house in Massachusetts. I'll e-mail you the instructions. Your money will arrive later today. Get it here as fast as you can." She hung up, giddy with excitement, and got out of bed. She needed to get to her office and have the money wired quickly, lest some Saudi sheik beat her to the statue.

Danielle popped on the television to catch some CNN, perhaps because Ali had planted the seed in her brain. She caught two pundits arguing over whether the CIA should be forced to comment on why the head of their organization was currently on leave. She smiled and texted Jeff Dennis:

CNN. You getting this?

Danielle sat on the edge of her bed smiling as she listened to one of the reporters drone on with great drama. ". . . and the American people have a right to know! They continually hide behind the veil of national security, when the rumors are that the director may have been involved in some *very* dark matters."

"And have you been able to substantiate any of the allegations?" asked the other talking head.

"Not yet, and of course it's very difficult because he is, in fact, the director of the CIA. But unnamed sources have leaked allegations of child pornography on the director's computer . . ."

"*What*?" exclaimed the other reporter. "Child pornography? When did *this* surface? This would be the most scandalous event in American history!"

The other reporter sat back smugly and tried to look like she had all of the answers but couldn't share it quite yet. "As I said, these are unnamed sources, but said to be very high up."

"High up *where*? Listen—you just dropped a bombshell that'll be talked about all day and night. Viewers are going to want to know more about this. Has he been charged with an actual crime? When did this become public?"

"Well obviously, it isn't public yet. I don't believe he's been formally charged yet, either. As I said, these are still considered rumors until we can substantiate the charges, but what we *do* know is that the director of CIA has been put on leave, and neighbors do confirm that FBI agents were seen at the house, perhaps to seize the director's computers."

The TV flashed to a neighbor's cell phone video of FBI SUVs and agents in front of the director's Virginia home.

Danielle cackled. "Jeff, you evil bastard! How's that feel, *Wally*?" she screamed at the television.

Her cell phone buzzed. It was a text from Jeff.

Saw the news Quite shocking!

There were too many smiley faces to count.

Back in their home, Director Holstrum held his wife as she cried against his shoulder.

"It's okay," he said quietly. "We'll get to the bottom of this."

CHAPTER 28

Oil Platform *Sunrise*

The corporate helicopter roared over the ocean toward the oil platform. Off in the distance, Apo and Bruce could see the ships, cranes, and dredgers that were building yet another new island in the South China Sea. Apo and Bruce sat in the rear seats behind the Bruneian pilot and copilot, having just come from the national airport in the capital.

It was loud inside the helicopter, but they didn't want their voices being heard over the internal radio system, so they took off their headsets, leaned close, and spoke loud enough to hear each other, but low enough that the pilots were out of earshot. Speaking against the Bruneian government or sultan was illegal, and neither of them wanted their pilot-babysitters taking issue with their conversation.

"Just what the South China Sea needs—another island claiming a twelve-mile international boundary," said Apo.

Bruce nodded. "If I had to guess where World War III was going to start, it's a toss-up between the Middle East and right here."

"Yeah, well, I'd rather we were fighting the Iranians before they get nukes than millions of well-armed Chinese with plenty of them."

"The Russians opening airbases in Iran will make it interesting, though. Can you imagine if Israel were to bomb the Iranian nuclear facility now? The Russians scramble MiGs,

101

Israel shoots one down, Russia and Iran declare war, the US and NATO defend Israel . . . would make for an interesting few weeks."

"Just a few weeks?" asked Apo with a grin.

"Yeah. First nuke from Iran hits Israel, it's all over. They respond and take out some Russians, Russia fires, we fire . . . Hell, these new islands may be the only things left on the planet with life on them."

"Maybe we should buy some beachfront property while we're here."

"I'm in! But I want a fishing boat. And we better plant some banana and palm trees now, so they're mature when we come back."

Apo pointed to the oil platform. "There she is. Damn, that thing is bigger in real life, huh?"

"Yeah, no kidding."

The pilot slowed and banked, and the helicopter descended to the platform. The pilot looked at his passengers and pointed to his headphones. Apo and Bruce put theirs on. In hard-to-decipher English, the pilot said, "No one answer radio. We land anyway."

"Okay, take us down, thanks," said Apo.

They landed on the helipad and slid their doors open. One of the members of the team was running toward them as they landed, looking extremely animated. They thanks the pilots and got out with their duffle bags, and the helicopter took off for the mainland again.

"Hey!" shouted Eric Hodges over the wash of the rotor blades. "Glad you're here, we have a big fucking problem!"

"What's up?" asked Apo.

"Jon went down to secure the nukes for recovery. When the bombs started coming up, the weight shifted and the jet moved. Jon went down and we lost audio."

"Jesus! Are you still monitoring his suit?" asked Apo.

They all started jogging toward the elevator to bring them down to the lowest deck where the team was assembled around the monitors.

"Affirmative," said Hodges as they ran. "Pressure is perfect—no suit breach, thank God. The rebreather is working fine. A few of the floodlights are broken, but we can still see a little, and we can see Jon's face. He's alive, but we think he's pinned under the wing."

The three of them ran off the elevator as soon as they hit the bottom deck of the semi-submersible. They found the team huddled over the monitors. Moose looked back and yelled at Apo and Bruce, "Hey. Hodges fill you in?"

"Yeah. No comms?"

"Not yet. Hang on."

Moose spoke into the headset. "Jon, we lost audio, but we can see you. If you can hear me, blink twice."

Jon blinked twice and the team gave a quick shout.

"Your pressure and air supply are both perfect. You can last down there for days. Can you move at all?"

Jon mouthed the words "my arms" very carefully. Moose confirmed it. "You can move your arms?"

Jon blinked twice.

"Look around you as far as your suit will allow so your cameras will show us what you see," said Moose.

It wasn't much of a view. Jon was pinned on his back and his range of motion was limited. The team above could see the wing over his legs, but that was it. It was dark outside the weak lighting.

"Where are the nukes?" asked Apo.

"Hanging maybe a hundred feet over him. We had started hoisting them up when he got pinned."

Apo stared at the screen.

"What are you thinking?" asked Moose.

"What if you drop the nukes back down close enough for him to grab a strap, and try and pull him out?"

"He's pinned under a ton of rusty metal. He grabs hold of that line and we start pulling—what if the suit breaches?" asked Moose.

Apo made a face. "Think he'd rather die in an un-breached suit?"

"Let's not go to last resort just yet. McCoy, get the strobe lights on the tower. We'll signal the *John Warner*. Maybe they can help us out."

Apo looked at Moose inquisitively.

Moose caught him up to speed. "Their skipper sent me a message. They're patrolling this sector. That sub's got all the latest bells and whistles. Maybe they can save our ass."

"At six hundred feet?"

"Who knows what they're capable of? But let's try before we just start tugging on him from way up here and pull his suit apart."

McCoy jogged off to get the lights on while Moose began talking to Jon again to keep him calm and let him know they were working on a rescue plan.

CHAPTER 29

Ranger Station, Labi Forest Reserve

Zyy and two of his clan had traveled through thick steamy jungle on and off for two days. They had stopped overnight only when it was too dark to travel. A torrential rain that night had prevented them from starting a fire, and it had been a wet, cold night that offered little sleep.

On the morning of the second day, the rain subsided and they ate the fish balls they had brought with them and drank rainwater from collectors they had fashioned from giant leaves. They continued their journey, winding up and down hills, following a stream they knew would lead them to the ranger station.

When they arrived at the small cabin that served as an outpost for the Labi rangers, they found "outsiders"—a term they used for anyone not living in the jungle. These outsiders were white photojournalists and spoke a language they didn't understand. When a ranger walked into the cabin, they excitedly began telling him the story of what they had seen. The ranger in turn was telling the people in the cabin with him.

The two outsiders were from Auckland and had been traveling Southeast Asia for almost a year, covering remote regions of the planet for NatGeo. Kevin and Valerie Jean were both twenty-six, and had met at St. Cuthbert's College. They'd been traveling the world together ever since.

"Quite a tale," said the young New Zealander, scratching his beard.

"Kevin, we could go with them, yeah? Not the story we thought we'd get, but it might be something huge," said his partner and girlfriend Valerie Jean. Her big blue eyes lit up with excitement at the idea of covering something akin to combat.

"Val, the poisonous snakes, spiders, and tigers are dangerous enough, no? Now you want to go traipse around a war zone?"

"Oh come on!" she goaded. "When have we ever covered anything like this? We can end up on the cover of *Time*!"

"We can end up *dead*," said Kevin glumly. "Fine. Fine. We'll tag along. But let's be smart about it, yeah?"

The ranger, an older man named Wie, spoke with Zyy and the two villagers for a while, and then used a satellite phone to call into the government office back in the capital, Bandar Seri Begawan. The minister of the interior's office, under the direction of Abdul Ali, had direct oversight of the park system.

Wie was informed that the minister of the interior wasn't in the office, but would get back to him with instructions on how to proceed. When Wie explained this to the New Zealanders and the villagers, none of them wanted to wait. Wie radioed his two other rangers, who were traveling within the park to check on campsites, and told them to return to the base immediately.

While they waited for the rangers, Wie began preparing for the trip. They had a speedboat that could get them to Kampong Aht in a few hours, although Wie planned on stopping the boat short of Aht and proceeding on foot to observe the village from a safe distance. With the help of the villagers and two journalists, Wie loaded the boat with supplies.

By the time they were finishing, the two other rangers returned from the forest. Wie reiterated the story that Zyy had told them, much to the horror of the two other rangers.

"If there are as many as they say, and they're heavily armed, we should wait for help," said one of the rangers.

"We aren't going to try and arrest all of them. We just need to confirm this first-hand, and then call in with our own report. We'll remain hidden, just like the villagers did," said Wie. "Let's go."

Reluctantly, the other two rangers followed the group to their speedboat. They exchanged nervous glances, but had no choice but to follow their boss. Between the three of them, they had three pistols. Not exactly an arsenal.

Once seated, they fired up the engine and roared off through the brown water heading upstream, south toward the unknown.

⊕

Jeff Dennis lived in a lovely brick house in an upscale suburb not far from Arlington, Virginia. The house was a four bedroom, although Jeff, on marriage number three, didn't have any children living in the home. Children one and two from marriage one, and child three, from marriage two, all avoided their estranged father at all costs. The man had never been around when they grew up anyway, spending all of his time in Washington, DC, around powerful people who could further his career.

He sat out on his patio watching the sunrise as he drank his coffee and read the news of the world on his iPad. It was a little brisk so early, so Jeff had pulled a sweatshirt on over his boxers and T-shirt. His wife, number three, was still fast asleep upstairs. Unlike wives one and two, this one was strictly an eye-candy purchase who would look good escorting him to important events around DC once he was a cabinet member. She was fifteen years his junior, with her own ambitions. The Mercedes convertible Jeff had given her when they had only been dating for four months had opened the negotiations on their future together.

Jeff was so close now he could *taste* it. Though he didn't like Danielle Reynaud any more than anyone else in DC, he understood her. She was power hungry and focused, just like him, and wasn't afraid to do whatever needed to be done to accomplish her goals. In his view, this was called leadership, and he would be joining her team in the White House next year. Getting rid of the few obstacles had been an enjoyable task, overall.

First, there was the Democratic challenger that posed a real problem in the primary. It had cost hundreds of thousands of dollars to get the dirt on him. The man had been so damn careful, and he was intelligent. But he had also purchased a home in the Caymans that no one knew about. With enough money to the right people, Jeff was able to figure out the home was actually purchased by a pharmaceutical company for almost three million dollars, and then sold at a two-point-nine million dollar loss to the senator a month later. That home on the beach was literally "the steal of the century." It was three hundred thousand dollars well spent from the campaign to make him "go away" before the primary.

Then there was the Republican opposition next fall. Jeff and his staff had carefully chosen the man they thought they could beat, and used all of their influence to make sure he was given the most television coverage by the media companies they had on their payroll. The one candidate who posed the largest threat in a general election had enjoyed a colorful childhood and college experience. It only took a hundred thousand dollars to find pictures and old friends who swore that Steve had sold them pot at Cornell, and had huge parties where several women came forward and said they had been groped or sexually assaulted. One of them claimed a rape from twenty years ago, which had cost Jeff a hundred thousand in cash, but also, money well spent.

The biggest problem had been Director Wallace Holstrum of the CIA. *That* bastard had been investigated the goddamn secretary of state of the United States! It was nothing short of treasonous. The fact that he found out the secretary was purchasing artwork stolen from countries that were listed as officially off-limits was beside the point. The secretary loved art, and she was merely saving it from those animals who would otherwise destroy it. What was the actual crime? Someone was going to pay ISIS for it, in any case.

Getting the kiddie porn on to Holstrum's computer had been *expensive*. That was a half-million-dollar job. He'd needed someone good—*really* good—who could keep his mouth shut. He found a twenty-one-year-old college student named Stephen Burstein living in Washington, DC, who had applied for an internship at the NSA. The young man was brilliant. Jeff had convinced him that they were testing cyber-security on the CIA's personnel to make sure foreign governments couldn't get into the nation's best-kept secrets. The young man was a patriot, which is why he wanted to work for the NSA in the first place. He was thrilled to have been chosen for this exciting, top secret assignment.

Jeff had written out almost twenty pages of documents for the kid to sign. It was legalese mumbo-jumbo that an Oxford professor would have a hard time understanding, never mind a young computer geek. Mr. Dennis had told Stephen it was standard for such top secret work, and basically just meant that divulging any part of the work could mean federal charges ranging from treason to espionage. While that terrified the kid, it also reinforced just how important the work was to the country. He signed and initialed it, in ten places, and then began his work. Although he didn't understand why such picture files were being used for the security testing, that decision was above his pay grade. He did as he was told.

One month later, when he read about the CIA director being under investigation, he was horrified. He immediately called the number he had used in the past for Jeff Dennis, a man he knew only as Mr. Kompy. The number was disconnected. He had no one else to call. The police? FBI? CIA? The documents he signed had been *very* specific. Any acknowledgement of his involvement in the top secret operation would land him in federal prison immediately. Stephen immediately went through his computer, his server, and his phone and deleted everything related to his special project. He emptied his bank account of the five hundred thousand dollars, dropped out of school, and moved to California while he tried to figure out what to do.

CHAPTER 30

Beirut, Lebanon

Carl arrived at the warehouse with his truck at the appointed hour. He was armed and prepared for anything. If Ali Sawaad decided he was taking the statue without paying for it, Carl wouldn't go down without a fight.

Sawaad was waiting for him at the warehouse when he pulled in, and Carl was relieved to see the man was alone. He pulled his truck back into the warehouse and cut the engine and climbed out. Sawaad greeted him in the traditional formal fashion, which Carl returned.

"I have a buyer and your money," said Sawaad with a smile. He leaned closer and asked, in a quiet yet dramatic voice, "You have more where this came from?"

Carl smiled. Greedy bastard. "You understand the risks involved, but yes. If you keep paying, I'll keep coming back."

Ali walked to a cabinet and pulled open a closet. Inside, there were two large duffle bags full of wrapped stacks of hundred dollar bills. Carl couldn't help but wonder if the US government had been ripped off somewhere down the line in Iraq, Afghanistan, or Syria for all this US cash to make its way here to Lebanon.

"Half a million dollars. A lot of money," said Sawaad.

"And a priceless treasure has a price," replied Carl. He opened the rear of the truck and showed Ali the goddess again.

"For a half million, you get the truck, too. I can take your car and leave it at my hotel."

Ali smiled. The truck would make things much easier. "Excellent," he said. "The keys to my car are in it. Just tell me where to find it."

Carl gave him the name of the hotel where he was staying and left with the cash. He didn't drive to the hotel, however. He went as fast as he could to a safe house in Ramlet al-Baida, west of the city on the water. From there, he'd be on a boat the moment the sun went down, headed south to Israel where a Mossad contact would help him to a private jet headed halfway around the world.

Ali Sawaad smiled at the gorgeous goddess. He opened his laptop and typed the message to his American customer.

Payment received. Shipment leaves tomorrow for New Jersey. Will send freight tracking numbers when I have them.

Ali hit the "send" button and then called for two of his workers who would help him make the crate and transport the heavy cargo to the pier for international shipping.

◆

Cheryl Cook's computer lit up to tell her she had another e-mail intercept from Ali Sawaad in Lebanon to the secretary of state's computer. She began reading her e-mail while at the same time, not far away in the same building, Darren Davis watched a GPS locator begin moving from a warehouse in Lebanon to the port.

CHAPTER 31

Oil Platform *Sunrise*

Apo and Bruce stood with the rest of the team on the deck looking at Jon on the monitor when McCoy back in the control room radioed over to Moose.

"Radar contacts heading this way. Looks like three ships in battle formation, skipper."

Moose and Ripper looked at each other. Moose's face turned red. "What the fuck? Seriously? *Now?* Someone get Hodges topside and get his ass up in the crow's nest to see what's going on. I doubt they're here to sink an oil rig."

Ray Jensen took off at a run to get their sniper. Ten minutes later, Hodges was at the top of the 450-foot-tall tower with his spotter scope.

"I swear I can see the curve of the earth from up here," he said in amazement as he scanned the azure water. "Skipper, I see three military ships. Looks like they're flying Chinese flags. They're red, anyway. I'm guessing destroyers or cruisers or something. Definitely military warships, and definitely on a beeline for us in military formation. Maybe two and a half klicks out. Not sure I can sink all three from here," he said, probably only half-kidding.

"Very funny. Keep an eye on them," said Moose. "McCoy, you copy?"

"Roger, skipper."

"If they make contact on the radio let me know. Out."

Ripper leaned into the monitor so he could see Jon's face. Jon was trying his best to find the torch that had been knocked off the arm of his suit, hoping it was underneath him or within reach, but wasn't having any luck. All he could do was move his arms in the cumbersome suit and hope he bumped into something, but he couldn't really feel anything through the thick padding of the insulation.

"How ya doing down there, buddy?" asked Ripper.

Jon blinked twice.

"Listen, you're doing fine. I called the president and got permission for you to pee in the suit."

Jon smiled, which made Ripper smile.

"We're waiting to hear back from a US Navy submarine. They're going to help us get you out, but it's going to take a while. I know you're probably hungry and thirsty and maybe even cold, but you just relax and sit tight. Maybe try and sleep to pass a few hours. We're monitoring you every second of the day, brother."

Jon mouthed "thank you" and Ripper continued to reassure him as best he could.

Hodges popped in on the radio. "Those three warships are closing fast. One and a half kilometers, skipper."

"McCoy!" barked Moose on the radio.

"Yes, sir!"

"Send a message to those ships. Tell them we're a Canadian oil crew from Interglobe Oil Exploration, and we're concerned they are getting too close."

"Aye, aye, skipper." McCoy tried channels ten and sixteen, and kept repeating the same message. *This is Canadian oil platform* Sunrise *to approaching ships. Please change your course . . ."*

The Chinese ships remained silent and on their same heading.

Back on the lower deck, Ripper turned to Moose. "Ya know, skipper, with those three ships out there, our sub can't surface. How are we gonna tell them about Jon if they can't surface?"

Moose nodded with an angry expression. "Exactly. They're flexing their muscles and there ain't a damn thing we can do about it."

Bruce interrupted. "Hey, Moose. I speak Mandarin. Let me try and get someone on the radio."

"Go!"

Bruce and Apo jogged up to the command center of the ship, where McCoy was still on the radio getting no response. Bruce motioned for the headset. "Hey, how about I try in Chinese, okay?"

McCoy smiled and handed it to him. "Have at it!"

Bruce tried channel sixteen, barking out in Mandarin. His radio call was immediately answered, also in Mandarin. McCoy looked at Apo and shrugged. They conversed back and forth in what sounded like a hollering match. After a few minutes, Bruce signed off the radio and nodded at Apo and McCoy.

"Okay. I think I talked some sense into them. This platform wasn't here on their last patrol, so they were coming to check us out. They thought maybe we were a new radar installation, but I convinced them we're drilling for oil. They're still coming through here, mostly just to piss off the Brunei government."

"They said that?" asked McCoy.

Bruce laughed. "No, I'm paraphrasing. They're on patrol, making sure they maintain free passage through this area that China claims as their territorial waters, even though the World Court in The Hague already said it isn't."

Apo shook his head. "It always seemed sort of insane, fighting over invisible lines on land, but out in the open ocean? Insane doesn't even begin to describe it."

"Yeah. Let's build an island so we can stick a flag in it." He shook his head. "The human race is whacked, my friends."

"In the meantime, with these idiots cruising so close by, our sub can't surface. We got a man down trapped at six hundred feet, and the *John Warner* is his only hope," said McCoy.

"Yeah, we know. He's gotta hang in there until the Chinese finish their patrol," said Apo.

"Easy for us to say from up here," lamented McCoy.

CHAPTER 32

Unnamed Tributary near Kampong Aht

The boat slowed, quietly chugging through the fast-moving brown water. They were going against the current, moving at less than ten knots as they tried to keep their engine noise quiet.

"There!" exclaimed Val, pointing to a body tangled in a fallen tree at the water's edge.

Wie steered the boat toward the body, slowing the engine to almost a stop. Their boat glided through the narrowing river until they grabbed branches from the fallen tree and cut their engine.

Val and Kevin quickly began photographing the body.

"Let's get a quick video," said Val. Kevin took the cover off of his small video recorder and Val sat on the gunwale of the boat with the corpse in the background.

"Rolling in 3 . . . 2 . . ." said Kevin, pointing at her instead of saying "one."

"I'm here in the Labi Forest Reserve in Southern Brunei, where reports of a mass murder—"

Wie jumped across the boat at Kevin. "No! No! You can't record this without government approval!"

"Wait! It's cool!" said Kevin, his camera still rolling to an uplink in his video "cloud" that went directly to a shared Dropbox folder with NatGeo. "I'll just tape it now and wait.

117

If the government says no, I can delete it. But we have to take the pictures as we find them! We won't get a second chance!"

This led to arguing between Wie and the two other rangers in Malay that Kevin and Val didn't understand. They went back and forth, obviously nervous about allowing any video that could make Brunei look bad. All media was controlled by the government, and any criticism of the ruler could lead to capital punishment.

"Look, we're just gathering facts and evidence. Your government is going to want to see this!" pleaded Val.

"That's right!" said Kevin. "Your own government will need this! We won't release any film without your approval, okay?"

Wie spoke again to the other rangers, and they reluctantly decided it would be okay to record the facts as long as they didn't share it with anyone before receiving government approval. Wie felt slightly more important now, having actual evidence to prove his patrol quickly responded to a report of danger.

With tacit approval, Val hopped back to her spot and Kevin kept filming.

"This is Valerie Jean Kozak reporting from the forest near Aht, Brunei. Aht is a kampong, or small village, just off the river here in southwestern Brunei, in the Labi Forest Reserve. This part of the country is isolated by thick jungles, and only a small population of indigenous people live here, in much the same way as they've existed for thousands of years. I'm here with cameraman Kevin Israel, accompanying three park rangers who are following up on a report of a mass murder. The three natives, who live in their own kampong near Aht, came across the carnage a couple of days ago, and we're here to see if the people responsible are still here, and if so, what their motives could have possibly been."

Kevin panned his camera and zoomed in on the body. It had been a young woman who had been shot at least five times that he could see through his lens. Mercifully, her long black hair covered most of her face.

"I'll be back with more information as we delve deeper into this ominous jungle." She paused.

"Cut!" shouted Kevin. "Great—that was *great*. Goddamn, Val. This is *real* reporting!" He gave her a quick hug and kiss, careful not to show too much public display of affection in such a conservative country. Even so, the others looked at them disapprovingly.

"Sorry, mates—just a little excited," Kevin mumbled.

The rangers didn't share their enthusiasm and looked anxious. The three natives spoke quickly amongst themselves and to the rangers. They didn't understand the camera concept and it was too difficult to try and explain. The Penan people were a primitive group, and even the concept of an engine on the boat was fairly amazing to them. They, like the rangers, were nervous.

After more discussion, it was decided to cut the outboard and paddle further up the river. The Penan knew a place where they could get out and follow a trail, which was getting close. The rangers and natives paddled with wooden oars, and Kevin kept his film rolling as he videoed their surroundings. They past several more bloated bodies in the water as they slipped through the brown river, Kevin getting close-ups of each one.

He could practically smell the Pulitzer.

He could *definitely* smell the bodies.

They paddled for another twenty minutes, tough work for a heavy boat against the current, and finally pulled the boat up into the muddy shoreline. The eight of them climbed out of their boat and followed Zyy into the unknown.

CHAPTER 33

Elizabeth Seaport, New Jersey

Chris and Julia sat in the parking lot of an abandoned factory near the seaport. Julia had a laptop open, watching the yellow dot on her GPS map. Chris sipped his coffee, suppressing a yawn.

"It's on the move," she said.

"So reassuring to know that a huge crate comes in from the Middle East and just cruises right through the seaport unopened," said Chris.

"Well, a K9 or radiological equipment isn't going to pick up a block of marble," she replied.

"I guess," he said, starting their engine.

When the box truck pulled out of the seaport with the GPS transponder in it, Chris and Julia got close enough to get the license plate and then dropped way back. They didn't need to tail the vehicle, they could follow it from anywhere, but they did want to know to whom the truck belonged. Julia sent the plate back to Dex Murphy, who advised them that the truck was registered to a Hussam Haddad. He had no criminal history but had overstayed a work visa and was currently living in the United States illegally.

"He's a nobody," said Julia, reading his information.

"Until he blows something up," said Chris quietly.

"Jaded much?" she asked with a smirk.

120

"As jaded as it gets. Over six billion people on this planet, and I only like about twenty of them."

"Glad I made the cut," she said.

"You're number one on the list," he replied. "He's heading to her place near Boston. Long drive. You might as well catch some Zs."

"I'm good. We can use the next five hours for you to tell me about how much you love me and want to marry me."

"Five hours might not be enough," he said.

"Oh, *man*. That was the right answer! You might win a prize!"

"While I'm driving?" he asked with an evil grin.

"You wish. Eyes on the road, mister."

Up ahead, a very excited Hussam Haddad sped along in the bumpy truck, anxious to get a thousand dollars cash for delivering the statue. His partner in the truck would get an almost even share of two hundred dollars.

CHAPTER 34

South China Sea

The USS *John Warner* was at mast depth observing the three Chinese warships in the distance. From his command chair, Commander Vince Norman made notes on the three ships being tracked. The crew was practicing a firing drill with torpedoes.

"Skipper, we've got strobes from the rig," said Master Chief Adams.

The skipper panned his joystick on his console and, sure enough, saw the lights flashing on the oil platform.

"Bad timing," he said to himself. He typed out an encrypted burst message to the team on the rig.

USSJW observes your strobe. Status?

McCoy was still at the console when the e-mail signal flashed. He was so excited he screamed out loud. *"Hey! Hey! I got 'em!"* he screamed into his headset.

"Who? The sub?" asked Moose from the lower deck.

"Affirmative, skipper! They're asking our status. They saw the strobes."

"All right, well, *tell* them! We've got a man down at six hundred feet and we need their help immediately!"

"I'm on it, out!"

Pete began typing as fast as his fingers would move.

Sunrise has one diver down, trapped at 600 feet. Diver is in an ADS 2000 Newtsuit. He has air and is conscious but can't get out from under the jet wreckage. Two broken arrows are secured and currently suspended at 500 feet from cables beneath our rig. Can you help us rescue our diver? We have no other means. He's been down eighteen hours.

McCoy hit "send" and prayed.

Back on the submarine, the commander read the incoming message and groaned. "XO!"

Commander Burdge hopped up from his own console and moved to the skipper's chair.

"The *Sunrise* has a SEAL diver trapped at six hundred feet in an atmospheric suit. He's stable but unable to extricate himself from the wreckage of that jet with the broken arrows. You have the bridge." He grabbed his PA mic and instructed his crew. "Attention on deck. Suspend all drills. We have a new mission. This is not a drill. US special operations has a diver down at six hundred feet. Rescue team meet in my ready room, out."

The skipper hustled back to his small ready room as it filled up with his rescue divers and support team. Within five minutes, eight sailors were crammed into the skipper's room.

"Gentlemen, we have a special operations team working on a clandestine mission off an oil platform in six hundred feet of water. That team is on station to recover two nuclear weapons from a downed aircraft. Their diver is trapped under the wreckage. He's wearing an ADS 2000 and has air, but he's been down pushing twenty hours. If the batteries go on his suit, he's a dead man. I need a plan put together to rescue their diver. There are also two nuclear devices suspended by cables which will have to be recovered, but not by us. Chief, if you've got ideas, I need them now."

Master Chief Karl White was the commanding officer of the sub's rescue diver team. The USS *John Warner* had a few tricks up her sleeve that older submarines didn't, including the ability to launch a small mini-sub for special operations with SEAL teams.

Karl and his team had practiced and drilled too many times to count for events like this. His answer was immediate. "Sir, I'd like to deploy the UUV first for reconnaissance. It would also reassure the diver to know that we're on station."

The Unmanned Undersea Vehicle was "the drone of the sea" and could do everything an aerial drone could do.

"Once we see his condition, we'll deploy the mini-sub with our own deep-water diver to cut him out. We'll have to recover him here and figure out about getting him to his team afterwards."

"Time frame?" asked the skipper.

"Put us on the diver and we're good to go. The UUV is ready to deploy and we can have the mini-sub launched in fifteen minutes."

"Okay, that's it. You're on." The skipper grabbed his phone that flashed up on the bridge.

"Bridge," replied his XO.

"This is the captain. Get us to 550 feet near Lima November. We're preparing to deploy the UUV on site followed by the mini-sub for a diver rescue. There are suspended cables with two nukes hanging from them that may not show up on our sonar, so keep back a thousand meters. Out."

"Aye, aye, skipper! Heading to Lima November, making depth 550 feet!"

The submarine silently angled nose-down and slipped into the dark world of the deep ocean, quickly heading to where Jon Cohen lie on his back shivering, staring out in the blackness, wondering if he was going to die.

CHAPTER 35

Kampong Aht

With Zyy guiding them through the thick jungle, the seven men and one woman moved as quietly as they could through the thick, steamy afternoon heat. The rain would come down in torrents, then quickly stop, only to return a short time later. The mosquitoes attacked them in clouds, and the mud tried to suck the boots off of their feet, except for Zyy and his two tribemates, who had never owned shoes.

No one spoke. Occasionally, Kevin would look at Val, or vice versa, to offer some silent encouragement in the form of a smile. Their enthusiasm overcame their fear and discomfort. They stopped several times for water or to rest, but for the most part they kept up their pace single-file through the jungle.

The sounds of the jungle grew so loud at one point that Kevin pulled his camera back out and began filming. Monkeys and birds were screaming overhead, and insects buzzed past their ears.

"We're heading further south . . ." Kevin whispered as he videoed. He was quickly told to be silent by an angry Wie, and he cut tape. Val shrugged. It would make for good B-roll or background. Oh well.

After almost two hours of arduous walking, the sounds of the jungle suddenly ceased, and Zyy squatted down in the trail. Everyone behind him stopped and also squatted down to wait.

125

Zyy cocked his head and listened, then whispered to his men, and finally to Wie.

Wie translated in a whisper to Kevin and Valerie Jean. "We're very close. We're going to move ahead and scout the kampong. You two wait here! No filming!"

The three villagers and three rangers moved ahead silently toward Aht. Kevin and Val looked at each other. She started to protest not going with them, but Kevin put a finger over his lips and held up two fingers. She smiled.

Two minutes later, he took off the lens cap and aimed it at Val. "Real quiet," he said. "Three, two . . ." he pointed at her.

"This is Valerie Jean Kozak reporting from the deepest jungle," she whispered. "We're just outside Kampong Aht. We're here to investigate the reported massacre of the local indigenous population known as the Penan people. Another tribe from a nearby village stumbled across the massacre and reported it to the local rangers while we happened to be at the station, and they've allowed us to accompany them on this dangerous journey.

"As we traveled down river, we came across multiple bodies that had been riddled with bullet holes, in an area that has never seen rifles before. Who would do such a thing to such peaceful people? Stay tuned as we try to uncover the mystery of the jungle massacre!"

"Cut!" said Kevin. He was so excited he could barely contain himself. "Hang on, I want to send this out now. Let me see if I can get a satellite uplink."

It took a few minutes, but sure enough, even in the deepest jungle of a third world country, he was able to broadcast a video off of a satellite thousands of miles away. "God, I love this new camera!" he said to Val. "That film's already at NatGeo and our cloud account! I have a guy at CNN I know, too. I'm sending him that clip to his mail. This is *real* news, Val! This could be huge! And no one has this story in the whole damn world other than us."

She beamed with excitement. "I'm a mess, though. It's not exactly a great first impression."

"Are you kidding me? You're gorgeous! And having some dirt on your face in the middle of the jungle makes you look like a war correspondent! This is great stuff!"

"I have dirt on my face? Seriously? Why didn't you say anything?" She wiped her sweaty face with the back of her hand and pulled her blonde hair behind her ears.

Kevin leaned in and kissed her. "You're beautiful. Stop it. Now come on, let's follow those guys before they get too far ahead."

The two of them jogged through the jungle, fighting thorned bushes and vines as they followed the footprints. They hadn't followed the trail for more than ten minutes when the sound of machine gun fire roared over the silence of the jungle. The two of them froze and quickly squatted down into the foliage. Kevin fumbled with his camera, slightly panicked as the gunfire grew louder and steadier. It sounded like an all-out war.

"Hurry!" whispered Val.

Kevin switched his camera to the "live" setting, which meant it would be uploading in real time as he shot the film. He was afraid he might not have time to sit and get a signal if they were on the run. Pointing the camera at her, he held up three fingers, then two, then pointed at her.

Val was whispering, close to the lens. "We're back, just outside of Aht. As you can hear, there's machine gun fire coming from the village. We're going to try and get closer and see what's happening!"

Kevin looked at her, horrified. "Are you fucking daft?"

It was too late. Val ran down the jungle trail toward the sound of the gunfire. Kevin, although terrified and totally against the idea, had no choice but to follow his girlfriend. They ran along the trail to the sound of the gunfire, which came to an abrupt halt.

"Shit!" said Val, ducking into the bushes. "There!" she whispered to Kevin. He pressed the "record" button and zoomed in on the village of Aht, built on stilts over the river. A large black flag with Arabic lettering fluttered in the breeze.

"Fucks's sake, Val! That's an ISIS flag!"

"Are you getting this?" she whispered.

"Hurry! We need to get out of here! Where the hell are our people?"

Kevin zoomed in on the flag, then pulled back and panned over to Val. She whispered into the lens. "This is Valerie Jean Kozak, reporting from Kampong Aht in southern Brunei in the Labi Forest Reserve. We've just uncovered what looks to be an ISIS training facility while investigating a report of a massacre of local villagers!"

"Hey!" whispered Kevin, pointing. He kept his camera rolling as a group of men with guns walked out of the jungle toward the village with Wie and one of the villagers. Wie and the native looked terrified, even from a hundred yards away.

Two Arabic-looking men walked out to the group, and they all began speaking rapidly with animated gestures. The man with the gun aimed at Wie pointed in the general direction of Kevin and Val.

"Shit. We need to get out of here," said Kevin, still filming live.

"Not yet! They have Wie. We need to see what they're doing."

What they were doing suddenly became very clear. One of the Arabic men grabbed Wie and held him by his arms from behind. The other man pulled a knife from his belt, grabbed Wie by his black hair, and slit his throat. Not satisfied with merely killing him, he kept sawing and hacking until he managed to severe Wie's head from his body. This brought a cheer from the other men as Hamdi held up the head.

The Penan villager pushed away from the soldier holding him and tried to run. He didn't get more than five steps before multiple AK-47s began firing and cut him down. This was also met with thunderous applause.

The same man, Hamdi, that had decapitated Wie quickly moved to the Penan man and cut off his head as well. The others quickly cut bamboo and shoved the poles into the ground, mounting the heads on top.

Kevin grabbed Val by the hand and pulled her along as he began running through the jungle back the way they had come.

CHAPTER 36

Chestnut Hill, West of Boston

"You buying me a house here?" asked Julia sarcastically.

"Yeah. Right after we steal that statue and sell it on the black market. Wow. There must be one golf course per capita up here."

"It's amazing. And this is just *one* of her houses?"

"Secretary of state must pay better than senior chief."

"There's no way we can follow this guy to the house. All of these places have gates and security guards and there are zero random cars just passing through. Jeez. Look at the size of these houses," said Julia, in awe.

"Gotta be every bit of twenty thousand square feet. All brick? Pool? Not too shabby."

Julia began typing a hundred miles an hour on her laptop.

"What are you doing?" asked Chris.

"One sec," she said, still typing. "Okay—I found one!"

"Found one what?"

"Found us a house. Twenty-six million. How much do you have saved up?"

Chris smiled. "Enough to pay the groundskeeper for two weeks."

"Okay, plus all my money, so that makes it three weeks. Should I call the real estate broker?"

"No. Call Dex. Give him the rundown. I'm cutting out of here. We stand out like a sore thumb. I knew I should have rented a Maserati."

"Told ya," she teased.

She called Dex's private secure cell phone back in Langley from her own encrypted cell phone.

"Hey Jules, where y'at?" he snapped.

"We are in a very nice neighborhood where Chris is going to buy me a house so I can have ten or fifteen kids. A place called Chestnut Hill."

"Yeah, that's her main residence. Look, just try and snap a picture of the truck going through the gate. Can you do that?"

"You got it, boss. Then what?"

Dex thought for a moment. "Then nothing. Go to Boston and have fun for a couple of days on the Company card. E-mail me the picture."

Julia smiled at Chris. "*We* have a hot date. One picture, and we're out of here."

She reached out and held his hand as they circled back to time their passing of the truck at the gate. Julia watched the GPS moving around the block and instructed Chris, who sped up and went around the corner. Julia casually fixed her eye makeup using her phone like a compact makeup mirror as they passed the truck, which she photographed.

"Best assignment we ever had," she said. "This is so much better than getting shot at in the jungle."

CHAPTER 37

USS *John Warner*

Chief White and two of his men set the UUV inside the chamber from which it would be deployed. The UUV weighed a hundred pounds, with most of the weight coming from the batteries, propeller, and lights. It could also be armed with explosives and used as a guided weapon, but in this case, it was for reconnaissance only.

The chief went through the checklist with his bosun, Charlie Decker, and once satisfied the UUV was ready to go, they closed the watertight vault door of the deployment compartment located just above the nose of the sub on the top deck.

They flooded the compartment and then opened the outside hatch remotely. Chief White sat at a console next to his assistant, Bosun Decker. Decker would be steering the ship, and Karl would be operating the camera for live video feed with a separate joystick.

The UUV had extremely powerful LED lights that didn't use much power, but lit up the black ocean for a distance of almost fifteen yards. Using the GPS location provided to them by the skipper, who knew the original location of the jet wreckage, they guided the UUV at twelve knots.

The USS *John Warner* remained motionless at 550 feet as the UUV dived deeper and traveled away from her. Back on

132

the bridge, the skipper watched the same video feed that Chief White was watching.

"Forty yards from our mark and closing," said Bosun Decker quietly. "Cables to our port side."

"Steady as she goes," replied the chief, now scanning back and forth with his camera.

"There!" The bosun altered his course slightly and sped to the downed jet. As he got closer, he slowed down and began focusing the lights near the wings. Dropping down lower, he cruised past the right wing and saw no sign of a diver. He moved around to the other side of the aircraft and dropped lower still.

"Bingo," said the chief. "Hold there."

The chief panned his camera around and zoomed in. "Up two feet and move closer so I can see his face."

The bosun moved the UUV up and around, and sure enough, the bright lights showed the face of a man inside his large helmet, squinting at them. Decker used the controls to wag the wings of the UUV at their downed diver. He smiled and pursed his lips, blowing them a kiss.

The bosun and chief both laughed out loud. "At least he still has his sense of humor," said the chief.

"Yeah, I'm not sure I'd manage to be so calm in his shoes."

The chief zoomed back and panned around. "Take me around, Charlie. Let's see how we're going to get him the hell out of there."

For the next thirty minutes, the UUV moved around the wreck examining the aircraft and how it was pinning their man.

"I don't think it's lying on top of him with a lot of weight, it's just that damn suit. It's so hard to move in those things. We get our mini-sub to him, I gear up with my suit, and I think I can drag him out."

"We have the inflatable jacks, too," reminded Charlie.

"Not a bad idea. We'll bring them, too." The inflatable jacks were similar to the ones firemen and first responders used.

They were wedged under an object and deployed, filling with air from a compression tank and lifting the object like a car jack.

"You ever dive six hundred, chief?" asked Charlie.

"First time for everything, Charlie."

"I'll go. I volunteer," he said.

Chief White patted his shoulder. "Thanks, brother, but you'll be steering the mini-sub. If you get wet, we have a serious problem."

Chief White hustled through the crowded sub back to the bridge, where he met with Commander Norman to go over the details. They discussed the mission, the location of the Chinese subs, and the hanging nuclear weapons, and put together a timetable that needed to happen immediately.

A few hundred yards from where they discussed the plan, Jon Cohen lie in the dark, his body now shaking uncontrollably, as he recited the twenty-third psalm.

CHAPTER 38

Jungle near Kampong Aht

Val and Kevin had run nonstop for fifteen minutes, hoping they were headed the right way. They stopped when they had cramped up so badly they simply couldn't run any further. They stood doubled-over with their hands on their knees, trying to catch their breath.

"They just fucking *murdered* them. I can't believe it," said Val.

"Insane. But that's an ISIS flag, Val. One hundred percent sure. *ISIS*. We need to get this video to the authorities, yeah?"

"Yes, of course. Do you think it's safe to stop here?"

"I'd feel better if we were further away. We'll catch our breath and go as far and fast as we can. God I hope the key's in the boat."

Val looked around. "Is this even the right way? I mean, I think it's the way we came. But are you sure?"

Kevin tried to fight the panic in his stomach. "I don't know. I think so. It feels like the same way, yeah?

Valerie wiped a tear. "I say we just keep going this way. It feels right to me. Do you think they know we're here?"

"I don't know. If they questioned Wie with a gun in his face, I reckon he'd tell them. But maybe they just killed him too fast to ask him. Damn. I don't know. Let's just go!"

135

The two of them started running again, heading back in the direction they thought they'd come from. After twenty more minutes of running, they stopped for water.

"Kevin? Are we lost?" asked Val.

His eyes were showing tears. "I don't know." He shrugged, trying to hold it together, but panicking in his chest. "Let me see if I can get a signal." He pulled his satellite phone and camera and turned them both back on. The satellite phone connected to the Garuda 1 satellite thousands of miles over his head, which provided satellite phone coverage for almost all of Southeast Asia. After a minute, he had a connection. The last call he had made on that phone was to the ranger station where he had met Wie. He hit redial and it just rang and rang.

"No one else is at the ranger station. I guess that was all of them."

Valerie shook her head and tried not to get upset thinking about the other six that didn't make it back. "When Wie called in to report it, he called the interior minister's office. Maybe we can reach someone there."

"Good thinking. The guy's name was Ali. Abdul Ali! That's it! Abdul Ali, Minister of the Interior. Let me search for a number!" Kevin spent a few minutes on his phone searching the Internet until he found the number for the interior minister's office. It took a few minutes of being transferred, insisting it was a national emergency, before he was finally put through to the minister's secretary, and finally to the minister himself.

"Minister Ali? Thank God! Listen, we have an emergency in Labi Park!"

The minister spoke perfect English. "Oh? What sort of emergency?"

"Did you get the message from the ranger station? A ranger named Wie?"

"I haven't spoken to him yet. I was told to call his office. I've been busy with other matters of state."

"Wie is *dead*! You have to listen to me, Minister Ali! There's an ISIS training camp or something out here!"

"ISIS? Don't be ridiculous," he said, trying not to sound rattled. If the sultan found out that the camp had been discovered, the sultan might make *him* the fall guy. He was suddenly very nervous.

"I'm not making this up! We saw the black ISIS flag! We saw the men with guns! They murdered three of your park rangers and three villagers who lived out here! We need help!"

"This is quite a story," said the minister, stalling as he panicked and tried to quickly come up with a plan.

"Listen to me! We're journalists, okay? I have everything on video! Give me an e-mail address and I'll send you the proof!"

"Video?" he blurted out. It came out sounding much louder than he intended.

"Yes! You need to call in the army or something! We're out here in the jungle and we need help!"

"How many of you are out there?"

"My girlfriend and me, that's it. They killed everyone else!"

Abdul was panicking. They had video. This could be a disaster. "Listen to me carefully. I'm going to try and get you some help, but I need to know where you are."

"We don't know where we are. We're lost I think. I know we're near Kampong Aht, and that's where the ISIS camp is now. They killed all of the villagers and your rangers, and they'll kill us, too." His voice cracked, and he took a deep breath, trying to be brave for his Valerie Jean, who looked every bit as terrified as he felt.

"Give me your cell number and I'll get back to you as soon as I can get you some help."

"Please, hurry," said Kevin. He gave the minister the number for his satellite phone and hung up. "What are you doing?" he asked Val, who was looking at her iPhone, which didn't have a phone signal out in the jungle.

"I have a compass on here. My phone doesn't work, but this does. Can you open a map on your satellite phone? Maybe we can figure out how we got here and backtrack."

Kevin squatted down in the ferns and pulled her down with him. "Okay, good idea. But we've got to be careful and really quiet. These buggers could be anywhere, yeah?"

"God, I wish I was in Auckland right now," said Val, fighting back tears.

"Yeah, me too. But we're not. So let's stay alive and use your compass idea. The minister's going to call back. Maybe they can send a helicopter or some troops or something."

"What about the Australian Navy? They always have ships out here. Or the Americans? What if we can get to a *real* army?"

"And how do you think we're going to do that? Just call the governor-general or something and ask her to send in the Royal Marines?"

"The video. Send that video to every news network on the planet. Hell! Let's do a live broadcast right now! Right here!"

"Jesus, Val . . ."

"I'm serious! Get that camera on live feed to the mailbox. We'll do it in one take, no editing, then shoot that film to every news agency we can think of. I'll beg for help. Someone will come!"

Kevin stared at her. It wasn't that crazy of an idea. What did they have to lose? He set up his equipment and took a quick scan around the area, which appeared desolate. The birds and monkeys were loud, which seemed to be a good sign.

"Quietly, yeah?" He pointed at her.

Val looked into the camera with tear-filled big blue eyes and began her broadcast, describing the mass murder at Kampong Aht, the capture and murders of their guides and rangers, and the proof that it was an ISIS camp, flag and all. She gave their approximate location and begged for help from anyone that could get to them. By the time she was finished, both she and Kevin were fighting back tears.

She closed the broadcast with, "Please . . . anyone who can see me. My cameraman and I are photojournalists from New Zealand. We don't want to die out here. There are hundreds of ISIS soldiers after us. Please. We're begging you. We need your help immediately! This is Valerie Jean Kozak, with Kevin Israel, in Brunei, signing off."

Kevin lowered the camera and gave her a long hug. "You were bloody fantastic. You might have just saved our lives."

"No—*you* are going to save our lives! Get that to every news agency on the planet."

Kevin sat on the wet ground and went through all of his professional contacts, sending the video clip they had just recorded. The heading of his e-mail said URGENT-LIFE AND DEATH. Someone somewhere should open that. Maybe?

"Now what?" he asked Val, having finished the upload.

"Now we get the fuck out of here," she said calmly.

The two of them stood up and began walking north following Val's compass, wondering if an army of terrorists was right behind them and if the river and their boat was in front of them.

CHAPTER 39

Oil Platform *Sunrise*

The mini-sub held its position over Jon Cohen. Chief White put on his heavy dive suit and full helmet. It wasn't an ADS 2000 like Jon's, but with a special gas mix that was piped in from the mini-sub via hose, he could stay at this extreme depth for almost an hour.

The mini-sub was pressurized and acted like a diving bell. The bottom hatch was opened inward, but the air pressure inside the sub kept it from flooding. In this fashion, Karl could drop into the ocean from the bottom of the sub. At six hundred feet, every procedure had to be executed precisely. There was no margin for error. Any mistake could kill all of them instantly.

Karl grabbed the nylon bag with the small pony tank attached to it and stood still while the other crew members checked and rechecked all of his gear. They gave him the "okay" sign, which he returned, and then he slowly dropped out of the sub. Once outside, he turned on the powerful lights and began swimming toward the lights of Jon's helmet.

⊕

The team stood together on the bottom deck of the platform, huddled around the video monitor wired to the ADS 2000. The sun was setting on a beautiful night in the South China Sea, with a warm breeze gently blowing. Although Jon couldn't see his friends six hundred feet above him, he could hear them. And although the team couldn't hear Jon, they could see him.

For almost ten hours, the team had taken turns telling dirty jokes to Jon, and when they could occasionally make him laugh, it was cause for major celebration on deck. Having run out of jokes, they decided to sing to Jon. None of them knew the complete lyrics for any songs, so they downloaded music videos from the Internet and did a horrendous karaoke on the deck. They found it much more entertaining than Jon, who was silently begging them to stop torturing him, but genuinely appreciated what they were trying to do for him.

They were in the middle of a Stones song when McCoy started screaming at them over the radio from the command center of the ship, where he was also watching the monitors. He was paying closer attention than they were down below while singing their brains out, and saw a difference in the amount of light on his screen.

"Hey! Shut the fuck up! *Look*! There's lights down there!" McCoy screamed into his radio.

Moose stopped singing and took a knee at the monitor. "Quiet!" he barked, as the team went silent and looked closer at the screen.

"Jon, you see anything? We see lights, we think."

Jon blinked twice and made a huge smile.

"Thank God," sighed Moose. "You see navy divers? A sub?"

Jon blinked twice again.

"Okay, listen. We can't see anything but your face. The other video feed went down with your lights. We're right here, though, brother. You're going to be okay. They're going to get you out."

Jon gave two long blinks and mouthed "thank you" with a smile.

For several minutes, they all sat in silence, quietly praying that the navy divers could save their friend.

When Karl made it over to Jon, he put his face directly over Jon's face and gave him a big smile while wiggling his eyebrows. Jon almost cried. He'd never been so happy to see another human being. He was cold, exhausted, and famished, and had never been so thirsty outside of desert training. The diver made a show of an imaginary watch and the "okay" sign, which Jon understood to mean, "Just give me a little time and everything will be okay."

He disappeared from view as he swam under the wing and set the jack near the wing tip, about fifteen feet from where Jon was pinned. He pulled the cord, and with an explosive burst, the jack inflated and raised the wing almost two feet on that side. That was the good news. The bad news was the jet started sliding in the downward direction, which meant it would slide off the jack in a moment. Karl quickly swam back to Jon and stood on the sand bottom. He squatted down and grabbed Jon by the straps near his helmet and, using every ounce of strength, began pulling a very heavy suit.

When Jon realized the diver was behind him and was trying to pull him, Jon used his arms to help. He shoved his claws into the sand bottom for traction and pushed as hard as he could. Over his head, the wing was sliding down toward his oversized boots, and he worried they'd get stuck. He pushed as hard as he could, no longer remembering he was exhausted or cold—he just wanted to live.

With Karl pulling and Jon pushing, they managed to clear the jet before it picked up speed and slid off the inflatable jack. The jet continued its journey after it cleared the jack and slid down the slope of the sand plateau until hit the edge and vanished, making its last flight to two thousand feet below sea level.

Jon lay on his back, laughing and crying in exhaustion and relief. The crew above had no ideas what was happening, but based on Jon's face, they were very excited that something good was happening down there.

Karl swam around in front of Jon and smiled, then motioned to him that he was going to get him to stand up—easier said than done. Karl, with Jon's help, managed to roll Jon slightly to his side. Once there, Karl did a squat near his upper body, grabbed Jon by the helmet, and stood up. Jon used his aching arms to push off the bottom, and between the two of them, they managed to get him back into a standing position.

The two men looked at each other and smiled in disbelief. Jon mouthed "thank you" and the other diver returned the smile with a "you're welcome." The original thought had been to bring Jon into their mini-sub, but with Jon clear and standing up, he could be returned to the surface if the winch was working.

Jon mouthed "up" to the other diver, who gave him a thumbs-up. At the surface, the team saw Jon's mouth say "up." His face was brightly lit from the other diver's lights, and they knew he'd been saved.

"Jon, did you say *up*? You ready to come up?" asked Moose.

Jon blinked twice and smiled.

"Up! You're coming up!" screamed Moose. "Okay, let's get our boy!"

Ryan and Ray ran to the winch and pressed the button that retrieved the six hundred feet of cable to the spool. Jon slowly began ascending. Karl swam up with him, escorting him to five hundred feet, and then, seeing he was okay, waved goodbye and returned to his sub. Karl passed the two giant nuclear bombs suspended mid-water on straps and cables on his way back to the sub. All he could think was "holy shit" as he swam past them.

Karl swam up the bottom of the mini-sub and was pulled inside by the crew. After the hatch was sealed and pressure adjusted, Karl began the process of decompressing in his suit as they adjusted the gas from the sub's controls.

"Outstanding," said Charlie as he guided the mini-sub back to the *John Warner*. He now had the delicate task of reentering the bay from which they had deployed. Space was tight on a submarine, and his entrance had to be perfect to slip inside the mother ship. There was total silence as he "parked the car in the garage."

CHAPTER 40

Sunset, The Sunrise

The team stood on the deck by the ADS 2000 retrieval system with their adrenaline pumping. Ray operated the winch, and the team leaned over the deck, staring at the ocean's silvery surface in the setting sun. The metal cable ran through the water as it re-spooled, and the team was yelling at Jon, even though he couldn't hear them from below the surface.

"Come on, baby!"

"You got this!"

A few minutes later, Jon's helmet breached the surface, followed by his Michelin Man suit, spinning slowly as he came up from the water. A cheer erupted from the team, and they reached out and grabbed his arms as the winch was brought over the deck of the ship. A minute later, Jon's feet touched the deck and the winch stopped, as Ray and Ryan immediately went to work taking apart the suit.

As the top half of the suit was lifted off, another cheer went up as they saw Jon's face for the first time. His lips were a little blue and he was shivering, but his smile was contagious. Ripper and Moose picked Jon up under his armpits and took him out of the suit legs, and McCoy wrapped a silver thermal blanket around him and handed him a bottle of water, which Jon drank instantly.

145

"Good to have you back, brother," said Moose, rubbing his shoulders and back and trying to warm him up.

"Holy crud, it's good to be above the water. I didn't think I'd see your ugly mugs again." His teeth literally chattered as he spoke.

"Get him inside," said McCoy. "He needs some hot food and a few more blankets."

"Call my mom. She'll send chicken soup," said Jon, forcing a smile. He was walking, with the help of Moose and Ripper, but he was exhausted from the cold and stress, and cramped up from being in the suit for so many hours. His lips were purple against a very white face.

"Hey, man, you might have set some type of dive record for most hours at six hundred feet," said Ripper with a grin. The group walked to the elevator and brought Jon to the deck where their rooms were located.

"I don't recommend anyone try and break it," replied Jon weakly. "What about the nukes?"

"They're still hanging below us," said Moose. "We changed mission priorities to rescue the world's worst diver."

"Sorry about that. Shit, man, I never even saw it coming. The weight coming off the jet made it shift—next thing I know, I'm on my back and can't move."

"I'm just busting your balls, man. You did great. We have the nukes ready for recovery, and you're still in one piece."

McCoy helped Jon to his small bed in his room. "Just lay down and warm up for a little bit. I'll bring you some food."

"I want to hear about the rescue, when you're up for it," said Moose. "Some dude in another one of these suits just walk up to you from out of nowhere?"

"No, it wasn't a Newtsuit. Just a deep-dive dry suit. I was flat on my back, and a face appears right in front of me, with some dude smiling and making faces at me. I thought I was narced out or something for a second. Man, was I glad to see him. I owe that sailor a beer or ten."

McCoy's voice came on over the PA system of the rig. "Moose to command! Incoming flash messages!"

Moose and Ripper exchanged quick glances and smacked Jon on his shoulders. "Okay, boy-o, we gotta go see what's up. Eat. Sleep. Take a hot shower, and we can debrief when you're ready."

The two of them hustled off to see what was so exciting in the control room.

CHAPTER 41

Langley

Darren Davis and Dex Murphy sat together in Darren's office working their way through yet another pot of Turkish coffee.

"If we give the pictures to Gallo, he'll have to follow up," said Dex, looking at the pile of photos on the table that Chris and Julia had taken. The images showed the various pieces of artwork stolen from Syria and sold through Ali Sawaad to the United States secretary of state.

"Don't bet on it. Those were gathered illegally, and Gallo has his head so far up Reynaud's ass he wouldn't do shit about it. What he *might* do is serve us a subpoena for breaking into her homes to take the pictures."

"Come on, Darren, we have the GPS in the statue! We have the money transfers! We can nail her ass to the wall."

Darren shook his head. "Look, the priority is getting the boss's head out of the noose. We show Gallo the photos, tell him we have her cold, and simply make a trade. He'll find evidence of a foreign government having planted the pictures on Wallace's computer, and we'll forget about the art that Danielle has 'saved from destruction' because of her noble concerns about ISIS destroying the artwork."

Dex shook his head. "It's bullshit."

"Of course it's bullshit! But with Danielle and the president and the director of the FBI all swappin' spit together, it's the best we're going to get. Besides, with the stuff we've got on her, she'll never be able to run for president next year."

Darren's inside phone rang, and he grabbed it. "Davis."

It was Tina Marie, one of his assistants from the Pacific Desk. "Chief, open your mail and play the video I just sent you. That operation in Brunei just got a little more interesting. I'm in my office if you need me."

Tina Marie had been instrumental in setting up the operation in Brunei, and had done all of the actual legwork to acquire the semi-submersible oil platform, set up the fake Interglobe Oil company, and take care of all the ground support for Bruce and Apo during the operation. She was reliable, and rarely bothered the boss unless it was important.

Darren looked at Dex and shrugged, then popped open the video from his mail. A pretty blonde with a New Zealand accent was pleading into the camera for a rescue from ISIS fighters in Brunei.

"Holy shit," blurted Dex. The two of them listened to the videos, and then projected the map software on to a large screen in the office. They zoomed in on the Labi Forest Reserve.

"No notation about Kampong Aht," mumbled Dex.

"Too small, I guess. But let me get our people on this. If this is legit, then we were right in our assessment of the sultan. If he's taking his country down the Sharia highway, then it's not far-fetched that he'd allow ISIS to operate in his country. There's no way they'd be there without the government knowing it. That country is tight as a drum. No way. If they're there, it's with the sultan's blessing."

"What do we do about those two reporters?" asked Dex.

Darren folded his arms. "Not sure. Our priority is the nukes. Especially with ISIS forces confirmed nearby. Jesus, can you imagine ISIS with twenty megatons? I'll check in with Apo and the team and see what the status is over there." He walked to his desk and sent a flash massage to his people on the *Sunrise*.

CHAPTER 42

Oil Platform *Sunrise*

Moose and Ripper ran all the way to the control room where McCoy was sitting behind the console with Apo and Bruce. Apo turned when he saw them enter.

"Things just got interesting," he said. "Flash message from Langley with an attached file. Watch this."

He hit "play" on the video, and Moose and Ripper watched the same video from Val and Kevin that Dex and Darren had watched only moments ago, halfway around the world. The woman was begging for help.

Moose shook his head and asked, "Boss looking to mount a rescue op?"

"Not exactly. He wants our status on the nuke recovery first."

"You message him back yet?" asked Moose.

"Negative. I figured we'd better discuss it together first." Although Apo was technically in charge of the whole operation, Moose was the team's commanding officer for all things combat-related, having taken over for Chris Cascaes when he retired from the team the year before.

"The nukes are ready to be plucked and sent off on their way. We just need a ship that can bring them aboard. Once they're up and out, we can fly out to wherever the hell those two reporters are. Do we *know* where those two are?"

"Not exactly. Labi Forest Reserve is seven hundred acres or so of thick forest and jungle. Assuming we could get a bird to take us, we have zero intel on the ISIS force we'd be facing. I'll ask Langley for some additional intel—maybe sat or drone photos—and tell them we're ready for the nukes to be extracted. As soon as the nukes are picked up, we can move."

"How's Jon?" asked Bruce.

"He'll be good to go by tomorrow. My guys are part fish. They're *supposed* to be underwater. You get us a mission, I'll have us ready," said Moose.

"Okay. I'll see about getting these nukes aboard a ship," said Apo.

"And let's just hope that the Chinese don't come cruising by while the nukes are being pulled up out of the water," said Bruce.

"It's our property, being recovered in international waters," said Apo. "Fuck 'em."

"Yeah, well, China says this water is *theirs* and I'm not so sure how nine of us will do taking on three warships," said Bruce with a shrug. "Besides, we're supposed to be Canadian oilmen—we'd have no authority to be touching nukes, American or otherwise."

Apo began typing a message to Darren Davis requesting as much information as they could supply on the ISIS camp and size of the force there. They'd be ready to mount a rescue if called upon—they just needed the ship to pick up the nukes.

⊕

Back in Langley, it was early morning. Darren and Dex were still in Darren's office discussing five different problems occurring around the world at the same time.

Just another day at the office.

Darren's inside phone rang again. It was Cheryl Cook.

"Hey, Cookie, how are we doing on our boat?"

"It's on its way. The high-speed special operations ship HSV *Dauntless* was on standby in the Philippines. The ship will be at the *Sunrise* by tomorrow morning, Zulu time, approximately seven hours from now. It has cranes to hoist the packages. The USS *William P. Lawrence* will provide an escort out of the South China Sea, as well as the submarine USS *John Warner*. PACCOM is looped in on the packages and understands the ship isn't to be stopped by the Chinese or anyone else."

Dex wrinkled his eyebrows, wondering what, exactly, the US Navy destroyer *William P. Lawrence* would do if it was engaged by the three Chinese warships that had been patrolling the area around the new artificial island. There was no question that the destroyer and submarine could sink all three ships; it was more a question about starting World War III over a piece of water that shouldn't even have "territories" marked on a map.

"Thanks, Cookie. Keep me in the loop as the ships gets closer to our oil platform. I'll inform the team that the ship is on its way." He hung up and looked at Dex. "I'll need to update the president. He'll need to give PACCOM the ROEs if the Chinese try and intercept the supply ship."

"It's going to be an interesting few hours," said Dex.

"The team reported in that they can attempt a rescue of those two Kiwis, assuming they're still alive," said Darren.

"Why us? Don't the Aussies have anyone in the area?"

"The president wants a clear statement to the sultan of Brunei, as well as everyone else in the Pacific region, that if ISIS shows up, so will we. I think it sends the right message."

Dex nodded. "Okay, I'll buy that. But we only have a team of nine operators. We have no idea how large this ISIS force is."

"Working on that now. I had PACCOM dispatch a drone off the *Ronald Reagan*. As soon as we have any intel on location and force size, we'll come up with a plan. In the meantime, I had IT trace the mailbox of the journalists that sent the video. We're trying to get a message back to them to let them know we're sending help. They just have to stay alive another day or so."

CHAPTER 43

Kampong Aht

Mohammed and Hamdi sat in their hut, completely horrified, as they listened to the minister of the interior, Abdul Ali, scream at them on their satellite phone. They had made contact to request their ship to Singapore and, instead of getting the details of the ship and truck convoy, were shocked to learn that two journalists from New Zealand had seen their camp and witnessed the murder of a park ranger and a Penan tribesman. Abdul Ali was furious.

"The sultan was gracious enough to give you safe conduct and a place to make your camp, and you repay him with your carelessness!" He had been screaming at them for five minutes straight. When he paused to catch his breath, Mohammed spoke.

"Your Excellency, this is most unfortunate, but they are but two people lost in the jungle. I will have my men find them. It won't be a problem, I swear it. We have another ranger that my men were preparing to execute. We'll make him guide us to these two infidels. This can't take us off of our schedule, though, Excellency. We need trucks waiting for us where the river bends near Kuala Belait. The trucks need to transport my men to the ship we discussed. I need my men on their way to Singapore by tomorrow."

"And I need those two reporters taken care of *now*! Or you can forget your trucks *and* your boat! The sultan will hold me responsible for your carelessness!"

"Yes, your Excellency. My men will find them right away. Please, though, I beg you, have the trucks ready. As soon as these two are disposed of, I need my men operational."

The minister hung up on him.

Mohammed stood up and stormed out of the hut, followed by Hamdi. They walked quickly along the wooden planks between the huts until Mohammed spotted his men down below. He screamed down to the field where the ranger was tied between two trees. The ranger, found a short time after the others, had been tortured for hours. In his agony, he had convinced Mohammed that the three rangers and three Penan natives were all of them. Now, Mohammed found out that there were two more. He was beyond furious.

At his instruction, the men cut the ranger down from the trees and dragged him across the field toward their leader. Mohammed and Hamdi climbed down the ladders to the ground below and grabbed the beaten man from his guards.

"Lying dog!" screamed Mohammed, punching the man in his face. The man collapsed.

Hamdi jumped down and straddled the man, punching his face three more times, breaking the man's nose and left cheekbone.

"Enough! I need him alive," shouted Mohammed. "Take ten men. Have this dog lead you to where those two other infidels are and capture them. I want them brought to me immediately!"

Hamdi grabbed the man and pulled him to his feet, pushing him into the arms of the other two guards. "You heard him! Get more men! This ranger is going to lead us to these two reporters!"

The ISIS fighters assembled a search party, armed with AK-47s, and pushed the ranger out in front of them. The ranger, beaten and terrified, had a rope around his neck like a leash, held by the man behind him. He was told to find the trail to the two reporters in exchange for his life, which was, of course, a lie. The ranger had previously been told he was going to be burned alive, and the mere possibility of escaping such a fate was enough to break him. He swore he would find the two New Zealanders, and led the group out into the woods.

The ranger, even in his horrid condition, was able to quickly pick up the trail where they had come in. The group began a slow run through the woods as Mohammed and Hamdi had the men back at camp assemble and prepare weapons, ammunition, food, and their exploding vests. Eighty of the men would be leaving by boat, heading north toward Kuala Belait. By the time they got to the point of the river closest to the city, these two infidels would be caught and tortured to death, which would satisfy the interior minister, and then the men could be transported by truck to the awaiting ship at Kuala Belait for Singapore.

It was a tight schedule, but as long as his men could find the two meddlers, they should be able to strike Singapore within forty-eight hours.

As Mohammed and Hamdi stood on the planks of their elevated huts watching the men below loading their small boats, a small drone flew in slow circles twenty-five thousand feet above their heads. Live video feed bounced off a satellite over Australia and shot the signal to another satellite over the Atlantic, where it was bounced yet again to a small screen in an office in Langley, Virginia.

CHAPTER 44

Langley

Dex Murphy sat at his desk watching the live feed from the drone. Two men appeared to be in charge, standing up on a catwalk between huts overlooking the camp. Facial recognition software was still working on one of the men, but the other man was confirmed to be Hamdi Fazil, a Pakistani national known to be responsible for multiple attacks in Afghanistan and Iraq against US troops as well as just about anyone else he felt like murdering.

Dex grabbed his phone and dialed Darren, who was on his way back from the White House. "Go," said Davis from the backseat of his bodyguard-driven SUV.

"Drone's on station. We have positive ID on one of the men. Hamdi Fazil. He's a mid-level murderer, most likely not running the show. We're still running a few other faces. Nothing else yet. Oh, and definitely an ISIS flag in the camp."

"Well, nice of them to hoist the black flag. Did they draw a big bull's-eye on the campsite while they were at it?"

"Not necessary. Just say the word and I'll have a B-52 remove it from the jungle."

"Would be nice, but no. The president isn't going to sign off on an attack on a sovereign nation with which we aren't at war and don't have permission to run an air strike. A covert rescue operation is a different story. What's the status of those two Kiwis?"

"No response from our messages. They're either on the run, dead, or out of batteries."

Darren grunted. "Well let's just hope they've been on the run and haven't looked at e-mail. Hell, maybe they can't get a signal from the jungle."

"They managed to upload the videos," replied Dex. "But you're right. They're probably just on the move and haven't looked yet."

"What's going on at the camp?"

"Video shows activity. Lots of men moving around. They're loading up a small flotilla of boats. Looks like they may be bugging out."

"So whatever we're going to do, we need to do it fast. What's the status of our broken arrows?"

"The *Dauntless* is en route. A few more hours before it arrives on station. Oh, and just to keep things interesting, the USS *William P. Lawrence* was buzzed by two Chinese fighters again."

"Jesus. What the hell is the matter with these people? Are they *trying* to start World War III?"

"I know, it's crazy. The *Lawrence* fired warning flares."

"Yeah, well one of these days, we're going to fire a warning Sea Sparrow, and we're going to have a real situation on our hands."

Dex smiled at the thought of Sea Sparrow surface-to-air missiles knocking out a couple of Chinese J-11s. "Interesting part of the world," he muttered.

"Our other nasty weapon should be arriving at the *Sunrise* any second as well," said Darren.

"What's that?" asked Dex.

"Carl Stone," replied Darren. "He's out of Lebanon. I sent him to help out the team."

"They already had nine operators. Ten against a hundred seems like overkill," said Dex.

Darren smirked. "Don't be so cocky. Let's find those two reporters and knock out that camp. I'm on my way back to the office. See if you can find out who's running the show over there in Brunei by the time I get back."

Half a world away, an HH-60H Sea Hawk helicopter was landing on the helipad of the oil platform *Sunrise*. The gray helicopter was property of the United States Navy, Special Operations Group, off of the USS *Ronald Reagan*, from where the drone had deployed.

The team was asleep, except for Hodges, who was on watch again. The sound of the rotors woke up the sleeping men, and they all scrambled out of their beds to the deck above. Most of them were barefoot, in boxer shorts, but all of them were armed.

The door slid open and Carl Stone hopped out. A crew chief handed him three large duffle bags and snapped a quick salute, and off they went.

Hodges stood nearby, waiting for the arrival. Eric, like the rest of the team, had met Carl Stone while in Mexico on a previous covert operation. Unlike the team, Carl wasn't military. He wasn't actually anything. He didn't exist.

"Hey! Good to see ya," said Eric as he helped Carl with his bags.

"Thanks. Got here just in time I think. You got coffee or Rip Its on this barge? I'm in my own fuckin' time zone. I started in Lebanon. Went to Israel. Got a flight to Japan. Japan to the *Ronald Reagan. Reagan* to here. All in less than twenty hours. I'm so tired I could puke."

"Coffee's on. Just made it."

The two of them turned to see the rest of the team stumble up the steps, half asleep.

"Welcome to the *Sunrise*," said Moose. "We haven't hit any oil yet."

"Well, we're gonna be hittin' *something* real soon," said Carl.

CHAPTER 45

Kevin and Valerie Jean had been running on and off for hours, and were now officially lost. They'd checked the compass and the map dozens of times, but the jungle was impassible in some places and they had to change their course several times until Val's phone died, taking their compass with it. They'd been very frugal with Kevin's camera and satellite phone batteries, and so they'd wandered off course until they were exhausted and starting to panic. When it became too dark to move, they slept for a couple of hours of terrified rest on the wet ground and then forced themselves up at the first hints of ambient light.

"Try the minister again," said Val, sitting on a fallen tree to catch her breath.

Kevin turned on his phone and saw his mailbox had gotten several new messages. At a quick glance, he saw several news networks that he was anxious to read, but a different one said *RESCUE* and caught his eye. He opened it and read it out loud to Val.

United States Special Operations Group has received your video. We will attempt to find and extract you from your situation. Please acknowledge your receipt of this contact. Include your communication equipment status and approximate location if possible. Taking a picture with your GPS tag on and forwarding it here will assist us in locating you. If being followed by hostile forces, stay on the move. Head northeast if possible for better terrain. Remain calm and quiet.

Preserve batteries once you respond and check your e-mail again at 0800 your time. If possible, call this number.

"Rescue? Oh thank God," said Val, feeling her eyes fill with tears of relief. "Try the number!"

Kevin dialed the number on his satellite phone and was shocked when a woman's voice answered.

"You've reached a special hotline, confirm your identity," said the voice calmly.

"Hey! This is Kevin Israel and Valeria Jean Kozak! You sent us this number!"

"Okay, Kevin. This dedicated phone line was set up specifically for you. Are you in a safe location and how much battery life do you have on this phone?"

"I don't know. We've been on the run for hours. We only stopped last night when it got too dark. We can't tell if they're following us. I've been careful with my battery. Should have a few hours left."

"Very good. I need you to turn on the GPS locator on your phone, take a picture of yourselves, and send it to this number. It will help us find you. Then I want you to turn off your phone to save batteries, and keep heading northeast, away from that camp, to higher ground. If you're walking uphill, you're going the right direction, do you understand?"

"Yes, ma'am. When can you send help?"

"That's being worked on now. You need to understand, it may take a day or two. You're going to have to tough this out. Stay on the move, and stay quiet. Keep walking uphill and don't stop for anything. We're gathering intelligence now and working on a plan for extraction. What can you tell us about the camp? Do you know the number of soldiers? Did you see weapons?"

"We could hear machine guns. There was a lot of them, but I don't know how many. We ran. They killed the rangers and the natives that lived out here. There was a little village—a kampong, called Aht. They murdered all of the villagers and took over the kampong and turned it into a training camp or something."

"Okay, stay calm. So you think, more than fifty? More than a hundred? Can you give me your best guess?"

"I don't know. Maybe a hundred. I don't know!"

"Okay. It's okay. Just try and remain focused. Do you have any questions for me?"

Kevin looked at Val and shrugged. "No, I guess not. I'll send the picture, turn off my phone, and check again at eight my time."

"Outstanding. Kevin, you and Val need to remain calm, stay on the move, and use your brains to stay alive. Don't forget to activate the picture location services on your phone. The GPS. We're going to get you out."

"Thank you. Thank you so much. I'm going to send the picture now."

He hung up and took a picture of Val with his location services GPS on, and sent it to the number. The two of them hugged for a long moment and tried not to cry, then grabbed each other by the hand and continued moving through the jungle.

Three kilometers behind them, a dozen men with assault rifles hacked through the jungle and arrived at the ranger's boat the group had used to head up the river to Kampong Aht.

"If the boat's still here, then so are they," said Hazrol. He smacked the beaten ranger in his swollen bloody face. "Find their trail!" he commanded.

The ranger led the group into the jungle, unsure of what to do, but hoping that staying on the move might keep him alive until he could figure out a way to escape. Behind him, the

ISIS fighters trudged through the slippery mud and vegetation, angry to be on a wild-goose chase in the steamy jungle instead of preparing for an attack on the infidels.

CHAPTER 46

Dex received the call right before he was ready to leave for the day. The two New Zealanders were still alive, and had made contact through the emergency number created just for them. The agent that took the call immediately gave the information to Dex, who threw his jacket off and ran over to Darren Davis's office. Darren was just back from the White House.

"We've got contact from the two Kiwis. They're alive and on the run."

"Good news."

"The drone's still up. Analysts say a hundred men, give or take. The village of Aht is tiny. It was a family clan of maybe fifty, tops. Looks like these guys came up the river by boat, killed all of the villagers, and just made it their own. Facial recognition software gave us the most likely ring leader. Guy's name is Mohammed bin Awad. Syrian gunrunner who's been a lifelong dirtbag. I confirmed with two of our agents that he's an up-and-coming ISIS commander, but in Syria and Iraq, not Southeast Asia. This looks like the makings of a large-scale operation. With Mohammed and Hamdi traveling all the way to Brunei, they've got something big going down. We're shaking the trees, but no one's heard of anything being talked about in the rumor mill."

Darren crossed his arms and tightened his face in thought. "Brunei. Why the hell would these two fly halfway around the world to Brunei? What's their target? Something economic? Hong Kong, Singapore, Tokyo? Or something governmental, symbolic, or religious? Jakarta? Manila? Hell, even Australia. Damn. We haven't heard *anything*?"

"*Zero* chatter."

"Damn it." Darren stretched his back and loosened his tie. "Just off the phone with PACCOM. The *Dauntless* is almost at the *Sunrise*. As soon as they have the nukes loaded, they'll head straight to Guam."

"Guam, huh? I was wondering what they're going to do with it."

"The Marines at Andersen Air Force Base have EOD that will take the nukes. They'll be brought into Naval Base Guam. Once the navy has the nukes, disposal is their problem."

"Long trip."

"Yeah. Over twenty-three hundred miles. They'll have escorts for most of it. We just need to get them out of the South China Sea without an international incident."

Dex pulled off his tie. "I was getting ready to head home. Guess I'll stick around and wait for the packages to make it onboard."

"Go home and visit your wife. Get some sleep."

"And miss the start of World War III? No way. Plus, if this whole plan with the secretary and FBI goes south, I might be the new director. I should probably be here."

"Fuck you. Make us coffee."

$\oplus$

Several thousand miles away, the HSV *Dauntless* skimmed through an amazing red sunrise that sent pink tendrils across an endless sky. The *Dauntless* was shaped like a giant steel catamaran. For a vessel the length of a football field, it was nimble and could hit over forty-five knots. The ship had a helipad and large crane at the stern, and in its lifespan it had performed everything from special operations support to hurricane rescue and relief operations.

"Contact the team on the *Sunrise*," said the ship's captain, Commander Jessica Coulter.

"Aye, aye, skipper," replied her radioman. He hailed the *Sunrise*, appropriately, at sunrise.

Back in the control room of the *Sunrise*, Pete McCoy grabbed his radio when the call came in. Both the team and Commander Coulter knew the cargo, as well as the secrecy required during the loading of the nuclear weapons.

"*Sunrise* here. I have your contact on my screen, two miles out. We will begin preparing the cargo for transfer. Over."

"*Sunrise* this is *Dauntless* Commander Coulter. Estimated time to docking alongside is fifteen minutes. I'll need assistance from your platform. We usually have a tugboat for this. Parking this vessel alongside will be interesting, to say the least. Over."

"Roger, *Dauntless*. Understood. We'll have all available hands on deck three, which should be close to your rail. Cargo will be prepped for transfer to your cranes. Out."

McCoy pressed the "All-Call" button on the console and spoke into the mic. "Now hear this, now hear this. *Dauntless* preparing to dock alongside in fifteen minutes. All hands on deck three to assist. Winch operator to deck one to prepare cargo."

McCoy smiled. It was the closest he'd ever come to commanding a US Navy ship, and he felt all-powerful speaking over the ship's public address system. The euphoria was short-lived, however, and he hopped up from his chair and ran down to deck three.

By the time McCoy arrived at deck three, everyone except Ray Jensen was already there, spaced out along the rail with heavy lines at the ready. They'd already put out the bumpers alongside the rail, and stood in silence watching the beautiful sleek ship slowly move closer. Ray was on the first deck, just above the waterline, operating the winches that were now bringing up two bombs large enough to vaporize their oil platform and the navy ship in a split second.

As the *Dauntless* came alongside, Commander Coulter used the twin props to expertly move within a foot of the platform without touching it. It was nothing short of amazing to watch a person who looked so tiny up in the bridge of a large ship move it with such precision alongside an oil platform so immense that it dwarfed the three-hundred-foot-long vessel. As she came alongside, the team began throwing lines to the sailors on the deck, and the dozens of sailors pulled the two vessels together until they were tied off and the engine was cut to neutral.

By the time the ship was docked alongside, Ray had brought the winch up all the way. He used the controls to move the small crane out away from the platform, and by so doing, the two giant eggs were suspended a few feet below the water.

Aboard the *Dauntless*, the crew had been briefed about their mission and sped into action. One of their sailors repelled over the side in a wetsuit and dropped down into the water as the ship's large crane deployed from the stern. While that sailor went to work immediately securing the straps around the nukes to lines from the crane, a small inflatable craft deployed from beneath the stern and four EOD techs roared over to the nukes with a sailor at the stern running an outboard.

The crane operator brought the two bombs up to the surface of the water as the small watercraft pulled up alongside. The EOD techs secured their raft to the bombs and jumped right into their mission—disarming two nuclear bombs while floating between two large vessels full of human beings.

The team had moved to the side of their platform, which gave them a view of the EOD crew down below. While normally they might take cover somewhere when a bomb was being disarmed, it made no difference where they stood this time. There was no hiding from a twenty-megaton explosion.

No one said a word as they looked down and watched the techs use small torches to cut open the now-rusted access panels. Once the bombs were opened, they went about their work methodically. Though the team couldn't see much from where they stood, they knew the men below were either going to successfully disarm the two nukes, or none of them would ever know they didn't.

Twenty minutes later, the EODs gave a thumbs-up on the first nuke. No one cheered or dared even breathe too loudly. That waited and watched in silence as the bomb techs went to work on the second nuke. Almost a half hour later, when the EOD team held up their hands in victory the second time, there were a lot of sighs of relief. Aboard the *Dauntless*, the crane began lifting the two bombs very slowly to the stern of the ship.

As the men watched, the bridge of the *Dauntless* began flashing signal lights at the men. Something was up.

McCoy, who had left the command room of the *Sunrise* unmanned to help below, ran as fast as he could up the stairs to the command center. Apo was right on his tail. They burst into the room and McCoy grabbed the radio.

"This is *Sunrise*. You hailing me? Over."

"Affirmative. Been trying to reach you. We have two inbound aircraft on my radar. Most likely Chinese fighter jets. Maybe four minutes out, over."

"Shit," said McCoy to Apo. "What do we do?"

Apo grimaced. "Nothing. Load the nukes and let them get underway."

"Understood. The second you have the cargo secure, we'll cast off and help you get underway. Over."

"Affirmative. We're going to try and get the cargo under cover before they pass overhead. Our escort is still a few hours away from our rendezvous point. Thanks for the help, out."

McCoy grabbed the all-call mic and hit the button. "Attention on deck. Two inbound aircraft, most likely Chinese fighters. We need to get this ship underway as fast as possible, and they need that cargo secured and concealed. Bridge out!"

Down below, Moose and Ripper were barking at their men just like the sailors aboard the *Dauntless*. The small raft roared up out of the water and raced to the stern where it slid up a rear ramp and the sailors hopped out to secure their boat. The sailor who had gone over the side was helped back up over the rail as the crane began lowering the two bombs toward the deck. More sailors appeared from inside with large dollies, which they positioned below the bombs as they were lowered. The instant the bombs were free of the straps, the crane moved away and the sailors pushed the dollies to a deck elevator where they would be lowered and secured inside the ship. The team onboard the *Sunrise* cast off the lines and gave a few waves to the other sailors, and Commander Coulter revved up the engine and blew the ship's whistle. A moment later, the *Dauntless* roared away from the oil platform just as two Chinese J-11 fighters took a slow pass overhead.

Six miles away, the USS *William P. Lawrence* closed on the *Dauntless*, aware that three Chinese warships were shadowing them from less than five miles off their stern. Three hundred feet below the surface, half a mile behind the *Dauntless*, the USS *John Warner* silently moved through the water column, watching everything in the water move on their sonar monitors. Eighty miles away, the USS *Ronald Reagan* altered its course to provide air cover if needed as the *Dauntless* headed toward Guam.

The South China Sea—three and a half million square kilometers, and suddenly very crowded.

CHAPTER 47

Labi Forest

The sun had only been up for a couple of hours and it was already sweltering. Kevin and Val pushed themselves to keep moving, trying to walk uphill wherever they could see a slope in their footing. Kevin stopped near a plant that had rainwater collected in a depression of a branch. He licked his lips and grabbed Val.

"Drink," he said, pointing.

"I'm okay. You drink it."

"There'll be plenty more, go on."

Val leaned in and slurped up the water, wishing it was a gallon more. Kevin licked some moisture off one of the large leaves and pulled a dark berry off, examining it.

"If you don't know what it is, don't eat it," she said, worried.

He nodded and tossed it away, feeling his stomach grumble.

"Okay, we have to keep moving," he said. He stepped forward and rolled his ankle on the root of a large tree, tumbling over, almost tripping Val as he went down. He rolled around trying not to scream out loud as he held his ankle, wondering if he had broken it. Terrified he had broken his phone or camera, he scrambled around in the ferns and grass until he located them both. The lens cap was missing from the camera, but other than that, they were unscathed.

"Are you okay?" asked Val, kneeling down and grabbing him by the shirt.

"My ankle. I'm an idiot. Jesus, it hurts. Let's take a break for a second. It's throbbing." He sat up in a more comfortable position and looked at Val. "Hey, let's do another broadcast while we're stopped. I'll tag the video with our GPS so the Yanks can find us easier."

"Okay, but I look like shit," she said, pulling her hair behind her ear.

"It adds drama," he said, forcing a smile.

Kevin powered up his camera and phone, using the satellite uplink to live broadcast the video directly to the Dropbox folder and mailboxes he had used earlier. He focused on Val and gave her the cue.

Val spoke softly. "This is Valerie Jean Kozak, on the move in the Labi Forest as we flee from ISIS forces that have murdered dozens of Penan tribesmen as well as several Bruneian forest rangers. To anyone that is seeing this broadcast, we need your help. We don't know how many or how close our pursuers are, but we do know that we can't be captured. Please, if you're seeing this, send help! This is Valerie Jean Kozak, signing off and praying for help."

Kevin stopped filming and hit the "send" button. "Okay, they should see that. I'll leave my phone and video on in case they call."

⊕

One of Interior Minister Abdul Ali's most trusted men knocked on his door and walked in with a bow.

"Minister Ali, I've been trying to find information on the two journalists, as you requested."

The minister stopped what he was doing and looked up from his desk. "Yes?"

"They just broadcast a message from Labi Forest requesting help. It was in a file that had the GPS location on it." He smiled.

The minister stood up from his desk and ran around to his assistant with a huge smile. "Excellent work! You have coordinates?"

"I have the actual location, right on the map. Come to my office."

The two of them hurried down the hallway to his small office, where his computer showed a satellite map with a small flag. The assistant rolled his mouse over the flag, and longitude and latitude coordinates appeared. Abdul pulled his phone and hit redial, which went to the last number—Mohammed bin Awad.

"Yes, Minister?" answered Mohammed, seeing the incoming number.

"I have the location of the two reporters, write this down!"

The ranger had walked along a trail for several kilometers, not sure when it was last used, or by whom. For all he knew, it could have been made by Penan people or a wild pig. What he *did* know was that every minute he was further away from the ISIS training camp and a horrible death.

The men behind him complained of the heat and bugs as they hacked through the jungle. Thorned bushes cut sweaty skin as AK-47s clunked along hip bones. Hazrol's radio squelched, and he pulled it off his belt.

"Hazrol," he whispered as he followed the long line of soldiers.

"We have their location!" sneered Mohammed. "They were at this compass point less than thirty minutes ago. I'm going to send it to your sat phone. If you hurry you can catch them in less than an hour!"

"Excellent. And what about the mission?"

"The minister has agreed to arrange for the trucks, now that we know where these two are. The men are loading into the boats right now. God willing, they'll be at the port and out to sea tonight. When you find these two, you can kill the man there, but I promised Hamdi the woman, alive."

"Understood." Hazrol opened his sat phone and looked at the screen. The GPS map lit up with a blue point showing their location and a yellow pulsing point showing their target. He smiled and told the men in front of him to stop. The line of men stopped walking, and Hazrol walked quickly to the front. He took the machete from the man behind the ranger and smiled at their captive.

"Your services are no longer needed," he said, slicing the sharp blade across the man's bare belly. His guts protruded out of the gaping wound, and Hazrol shoved his hand into the coils of bloody intestine and pulled them out. He let go and watched the man hit the soft earth, screaming ungodly sounds. He handed the machete back to the soldier, wiped his hands off on his pants, and shouted "Follow me!" as he ran through the jungle following the flashing yellow dot on the map.

CHAPTER 48

Langley

Darren and Dex sat in a conference room drinking coffee, watching the video screen. Tina Marie had just showed them the most recently broadcast message from the two reporters in Brunei.

"It was recorded at ten in the morning Zulu time. They're exactly twelve hours ahead, so that's only thirty minutes ago," said Tina Marie.

"Were they told to broadcast another video?" asked Darren.

"No, sir. They weren't supposed to check in for several hours after their 0800 message. I think they're getting tired and scared."

"Yeah, well if the wrong folks are seeing this, they have reason to be scared. We need to get the team on the move."

Darren pulled his secure phone and pressed the contact for Moose.

"I was just going to call in, chief. The *Dauntless* is underway with the packages. We're trying to monitor things here from the control room's radar and sonar. Considering we're out in the middle of nowhere, this sure is a busy place."

"Explain," said Darren.

"I've got an island being built less than one klick away, two Chinese J-11 fighters buzzed us and the *Dauntless* twice already this morning as she was taking off, and Hodges is way up on top of the tower telling me he can see Chinese warships cruising around nearby. They got the whole ocean. They gotta be right in my fucking lap?"

"Well, yeah, that's sort of the point. Excellent work on the recovery. You have a new mission."

"The two reporters?"

"Affirmative. Satellite and drone intel came up with two names. Mohammed bin Awad and Hamdi Fazil. Awad's an up-and-comer. Hamdi's just muscle. They organized a force of about a hundred hostiles, but we don't know their target yet."

"Maybe it's just a training ground?" said Moose.

"Not halfway around the world from home. There's a target out there somewhere. Depending on how sophisticated they are and how much support they have, they may know they've been compromised. How fast can you have your team ready for a search and rescue op?"

"We're ready now, although we packed light for this mission. If we're facing a large force, I'd like some heavier weapons and more ammo. Can you have our transport bring us a shopping list if I send it to you?"

"I should be able to make that happen. Your transport will come from the *Reagan*. Probably be at least an hour if they can scramble fast. That gives you almost no time to come up with your plan. I'm sending you satellite images and last location of the two reporters. You can decide the best approach and just tell your bird where to take you. I'll have it all set up."

"Roger that, chief. We'll be ready."

Moose called Ripper into the control room up top, and the two of them began pouring over the maps and images that Langley had sent. They had a pretty good idea of the location of the two reporters based on their last recorded GPS, but didn't know how large a force was tracking them. The jungle was so thick where they were, even a drone couldn't see through the canopy.

"If they keep heading up to higher ground, there's a little clearing here. We can intercept them here," said Moose, pointing to their screen.

Ripper nodded. "What about the camp?"

Moose shrugged. "Right now, it's just a search and rescue. The last real-time shots of the camp show them on the move. They're either sending everyone out after the reporters, or they're heading out to wherever their target is. Langley thinks they have something big planned, otherwise why head halfway around the world to set up a camp here?"

Ripper looked at the satellite and drone images of the camp. There were a lot of enemy fighters packed into boats on the water. "The river doesn't follow the escape route of the reporters. If they're heading in the direction that the boats are all facing, they're going downstream, headed northwest. The reporters are moving to higher ground northeast." Ripper pointed to where the river emptied into the South China Sea. "They could follow the river to Panaga, Kuala Belait, Sungai Teraban, Seria—they'd have a lot of options once they get north. What's there worth destroying?" asked Ripper as he zoomed in on the map.

Moose studied the screen. "If they want to disrupt oil production, they could hit pipelines, the docks here and here, or the port where the tankers load. There's financial offices here and here. It doesn't seem right, though. Everything Langley says points to the sultan instituting more Sharia law and harsher penalties for noncompliance. Why would ISIS want to hit what looks like a friendly host nation?"

Ripper made a face. "So then they're not hitting anything. They're catching a ride out."

Moose nodded. "I think that's a much more likely scenario. They grab a ship to beat feet because maybe they know that *we* know they're there. That broadcast has already hit news networks and the web. They have to know that their location is compromised." He thought a moment. "So where would they go?"

"Either to a new camp or to their target. You know, there may be an airfield out there, too."

Moose nodded. "Langley said there was zero chatter about possible targets out here. They got a big fat zero. But Darren thinks it's something big and coming soon. No intel—just his gut. But the man's usually right."

Ripper sat back in his chair and folded his thick arms. "Well, we've got about ten seconds to come up with a plan and unass this rig. We just leaving it?"

"The *Sunrise*?"

"Yeah."

"Yup. The CIA brought it in from somewhere. They'll bring it *out* to somewhere. Not our problem. Tell the men we're leaving and to assemble on the helipad in forty minutes. We're heading into combat, so full battle rattle with Kevlar, I don't care how hot it is. The inbound bird will have extra ammo and some heavier weapons I requested. See you in thirty."

Ripper smacked Moose's massive shoulder and hopped up out of his chair. "This is good," he said to himself out loud, nodding his head.

"What's good?" asked Moose.

"Going back out into the jungle to kill some ISIS fucks. I kind of hated being on this floating metal target that doesn't move. If I wanted to be an oilman, I would have moved to Midland, Texas, with my brother. Let's go spread some seven-point-six-two freedom."

Moose shook his head. "There's something wrong with you, which is why I love you. Get moving."

Ripper froze. "Wait!"

"What is it?" asked Moose, seriously concerned.

"McCoy got to do it twice. I always wanted to do this!" He walked over to the all-call PA button and smacked it. "Now hear this! Now hear this! This is your almost-captain speaking!

Gear up, you meat-eating fish! We're going to go rescue two reporters and get a chance to maybe separate some terrorist heads from terrorist bodies! Grab all gear and assemble on the helipad. You have forty minutes from now. Full battle rattle and Kevlar! Go!"

He leaned back against the wall and smiled, much goofier than his normal serious face. "Man, that was so cool. No wonder the skippers all walk around like they have a stick up their ass."

Moose shook his head. "Seriously, dude. When we get back, I'm sending you for a psych eval."

"Oh, come on! Like you don't want to do it." He made a face and walked out to get his gear up.

Moose sat in the control room, staring at the all-call button, wondering what he'd even say.

Four hundred feet below the surface, the USS *John Warner* tailed the HSV *Dauntless* and the Chinese submarine that followed her in three hundred feet of water. The high-speed *Dauntless* was pulling away from the noisy Chinese submarine, which was completely unaware that the United States' newest *Virginia*-class sub was behind her.

"Maintain course and speed, Mr. Burdge. Master Chief Adams, is it me, or is that the noisiest damn submarine in the ocean?"

The master chief looked back over his shoulder at the skipper. "Maybe we're just spoiled, skipper. But yes, sir. I could follow this pig from fifty miles out. If we had windows, we'd probably see black diesel exhaust."

The skipper laughed. "Stay on her. Surface ships closing?"

"Negative. Those same three ships are maintaining their parallel course three miles out. And it *is* parallel. Every time the *Dauntless* moves by a few degrees, so do they."

The skipper nodded. "They're just sending a very clear message—letting the *Dauntless* know that they're there. You know what's so damn cool, though?"

The master chief smiled. "*Yes, sir*. That no one knows *we're* here!"

CHAPTER 49

Two US Navy Sea Hawks sped over the South China Sea just above the water. Far above, the *Reagan* had also deployed a radar-jamming plane that would be escorting the two birds into Bruneian airspace. While the Sea Hawks were capable of carrying eleven soldiers, the team had requested additional weapons and ammo, and the commander of the *Reagan* had been generous with the requested arms. The additional gear meant a second bird to give the team a little room to reassemble their individual kits, something not usually done while on the way to the mission target.

With one bird hovering, the first touched down on the pad, and Moose directed half the team into the Sea Hawk.

"Let's go, people! McCoy, Jensen, Apo, Batman, and Cohen! Chalk one!"

The assigned men ran to the door as it slid open and piled in. By the time the bird was moving out to make room for the second, the men inside were already opening boxes and pulling weapons and ammo.

Moose watched as the second bird set down gently on the oil platform. He grabbed Ripper and yelled into his ear above the rotor blades. "Did we remember to turn off all the lights and water?" He smiled and smacked his friend's shoulder, then yelled to the remaining team.

"O'Conner, Hodges, Stone, Ripper, on me in chalk two! Sayonara *Sunrise*!"

They didn't have much time to gear up as they flew over the water at 150 knots. They quickly grabbed extra ammo, including grenades. Ripper pulled an M249 SAW out of one of the crates and loaded it. McCoy, their acting medic and radio operator, put together first aid supplies lest the two reporters need medical attention, or any of them become wounded during anticipated combat, as well as extra batteries for the radios and phones.

They finished getting ready, double-checked their gear and communications equipment, and then sat back and watched the water go by. The crew chief spoke to them over their radio headsets.

"Time to target, ten minutes. We'll be on station over international waters while you're finding your package. If we get low on fuel, we'll have to go back to the ship, refuel, and return. That means an extra hour for the round trip and refueling, so grab them fast, or prepare to hunker down for an hour."

"Roger that. Finding these two make take more than a couple of minutes, and they have company on their tail. If we can't dust off in time, we'll keep heading north."

The crew chief gave them a thumbs-up. The two helicopters banked hard, having gone a bit out of their way to avoid populated areas along the coast. Now over land, they turned southeast and roared over the treetops hugging the earth to avoid being spotted. Over their heads, the navy pilots were jamming Bruneian airspace in the area.

The lead pilot's voice came over their headsets. "Thirty seconds!"

The birds slowed their speed and banked again, this time moving around some very tall trees and finding a small opening in the canopy over a river. Stones in the riverbed could be seen in the shallow water. The lights inside turned green and the crew chief slid the side doors open.

"Good luck!" shouted the crew chief as the birds hovered just a foot over the water.

Moose was the first one out of his helicopter, hitting water only a few inches deep. In less than a minute, all ten men were on the ground, running full speed into the jungle for cover. The Sea Hawks disappeared quickly as the men squatted in the ferns, taking their weapons off safety.

McCoy had a small tablet out and was looking at the pulsing yellow dot on the screen. "Less than half a klick, skipper. Due west."

The men fanned out in the woods and moved in complete silence, walking down a gentle slope in the thick tropical air. McCoy typed on his tablet and sent an e-mail to the reporter's mailbox. He called the satellite phone number Langley had supplied, but it went right to voice mail. He looked at Moose and shook his head, then whispered into the phone, "Rescue team is on the ground. Keep heading uphill and call this number back."

The team began running.

◈

Hazrol led his men in a single column as they jogged through the jungle following the GPS position on their screen. He slowed down as they got closer. "I want the woman alive!" he ordered his men. The men fanned out and moved slowly and quietly through the woods. When they arrived at the location on his screen, they stopped and began looking around more thoroughly. Hazrol squatted down and picked up the lens cap of a camera and smiled. They were close.

◈

Kevin and Val were standing, doubled over, as they tried to catch their breath. They'd been running all morning, and even though they were young and fit, they were also exhausted and without proper food and water for over twenty-four hours.

"We've got to keep moving. How's the ankle?" asked Val.

It was purple and throbbing, but stopping to rest wasn't an option. "I'm okay. Let me check in, one sec." He pulled his sat phone and turned it on. He had a new voice mail. It was a man's voice saying the rescue team was on the ground.

"Oh, thank God," he said, closing his eyes for a moment. "Val, they're here! They're on the ground looking for us!"

"What did he say?" she said, now energized with an adrenaline rush of hope.

"Uphill. We just keep heading uphill. I'll call him back."

The two of them began running again, Kevin's gait awkward as he limped, but he never complained as he used trees and plants to pull himself along through the jungle. He hit the call-back option on his phone and listened to it ring as he stumbled through the woods.

"Special Operations, McCoy here, go!" said the voice.

"Thank God you're here!" said Kevin, stopping to catch his breath. "We've been running for two days. I have no idea where we are."

"It's okay. Leave your phone on now, okay? I can track you. How much battery life do you have?"

"At least an hour or two, I think."

"Okay, good. You and your friend, are you injured?"

"No, no, we're okay. I rolled my ankle and it's slowing me down, but we're on the move, heading uphill."

McCoy was looking at his tablet at a map with Moose and Ripper standing over him. Moose pointed to the river.

McCoy nodded and spoke into the phone. "Listen to me. If you keep heading the way you're going, you should come to the river again. It winds around all through the hills up here. We're very close to it ourselves. When you get to the river, we should be able to get you out. Our helicopters can get in there where the river gets wider."

"Okay. How far is it do you think?"

McCoy squinted at the map. "Maybe half a kilometer. Just keep heading straight up the slope."

McCoy heard Val in the background of Kevin's phone as she whispered, "Shh!"

Kevin's panicked voice hissed into the phone at McCoy. "They're right behind us! We need to *run!*"

Hazrol and his men had an easy time following the two reporters. Kevin had been using plants and trees for support as he ran, and he might as well have left a trail of spray-painted arrows behind him. The broken trees limbs and torn leaves had led them for hours straight after the pair of infidels.

"There!" shouted one of the men, pointing up the hill.

The man next to Hazrol raised his rifle.

"Wait! The woman has to be taken alive! Get them!"

The men began running up the hill toward where they had seen a brief flash of the reporter's shirt moving through the woods. They were screaming with excitement like a pack of hyenas after a wounded animal.

CHAPTER 50

Mohammed and Hamdi waved and shouted blessings and encouragement to the men as the small flotilla took off downstream. Eight small motorboats carried sixty men, each armed with an AK-47 and an exploding vest filled with Semtex and ball bearings. The vests would be turned on the morning of the assault and could be detonated manually by the wearer, or would simply explode via a timer. The plan was to have each man at the correct location in Singapore a few minutes before noon, and then, at exactly noon, all sixty men would simultaneously turn into human claymore mines. If discovered by authorities before noon, the wearer could simply pull the cord and manually detonate. The wearers weren't informed of the timers, and in the event that they chickened out, they would still martyr themselves.

The boats disappeared around a bend in the chocolate-colored river, and Mohammed and Hamdi returned to their hut to call Hazrol and check on the status of their two reporters. Hamdi had mentioned *mut'ah*, a temporary marriage, on more than one occasion to Mohammed, something permissible under Sharia law, and Mohammed was now considering it himself. He had seen the video, and the blue-eyed, blonde-haired woman was quite beautiful. Perhaps he'd enjoy the woman first, before Hamdi—a privilege of rank. Mohammed knew Hamdi would most likely kill her during the marriage anyway, as the man wasn't quite right.

185

Once the boats were gone, Mohammed made the call, but it went to voice mail. Whatever was happening would remain a mystery, at least for the time being.

Fifteen thousand feet above Mohammed's head, a small drone made quiet circles, feeding video real time to Langley, Virginia, half a world, and perhaps a few centuries, away.

"Darren, it's Dex. Cookie just called in to tell me they have Mohammed on drone video surveillance again. I'm watching it right now. Check your monitor. Those two are back at camp with a small group of men. Most of them are heading downstream in small boats. I can have a Raptor on station in less than forty minutes and we can hose the whole armada."

Darren was putting on the video feed as he listened to Dex. "I told you, the president won't allow an air assault inside Brunei. If the team can get in and out unseen, we're green light. But that's it. If these boats leave shore, that's a different story. Plenty of options if they go out to sea."

Dex was frustrated. "Well, we have the drone over the camp watching the two ring leaders. I either have to re-task the drone to follow the boats, or we risk losing them."

Darren thought for a moment, and then said, "Keep it on Kampong Aht. Get another air asset off the *Reagan* to start following the boats. We know they're heading downstream. We'll find them."

"What if they get off somewhere? We'll never have another shot at them," said Dex, starting to get wound up.

"There's nothing out there worth blowing up until they get to the coast. By then, we'll have them tracked again."

"I hope so," mumbled Dex. "What's the plan for Mohammed and Hamdi and their little group of choirboys?"

"Once the team extracts the two civilians, we'll have them find the camp and destroy it."

"Assuming they find them. I've been trying to reach them with no luck."

"The team or the two reporters?"

"Both."

$\oplus$

Moose and Ripper had split the team into a hammer and anvil. They took Hodges with his sniper rifle and O'Conner and sprinted right to flank the reporters and their pursuers. Once they had the two civilians secured, they'd force the enemy back toward the rest of their team, who'd be ready for them.

The four of them sprinted down the hill full speed. Moose and Ripper looked like NFL linebackers when they got a head of steam up. They didn't bother going around small shrubs and saplings, they barreled right through them. Hodges and O'Conner followed the two of them like running backs following blockers.

"Dead ahead!" Moose warned in a hoarse whisper.

All of them hit the ground and continued to crawl forward looking for cover and concealment. They could see movement in the heavy foliage, but it was impossible to see who it was. They had weapons at the ready. Moose had the bipod out under the SAW, and Hodges popped off the lens caps on his sniper rifle as he started slowing his breathing as he focused on the leaves whipping around down the hill.

Hodges scanned through his scope and finally smiled. "It's our two civilians, twelve o'clock, headed to our nine o'clock. They're making for the river."

Moose decided to take a risk and yelled at them. "Over here! Over here!"

Fifty yards ahead, in thick foliage, Kevin and Valerie Jean heard the American voice. Kevin grabbed Val by the arm and pushed her in the direction of the voice. "Go!" he screamed. "Run!"

Their pursuers had closed on them, now only another fifty yards or so behind them. If they wanted them dead, they'd already have been shot, but clearly they wanted them alive. Kevin and Val knew all about what happened to ISIS prisoners, and would prefer death to capture. Kevin ignored the pain in his ankle and sprinted with Val as fast as he could, his lungs burning.

Valerie Jean was the first to appear through the foliage, sprinting straight for the team, who were camouflaged and hidden in the ferns. She didn't see them until Ripper stood up and waved at her. "Here!" he snapped at her. She burst into tears of joy and screamed at him, "They're right behind us!"

The team stayed where they were in their firing positions and Ripper just kept shouting at her to run faster to him. Kevin appeared behind her, a second later, running clumsily on his swollen ankle. When they were close enough, Ripper jumped out and grabbed them both and pushed them to the ground.

"Stay down! Do not get up for any reason!"

Hodges spoke into his throat mic to the other half of the team. "About to go kinetic. Prepare for assault. Out." He lined up his target, the first of the line of men racing through the woods, and took a slow, steady breath.

Hazrol was screaming at his men to run faster. They could see the pair they were chasing on and off for the past five minutes, but had failed to catch up to them. Carrying their weapons and ammunition had slowed them down slightly— and perhaps terror had made their quarry faster.

Hazrol was yelling at the man in front of him to move faster when the man's head exploded into a cloud of blood and brains. It took Hazrol a second to process what had happened. One second, the man was there chopping through the foliage as they ran up the slope; the second, the man's head was just gone. He was still staring at the body that was dropping when his own head was removed from his body.

The men behind Hazrol saw their leader's head removed by the sniper's bullet and stopped their advance. A third shot rang out, hitting yet another of their men, who exploded in blood before spinning off into the foliage. The remaining men panicked. The eight of them turned around and started running without any plan—they were just trying to get away as fast as possible.

Moose opened up with the SAW and the woods around the men began coming apart. Leaves and branches were dropping out of the jungle as a hundred rounds zipped all around them, dropping two more of them. The red tracers added to the ISIS fighters' terror as they ran away. They were getting further away from the sound of the SAW when they ran into the second half of the team. Apo, Carl, and Bruce were the only men that weren't wearing jungle-camouflage BDU fatigues. They were in khaki cargo pants with T-shirts and Kevlar vests, looking like they could easily remove their vests and go out for lunch. Their marksmanship gave them away, however. They each began firing two-round bursts and killed five enemy soldiers before they even realized they had run into an ambush.

Jon fired his M4 from behind a fallen tree and took out the last enemy soldier. The woods went completely quiet and nothing moved. Blue smoke hung in the air and the smell of gunpowder filled the noses of those people still able to breathe.

McCoy scrambled over to the two reporters. "Hey! We got you, you're safe!"

The two of them hugged him and began thanking him over and over. "We didn't think anyone would come," said Val, overcome with adrenaline and relief. She was shaking.

"We happened to be in the neighborhood. Are you hurt?"

"No, we're fine, thanks to you," said Kevin.

"He's not fine," said Val, reaching for his leg. "I think his ankle is broken."

"Yeah?" asked McCoy. "You ran through the jungle on a busted ankle? Maybe you can join up with us. We like that sort of attitude."

Kevin forced a smile. "That attitude is called total fucking terror, mate. From now on we're covering flower shows in Brisbane."

Moose looked at McCoy, who gave Moose a thumbs-up. "Ankle, but mobile enough. We're good to go."

Moose touched his throat mic. "Moose to Apo, we're coming in, don't shoot, over."

Apo's voice came back on the radio. "Area is secure. Weapons safe. Out."

CHAPTER 51

Langley

Dex and Darren were in the Ops Room with Cookie watching the drone feeds when the radio came in from their team. Though they could only see the camp at Kampong Aht and the ISIS boats moving downstream on the river, it was really the rescue they were trying to monitor. The foliage had made observing visually impossible, so they sat on pins and needles for an hour waiting for word back from their team.

Moose's voice finally came in via sat phone. "Company One, this is Rescue Actual. Package is secure. Preparing for exfil, over."

Darren, Dex, and Cookie all exhaled with relieved smiles. Darren spoke into his phone. "Roger, Rescue. Outstanding. Over."

Dex looked at Darren with a raised eyebrow. "Well that was our good deed for the day. Now what about the evil deeds?"

Darren nodded. "Agreed."

"Rescue Actual, once packages are secured, are you able to Charlie Mike to Kilo Alpha?"

Moose looked at his team of warriors. The boss had just asked him if they could continue mission to Kampong Aht once the two civilians were secured. His men were one hundred percent badass, but they also didn't have much information on the enemy force.

191

"Company One, do you have additional intel on target, over?"

"Affirmative. Target has split in two. Kilo Alpha has two HVTs and approximately a dozen tangos. Larger force is on the move north by water. Destination unknown, but possibly to target along the coast or for exfil by boat or plane. We can supply target coordinates if you're good to go. Over."

"Send coordinates and intel. We're waiting for medevac, out."

Moose handed McCoy the phone and called his team over. The two civilians were nearby, eating MREs and drinking water with Kevin's foot elevated on a tree stump.

"Boss wants us to Charlie Mike to two separate targets. There's the camp at Kampong Aht with a small reserve force guarding two high-value targets, and the main force on the move. The larger force is traveling by boat downstream, heading north. They can be at the coast in a few hours. They're either attacking a target along the coast, or they're looking for a ride. We'll need to split into two groups and hit both simultaneously after these two are secured."

Apo spoke up. "Bruce and I can hit the camp."

Carl nodded. "I'll go with them."

Moose nodded. "Good. Three of you should be enough to handle the camp. McCoy, open that e-mail from Dex and show them the two HVTs. Mohammed bin Awad and Hamdi Fazil. This is not a capture mission."

Carl looked at him with a raised eyebrow, as if to say, *"Are you kidding me?"*

"I'm not real big on those," he said quietly.

"The rest of us will head north by helo and drop in here. We'll ambush the boats as they come up around this bend."

McCoy pointed to his headphones. "Moose, birds inbound. I requested a third for medevac straight to the *Reagan* for these two."

"Excellent. Prepare to unass this mosquito factory."

The team went into fast motion gathering gear and securing weapons. Assisting Kevin, they led the two journalists down near the water where the trees wouldn't be in the way of the Sea Hawks' rotors. When they heard the birds inbound, McCoy grabbed his radio just as the pilot's voice came on.

"Rescue One, stalkers inbound, over."

"Popping smoke."

"Roger, I see green smoke."

"Rescue One, that's me, over."

"Bird One will be medevac. Over."

McCoy relayed the information to Moose, and he and Ripper grabbed Kevin and helped run him out into the shallow water with Val close behind. As the bird hovered over the water, the side door slid open and a navy corpsman leaned out to pull Kevin in with Moose and Ripper lifting him off the ground. Once he was aboard, Moose grabbed Val and picked her up as if she was weightless, handing her up to the corpsman.

She surprised him with a kiss on his cheek. *"Thank you! Thank you all!"* she screamed over the noise. The corpsman pulled her in, slid the door closed, and the bird nosed down as it moved forward before roaring off over the trees.

The second bird came in straight behind it. This one had the door already open with a door gunner leaning out. He waved his arm, and Apo, Bruce, and Carl raced out of the jungle with their weapons, climbing up quickly with a wave goodbye to the team, and off they went. The third bird came in straight behind the second and repeated the procedure for the team headed north after the larger ISIS force.

The first and third helicopters raced north single file. Apo, Bruce, and Carl headed west toward Kampong Aht. The crew chief in their helicopter handed them headsets so they could speak without screaming at each other. He smiled at their two-day beards and dirty civilian-style clothes with Kevlar vests over their T-shirts.

"Y'all don't exactly look like a SEAL team," he said with a smile.

"You must have us mistaken for someone else," said Apo dryly. "We're insurance salesmen heading to a small sales conference in this little town called Aht." He never smiled, which removed the crew chief's smile as well.

"Whatever you say," he replied with a shrug. "Time to target, fifteen minutes. You're being dropped here," he said, pointing to a small map. "Aht is here. Just follow along the river west."

The three of them nodded, then sat back and closed their eyes for a few minutes' rest. They'd just come from a firefight, and the post-combat rush had left them exhausted until the next adrenaline rush.

Further north, in the first helicopter, the medic tried to remove Kevin's boot. He howled so loudly, the medic popped a syringe into his thigh to kill the pain. He waited and then pulled the laces out before opening the boot and sliding it off with Val's help. When he slid the dirty wet sock off, the purple and black ankle showed the lump where it was broken. The medic wrapped a small ankle brace around it to immobilize it, as Kevin leaned his head back and groaned, now woozy from the pain meds.

"Looks broken," said the corpsman.

"He ran on that for two days, almost nonstop," said Val, rubbing his shoulder. Tears welled up in her eyes. "Never even complained, tough guy," she said with a proud smile.

"Fear's an amazing thing. Thanks for coming to get us," Kevin said to the corpsman. "Hey Val . . ."

"Yeah?"

"Since we're alive and all, you want to get married?"

She leaned over and kissed his sweaty, dirty face. "I do," she said.

The corpsman laughed. "I've been in the navy six years. This is a first!"

The trailing helicopter banked hard left and stayed over the treetops racing at 150 knots toward the river near the coastline. Inside, the team quietly cleaned weapons as they prepared for their next little war.

CHAPTER 52

Langley

"Mr. Davis, Mr. Gallo is on line one," said Susan.

Darren looked at Dex and smiled. "This should be interesting." He punched the button on his phone so it went to speakerphone. He put his finger over his lips as he looked at Dex and said, "Good evening, Bill."

"Hey, Darren. Returning your call, what's up?"

"Your guys break the computer hack yet?"

Bill paused. "Investigation is ongoing. Hard to say where anything came from. The local guys who were swapping illegal picture files seemed to share through a Dropbox-type system, and we have *them* nailed down cold. Wallace's file didn't go through that Dropbox, so we have no idea how it ended up on his computer."

"Well, I think we have hard answers for you. Maybe you can stop by."

The FBI director paused, his anger building. "What do you mean, *you* have answers? You know the CIA isn't allowed to be part of this investigation."

"It's high level, Bill. Involves foreign perps connected here at home. Pretty alarming stuff. You really need to come over. This isn't for a phone. Even a secure one."

Bill didn't like being baited by the CIA, but he liked the CIA's involvement even less. He needed to nip this in the bud. "I'm on my way," he mumbled and hung up.

"Today's the day?" asked Dex.

"Why not? Poor Wally is home wondering if he's getting arrested or fired. This bullshit's gone on long enough."

The two of them continued to monitor the movements of their team for almost forty-five minutes until Susan called them by intercom. "Director Gallo is here to see you, sir."

Bill entered the room, not particularly pleased to see Dex Murphy in the room with Darren.

"We all staying for this?" he asked.

"Yes. Have a seat, Bill. Dex and I have an interesting story to share with you."

Bill sat down, looking annoyed.

Darren pulled a file from his desk and opened it, then handed a bundle of photographs to the director. Bill looked at picture after picture of statues, pottery, and ancient jewelry.

"What am I looking at?" he finally asked.

"Middle Eastern artifacts stolen from museums and parks all over Syria and Iraq. Some are Greek, some are Roman. All are basically priceless pieces of art. ISIS has been funding their war with the sales of art and oil."

"Tell me something I don't know," said Bill, now even more irritated.

"Well, it seems as though the secretary of state, your friend Danielle Reynaud, has been buying this art from a man named Ali Sawaad in Lebanon for almost two years." He let that hang in the air for a minute. Bill glanced down at the pictures again.

"Where were these taken?" he asked.

Darren stifled a smile. "These pictures were taken in the secretary's various homes. We have money transfers from her office to his bank in Lebanon."

"And how would the CIA be able to get a search warrant to look inside the secretary's home without me being notified, Darren?" His voice quivered with anger.

"Oh, we *wouldn't*," Darren replied softly.

The FBI director leaned into the table, his face now red. "Are you telling me that you broke into the homes of the goddamned secretary of state? Because if *that's* what you're saying, I'll arrest you myself! What the fuck do you think you're doing, Darren?"

"Wait. It gets even better," he said, now smiling. He turned his computer monitor around so Bill could see it. It was a GPS map showing Chestnut Hill, near Boston. He pointed to a glowing dot. "That's a GPS transponder, Bill. It was planted in an ancient Roman statue stolen from the country of Syria by ISIS, who then sold it to an illegal art dealer who was really CIA, who sold it to Ali Sawaad, who then sold it to Danielle Reynaud. So basically, the secretary paid a half million to ISIS to fund terrorism. But wait! It gets even *better*, Bill." Darren was now on a roll and getting wound up and angry. "That piece of shit didn't even have the decency to fund ISIS with her *own* money—no, she used a government account that's supposed to fund confidential informants to help us in the war on terror, not *fund* it, Bill!"

Bill's face fell. He was so stunned he was dizzy. While he wasn't particularly a fan of the secretary's ego or attitude either, he had hitched his wagon to her rising star and now felt sick to his stomach.

"Your people put the transponder in that statue?" he asked.

"Bingo. And you know what? A day after that statue was given to Ali Sawaad, Sawaad knew exactly who would pay a half million US to buy it. Go figure. He called his best customer, *immediately*. A few weeks later it's in New Jersey from Lebanon, then trucked to her place in Chestnut Hill. And while the pictures I showed you are inadmissible in a court of law, you're pretty damned compelled to get a search warrant for that statue now, aren't you?"

Bill sat and stared at the photos, speechless.

"Of course, this country has already had a pretty big embarrassment, hasn't it, Bill. Imagine, the director of the

CIA being investigated for kiddy porn charges—just about the worst accusation on the planet. Hell, you don't even have to be guilty, you just have to be *accused* and your best friends go running for the hills. You'd have a better chance of your friends coming over to your house to visit you if you had Ebola."

Bill looked back up at Darren. He was ashen.

"I think maybe the country would be better off if it was spared these two embarrassments. Don't you?"

Bill cleared his throat ever so slightly. A tell, to a poker player. "We had a name come up in the investigation. Wallace's investigation." He stared at Darren trying to read his face. The CIA had moles everywhere—did Darren already know or not? Bill continued, his voice now quieter. "If someone was to be arrested for planting those files on the director's computer, the public would be satisfied that an arrest was made, the culprit was found, and the director would be cleared. The bureau would have a successful investigation, and the CIA would have a director back to work."

"This is what I call interagency cooperation, Bill. What's the name?"

Bill looked at him, still unsure if Darren already knew. "Jeff Dennis."

Darren's face told Bill he hadn't known. "The secretary's campaign manager?"

"Well, 'political advisor.' But, yeah. Future campaign manager. The hack went from his office to Holstrum's home computer. Dennis wouldn't have done it himself—he's no IT guy, but you can be sure he ordered it done. It's a conspiracy charge. He's done."

Darren glanced at Dex, then back at Bill. "Like I said, the country doesn't need a long string of embarrassments. The director can return to work after you make the announcement about your successful apprehension of the suspect. I'm sure the secretary of state knew nothing about it. It may hurt her politically, but she'll most likely avoid any official problems."

Director Gallo cleared his throat again. "It would seem to be in the best interests of the country to make it all go away quietly. Director Holstrum is officially cleared. I'll call him personally."

"Thanks, Bill, but just the same, I'll call him myself." They locked eyes for a second.

"Sure. That's fine. We done here?"

"Almost. Reynaud is in possession of artwork that doesn't belong to her. The taxpayers own it. She's going to donate it to the Smithsonian Museum. All of it."

"I'm sure when she realizes it's stolen artwork and her art dealer was operating illegally, she'll want all of it out of her house," said Gallo. He stood, silently looking at Darren.

Darren Davis extended his hand and shook it firmly. "Always good to work with you, Bill."

Bill left the office and Darren and Dex exchanged a satisfied smile. "I should have had Chris bug her houses. I'd give anything to listen in on the next few phone calls between her, Jeff Dennis, her attorneys, and the FBI."

"A part of me wants to jump up and high-five you," said Dex. "But mostly I just want to puke in your trash can."

"Use your own," replied Darren. "And when you're done, we'll check in on our boys. I have a very happy phone call to make, first."

CHAPTER 53

Apo, Bruce, and Carl moved silently through the jungle toward Kampong Aht. Their helicopter had dropped them far enough away to avoid the sound of the aircraft reaching the tiny village, leaving them with a pretty good hike toward the village.

They were the "anti-team." While Moose and his original team looked every bit like SEALs or some type of elite special operations commandos with their gear, uniforms, buzz cuts, and shaved faces, Apo, Bruce, and Carl moved through the jungle in civilian-looking cargo pants and hiking boots, with their Kevlar vests simply put on over T-shirts. They did wear web belts with plenty of weapons and ammo, but with longer hair and Apo's beard, they looked more like cartel hit men than US spec ops. They could have also cared less what anyone thought of their looks. They were professional, fearless, and quite lethal.

Carl, the oldest of the group, spoke quietly as they jogged down the slope toward the village. "Bruce, you're lucky. Back when I was your age, out in the field, killing terrorists, we had to run uphill in both directions . . ."

"Yeah? But still, your age has its advantages. Your AARP card gets you discounts on ammo, and if we get stuck out here, you probably know how to make stone tools and fire and shit."

"True. All true."

Apo was out on point and held up a hand. They stopped their banter and squatted down into the ferns. Apo signaled them forward, and they moved up until they saw what had

201

stopped Apo in his racks. The body of a Penan tribesman was in the trail. The man had been machine gunned and left to rot, and the jungle's janitors had already gone to work on the body, feeding on the corpse so as to make its appearance disgusting.

They exchanged glances. They were now officially in "Injun Territory" and switched the safeties off and laser gun sights on. They fanned out and moved off the trail, now moving slowly and quietly in combat mode. The fun and games were over.

Mohammed and Hamdi paced angrily around the catwalks of the elevated village. They'd been unable to reach Hazrol and had no idea what was taking them so long. Interior Minister Abdul Ali had been emphatic about killing the two reporters, and failure to do so could mean the end of their mission. They needed those trucks and a ship at the ready.

Down below, the dozen men left behind to train the next group of martyrs performed daily chores. They fetched fresh fish from the Penan traps in the river, gathered firewood, cleaned weapons, and generally tried to kill time.

Apo held up two fingers and pointed. Apo and Bruce fanned out and snuck forward through the wet, soft moss and ferns. The three of them scanned the area to see who else was around. Apparently, it was just two low-level flunkies, gathering wood. They walked and chatted loudly, confident of their ownership of all around them. One of them had a machete, which he used to chop off branches. The other man was carrying a load of deadwood he had gathered.

Apo and Carl were the closest to the two men and circled so slowly they barely appeared to be moving. They maintained visual contact with each other as they moved through the ferns and grew closer to their quarry, waiting patiently for the right second. When both enemy soldiers had their backs turned and were focused on gathering more wood, Apo and Carl leapt out like jungle panthers, armed with KA-BAR knives. Each of them stabbed and slashed their targets so many times, both ISIS fighters were dead before they hit the ground.

The three of them moved forward, scanning in every direction and listening to the sounds of the jungle. Monkeys and birds chattered and insects buzzed. They were still undetected. When they reached the edge of the jungle, they could see the village in a small clearing. Perhaps twenty or so huts were built on stilts just above the water, with bamboo ladders leading to the primitive canoes below. The huts were also made from bamboo, with thatched walls and roofs. The design probably hadn't changed in a thousand years.

Apo pointed to a satellite dish placed on top of a thatched roof. Okay, perhaps *that* was a new addition. The three of them all instantly concluded the hut with the dish was the command center, or at the very least, the communications center. It would have to be hit before any alert went out. The problem was, it was situated across open ground from the jungle.

Bruce signaled to the others. He pointed to himself, then the river, then made a signal of swimming. He'd swim to the ladder and attack from the water. Apo and Carl nodded. They'd move around in the jungle and attack from the rear of the village once Bruce was in position. If they were detected, at least it would draw attention from Bruce's assault.

Bruce crept left toward the river as Apo and Carl moved to the right to circle behind the hamlet. Apo and Carl hadn't gone more than forty yards when they came to another clearing. The fighters had made a rifle range in the back of the village by clearing the woods and constructing a few earthen berms. Crossing the opening would be a problem, but four of the ISIS fighters were preparing to take some shooting practice, which might offer a solution. Apo whispered into his throat mic to Bruce, so softly it was barely audible.

"Batman, four tangos about to take rifle practice. When you hear shooting, it isn't an assault, but will mean four less tangos. Hoping their buddies will think it's just them shooting. Charlie Mike. We're kinetic in a minute."

"Roger. Out." Bruce kept crawling toward the river.

Apo and Carl knelt at the edge of the jungle, not more than twenty yards from where the four men pushed magazines into their AK-47s. As Apo and Carl examined their battle space more carefully, they realized that the fighters in front of them had taken bodies from the village and tied them to poles out in the berms. They weren't shooting at silhouette targets, they were shooting at dead civilians. Seeing their animal behavior made killing them that much easier.

Carl and Apo sat patiently and waited for the four men to take firing positions. The ISIS fighters laughed with each other and made jokes, and then the four of them raised their weapons. The instant they began firing, Carl and Apo also fired, hitting the four men twice each before they raced forward to make sure they were dead. Three of the four were already dead; the last man was gasping until Apo slit his throat. They ran across the clearing and made it behind the village on the other side of the rifle range.

"Batman. Four tangos down. In position. Over."

"Roger. Heading into the river. Out."

Carl and Apo moved into their assault position at the edge of the forest and waited for Bruce.

CHAPTER 54

The team sat on the edge of the helicopter's floor, feet on the rails, as the gray bird roared north over the river, below the tree line. The crew chief was watching a tablet with real-time satellite images of the flotilla further north. The copilot had the same information up front. When the helicopter was within two kilometers of their target, it swung up and out away from the river and made a large loop to get ahead of the boats.

Once the Sea Hawk had gotten ahead of the incoming boats, it dropped down to the water again, and the team jumped down with splashes into the waist-deep, brown river. The helo roared off north to refuel at the *Reagan*, and the team moved quickly out of the center of the river to both sides where they quickly took up positions of concealment.

Moose deployed the legs of the SAW on a fallen tree, with Ripper and Jon nearby. On the other side of the river, McCoy, O'Connor, and Jensen found positions in a series of boulders, and Hodges quickly climbed an ancient tree with limbs draped in vines and moss that hung over the water. He lay prone on a branch bigger than most trees, completely concealed in the foliage and moss.

They waited for ten minutes, and the boats appeared, chugging along the river with outboard motors. There were eight boats, full of heavily armed men wearing explosive vests.

Up in the tree, Hodges focused on the first boat. He squinted and tried to confirm what he thought he was seeing. He shook his head in disbelief. "Overwatch to Moose. Tangos are all wearing explosive vests, over."

205

Moose looked at Ripper. "We need to take them out quickly before any of them can detonate manually," he whispered. He watched the boats getting closer. Originally, the plan was to wait for the boats to get right between them before shooting, but with the fighters all wearing exploding vests, that would put them too close to the ambush team. They'd have to take them out before they were right on top of them.

"Overwatch, helmsmen are yours. Stop those boats when I open up. Everyone else, pick a boat. My side of the river will start from the front, McCoy's side work up from the rear. Do not let them get close with those vests. Prepare to assault."

They sat in silence, hearts now pounding, as the eight boats moved along the slow current at perhaps ten knots. When Moose opened up with his SAW, the tracers began lighting up the river like a swarm of bugs.

"Fire! Fire! Fire!" commanded Ripper as Moose began taking apart the lead boat. Up in the tree, Hodges killed the man operating the outboard on boat two, trying to create a traffic jam in the river to slow the other six boats. His .338 Lapua Magnum round hit the man center-mass, blowing his chest open and flipping him off the back of the boat. On the other boats, it took a moment for the ISIS fighters to realize they were under attack. They fumbled and pulled up their AK-47s, firing blindly in the direction of Moose's tracers.

Boat three roared around the first two boats, the lead boat now sinking with its occupants dead or dying in a hail of SAW rounds. The tracer rounds made the boat look like it was inside a fireworks display. Boat two was stopped in the water because no one was at the outboard, and every time one of the men tried to jump back there, he was killed. As the third boat sped past the first two, McCoy and his team on that side of the river opened up with deadly accuracy.

By now, the other five boats realized they were under attack and began taking action. The last boat spun around and took off upstream in retreat while the other boats gunned their engines and roared up out of the water, their bows now high with the fighters trying to return fire and hang on at the same time. Their accuracy was hampered in the erratic movement of the boats that were swerving around each other in a torrent of incoming fire.

Hodges fired a round through the engine of the third boat, which came apart and died. The men on board continued firing at Moose's position, from where they could see tracer rounds, but McCoy's team began taking them out from behind. It seemed as though the ambush might be over quickly until boat five's commander began screaming at his men as he opened the throttle on his outboard, making a beeline for McCoy's side of the river.

The boat commander had seen McCoy and his team take out the boat directly in front of them. As his boat roared toward their position on the bank of the river, Hodges tried his best to take out their engine, but he was in a bad position. McCoy fired his weapon and screamed at his team to take cover, but the men ignored the warning and kept firing at the boat in an attempt to protect each other. When it was almost on top of them, their commander screamed *"Allahu Akbar!"* and he and his men pulled their cords almost simultaneously.

The explosion was deafening and deadly. Hundreds of ball bearings tore through the battle space, cutting down trees and foliage that had provided cover. Ryan O'Connor and Ray Jensen were both blown backwards as the logs and trees they were using for cover disintegrated. McCoy had managed to get behind a large boulder and escaped injury, as did Hodges, high in the tree. Several ball bearings buried themselves deep into the branch's underside where he was lying, but the size of the branch had saved his life. Boat six used the explosion to roar past them down the river at full speed.

McCoy, acting corpsman, leapt out from behind the boulder and grabbed Ryan by his vest. As he began pulling him to safety, he could see Ryan was dead—killed instantly by a ball bearing that had hit him right above his left eye. McCoy screamed out in shock, but he still had a man down in the field and had no time to mourn the loss of his friend. The enemy soldiers in the boats were still laying down heavy fire as they tried to head downstream past the ambush. McCoy stumbled over Ryan and crashed through some downed saplings, ignoring the heavy fusillade of gunfire until he got to Ray Jensen. Ray was on his back, trying to get to the pressure bandage that all of them carried in their front right pant pocket to stop the bleeding in his thigh. His vest had stopped two ball bearings from killing him, but not before they broke two ribs.

McCoy pulled the pressure bandage and tied it off tightly. "Stay down! Stay down!" he screamed as he stopped the bleeding.

"O'Connor's hit!" Ray said through gritted teeth.

"Ryan's gone, man. He's gone. You stay down!" He handed Ray a morphine syringe. "If it hurts too much, pop this." With that, he was gone, stumbling forward toward the river, his M4 popping off well-aimed rounds at the men in the boats.

Ray ignored McCoy and crawled through the incoming fire. He had lost his assault rifle in the explosion, so he pulled his sidearm, determined to stay in the fight. He belly-crawled in agony, and began firing at the boats.

On the other side of the river, Moose reloaded his SAW and took apart another boat as it tried to maneuver around the sinking wrecks in its way. He poured heavy fire into the outboard, even as its occupants concentrated their fire back at him. Ripper and Jon also fired at the boat. Finally, Jon shouted, "*Fuck this, fire in the hole!*" and leapt up and threw a grenade into the boat. One of the men in the boat saw it and tried to dive out, but he was hit by Moose's fire and fell back in just as the grenade exploded. The grenade set off the exploding vests and every boat still floating came apart in the fiery blast.

The team stopped firing as they took cover, and when they peeked back out, it was over. One boat had headed back toward

Aht, on the run south, and one boat had made it past them headed north on its mission. The others were now floating north in pieces or at the bottom of the river. A few bodies and body parts floated away downstream as well.

Moose looked over and saw Ripper and Jon, who both gave him a thumbs-up. He got on his radio. "Sitrep! McCoy!"

McCoy had run back to Ray to check on his bleeding. He spoke into his mic. "Two men down. O'Connor is KIA, Jensen is stable, leg wound. Need evac ASAP. Hodges, you okay?"

"I'm good. Scanning the river. All clear. We lost two boats. Coming down, out."

Moose, Ripper, and Jon ran through the waist-deep water, being careful to check for any enemy survivors who could still pull their detonation cords. They made it across quickly and found Ryan first.

"O'Connor!" screamed Jon when he saw his friend. Ryan was on his back, dark blood pooled under his head. Jon checked his pulse even though he knew his friend was done. He bowed his head and said a quick goodbye, then ran over to McCoy and Ray. McCoy was putting a second pressure bandage on Ray's thigh.

"How ya doing, bro?" asked Jon as he took a knee next to McCoy. Moose and Ripper came up behind them, but stayed on guard looking for movement anywhere around them.

"Hurts like a bitch," said Ray, "But I still got all my junk."

"Yeah, good thing your dick is so small; on most guys it would have gotten blown off."

McCoy tied off the bandage. "You'll be okay, just don't move any more than you have to. Moose?"

"On it," he replied. He pulled the radio off McCoy's backpack. "Rescue One to Eagle One, request immediate medevac at insertion point. One wounded, one KIA. Need immediate dust-off, over."

"Rescue One, this is Eagle One, inbound. On your poz in fifteen. Out."

Moose tried Apo next, but didn't get a reply. He made a sour face. Apo and his team would have another boat heading their way within the hour. He and Ripper knelt beside Ryan. Moose gently closed Ryan's eyelids and picked up one of his dirty, bloody hands, which he kissed before laying it across his dead teammate's chest.

"So sorry, buddy. Rest easy, sailor," whispered Moose.

Ripper quickly wiped away a tear. His string of profanities were inaudible.

CHAPTER 55

Kampong Aht

Mohammed and Hamdi were still inside their hut when the sat phone finally rang. Mohammed answered quickly. "Yes? Tell me what's happening!"

He was assuming it was Hazrol with news on the two New Zealanders, but it was a panicked commander from his martyr brigade. "We were ambushed! There were soldiers waiting for us down river. They attacked us by the hundreds!"

Mohammed was stunned. How was it possible? Had the sultan double-crossed him? "Bruneian army? Police? *Who* attacked you?" he shouted. Hamdi's face fell as he listened in on the call.

"I don't know. It happened so fast. Commandos, not police. They were everywhere!"

"So what happened? Where are you? Did you get to the port? How many casualties?" He was rattling off too many questions for the terrified commander to answer.

"We're returning to camp. I don't know if anyone made it past the ambush. We were the last boat. We saw at least two sink. They ambushed us from everywhere! We turned around and got away!"

Mohammed felt sick in his stomach. "No, you idiot! You can't come back here! You'll lead them right to this camp! Turn around and go back!"

The boat commander was shocked. He couldn't turn around—that was impossible. "But Mohammed! There are hundreds of them! There's no way past them!"

"I don't care! Find a way! If you come back here, I'll kill you myself! Don't be a coward! Attack! Attack!" He hung up and stared at Hamdi. "This is no good. These cowards will lead whoever attacked them straight to us. Assemble the men. We'll need to leave here and find a new camp."

⊕

Bruce "Batman" Wei had floated silently to the bottom of the bamboo ladder and climbed up to the plank walkway that connected the thatched huts. On the other side of the village, Apo and Carl sat waiting for targets of opportunity. They had six enemy soldiers down, and perhaps six or ten left somewhere in the village. As Bruce slowly crawled over the plank, he readied his Uzi and moved forward, trying to see, hear, or even smell his enemy.

It was painstakingly slow to get to the first hut. He peered inside and saw one of the fighters sneaking a nap inside. Bruce pulled his KA-BAR knife and moved to a squatting position, then moved forward in a low crouch. He checked to make sure the man was alone. In two long strides, he crossed the room and slit the man's throat, then plunged it several more times into the man's heart. He wiped the knife and whispered into his mic.

"I'm inside. One down. Out."

Apo tapped his mic twice to let him know they heard him, without speaking.

Bruce peered outside the hut to the one across the plank floor and saw nothing inside. He quickly stepped across and cleared the room, then moved on to the next. It was three more empty huts until he was across from the one with the satellite dish. He heard a loud voice inside.

"We need to know how many boats made it! Even if we can only hit half of our targets in Singapore, it will be enough to be successful. But how many made it?" Mohammed was shouting.

"When they get to the trucks, we'll have a number," said Hamdi. "We just have to be patient. I'm sure some of them made it to the port . . ."

"If we don't capture those two journalists, Minister Ali won't give us the damn trucks *or* the ship!"

Hamdi nodded. He was equally frustrated. He wanted that blonde reporter for his own use, but even more importantly, the mission to Singapore had to be carried out.

Bruce listened from outside. His Arabic language skills were good, and he got almost every word. He was fortunate that the two men inside were screaming. He whispered to Apo. "Target is Singapore. Boat at the port. Out." He quickly and silently moved across the plank walkway to position himself just outside the doorway of the command hut.

"If we tell Abdul Ali that we killed the two reporters, he wouldn't know otherwise until after he supplied the trucks and boat. If any of our men made it, our mission would be complete. We can find those two later."

Mohammed thought about that. It wasn't a terrible idea. "But who attacked our men?"

Hamdi made a face. "The sultan wouldn't do it. Who else could do it without his authority?"

They both knew the answer. Only the Americans would dare launch a counterterrorism operation inside a foreign nation.

Mohammed pulled out his sat phone and called the minister of the interior's private cell phone. Abdul Ali answered immediately.

"The two reporters are dead."

"Excellent, the sultan will be pleased."

"Are the trucks and ship ready?"

"As promised, they're waiting for you."

"Very well. We're moving camp, I'll check back with you later." He hung up before Ali could ask him any more questions. "Assemble the men!" barked Mohammed. He tried calling Hazrol and once again got no answer. He tried several of his commanders and also got nothing. On his fourth call, one of them picked up.

"Mohammed! We were ambushed!"

"Yes, I know. Where are you?"

"Almost at the place where we get off this river and find the trucks. What happened? Who were they? Almost everyone else is dead."

"How many of you made it?" asked Mohammed.

"Only our boat. Eight of us."

Mohammed was so angry he wanted to throw the phone. "Then you must make sure to hit your targets. We're counting on you to complete this mission! Only you can do it, God willing!"

"We won't let you down. As long as the trucks are there to bring us to the ship, we'll make it."

As he finished his call, Hamdi left the hut to gather the troops to break camp. As he walked out of the hut, Bruce stepped behind him and shoved his KA-BAR knife into the man's lower back, then pulled it out to strike again. The large man was much stronger and faster than Bruce expected. Instead of dropping from the knife thrust, he spun around and crashed into Bruce, sending them both into the thatched wall of the hut. The wall collapsed under their weight, pulling part of the thatched roof down as well. Mohammed was knocked down by the roof collapse but managed to grab his AK-47 as he tried to understand what was happening. Bruce used lightning-fast hands to chop and strike at the much larger opponent. He shoved the knife into Hamdi's throat and yanked it sideways as he spun away from the man's crushing bodyweight. The man's throat opened in a gush of gurgling blood, and Hamdi died with eyes wide open and foam coming out of his mouth and nose. As Bruce hopped to his feet, Mohammed fired his AK-47 on full automatic, spraying Bruce with a deadly torrent of bullets, flipping him off the plank walkway where he fell twenty feet to the soft earth below.

Apo and Carl heard the gunfire from the huts and knew it was the sound of an AK-47. They charged out of the tree line, just as three men who'd been gathering food ran up from the other side of camp. They spotted each other simultaneously, but Carl and Apo were faster. They fired their weapons and dropped the three men, never breaking stride as they raced across the open ground to where Batman lay on the ground.

Apo knelt next to Bruce and rolled him over onto his back. He had too many bullet holes to be able to save him. Bruce was bleeding out fast. Apo pulled a pressure bandage from his cargo pant pocket anyway and shoved it against his chest just above the vest and below his throat. Bruce was wheezing and coughing up blood. He knew he was dying.

"Singapore. Boat taking them to Singapore. Minister Abdul Ali is their contact . . ."

"We heard you. Save your breath. We'll get them. You just hang in there."

"Mohammed. Up there."

"Just relax. We'll get you out of here as fast as we can."

"I'm dead, brother." And just like that, Batman closed his eyes.

"*Fuck!*" Apo let go of him and started running after Carl, who had already headed for the bamboo ladder to the raised huts. Three more men came running across open ground from the far side of camp, having heard the gunfire. Apo saw them and dropped to a knee, and then fired accurately. All three men dropped quickly.

Carl reached the top of the ladder and crawled over onto the planks. He saw the command hut partly collapsed, with a big man bleeding all over the planks partially out of the hut. It was

Hamdi. He drew up his M4 and moved closer, but the hut was empty. He scanned around for Mohammed, but didn't see him.

A figure jumping into the water at the other end of the raised hamlet caught Carl's attention. The man splashed into the brown river and swam quickly to a small Penan canoe and climbed in. He grabbed an oar and started paddling as fast as he could, heading downstream. Carl sprinted to the end of the plank catwalk and took a firing position, then opened up on the target in the water below. Mohammed fell back into the canoe as three rounds went through his back and out his chest. He reached clumsily for an oar as it fell out into the water, his hand grabbing empty air in desperation.

Carl leapt into the waist-deep water below the catwalk, remaining on his feet as he splashed and fired after the canoe. Although the canoe drifted with the current, the water was still shallow and slow, and Carl managed to catch up to it. When he was alongside, he fired another two rounds into Mohammed's head. The man was quite dead.

Carl splashed back out of the water at a full run, weapon at the ready as he scanned for more enemy soldiers. There were none. They had killed everyone in the camp. He ran back and found Apo kneeling next to Bruce. When Apo saw him, he shook his head. Bruce was gone.

Carl climbed quickly back up the bamboo ladder to the command hut. He searched around and grabbed a laptop and two satellite phones, then called in on his radio.

"Rescue Two to Eagle Two. Request immediate evac from Aht, over."

"Rescue Two, we are inbound, fifteen minutes. Will advise when to pop smoke. Out."

CHAPTER 56

Langley

CIA Director Wallace Holstrum entered the conference room and was greeted with a standing ovation. He smiled, looking weary. He glanced around at the people in the room and took a deep breath.

"I don't really know where to begin, other than to just say a heartfelt thank-you. To think we live in a time where the politics of this country have sunk to this level is more than alarming. Apparently, there's no limit to any of this. I could have been accused of almost anything else and wouldn't have given a shit—but this? It was beyond upsetting. My wife didn't sleep for a week. Mr. Dennis's arrest only makes me feel slightly better."

Wallace looked at Darren and Dex. "I know a few of you worked very hard to get me cleared, and I appreciate it with all my heart. And now, it's time for me to get back to work. I've had several briefings already, but I want to know what's going on with Brunei. Darren?"

"Yes, sir. First, welcome back. I'm sure as the criminal case on Jeff Dennis unfolds, other parties will be named, which should offer you more satisfaction. Regarding Brunei, the mission is ongoing. Yesterday, one of our teams hit Kampong Aht and eliminated two high-value targets. Mohammed bin Awad and Hamdi Fazil are confirmed dead. The rest of the fighters at the camp were also eliminated. Unfortunately, we lost one of our

217

own, Wang Wei. The elements of the ISIS group that were en route to their target were also almost completely eliminated. We lost one team member, Ryan O'Connor, and have one wounded, on his way home. Ray Jensen. The rest of the team is aboard the *Ronald Reagan*, awaiting intel and orders. We believe two groups of ISIS fighters survived our contact on the river. One is upstream somewhere, maybe headed back to Aht, and one made it north to the port. Bruce was able to gather two important pieces of information before being killed. First, we know the target is Singapore, and second, we know the ISIS contact is the Bruneian interior minister, Abdul Ali."

Wallace listened to every word. He'd been out of the loop for almost a week, and his morning had been insanely busy trying to catch up on fifty different situations around the globe.

"We have Carl and Apo attached to the team?" asked Wallace.

"Yes, sir. Everyone was brought to the *Reagan* together," said Darren.

Wallace drummed his fingers on the table. "Apo met with the Bruneians to set up the oil deal, right?"

"Yes, sir."

"Maybe he can meet with Abdul Ali. Maybe squeeze a little information out of him?"

Darren made a face. "They'd have to do it in Brunei. Getting in wouldn't be hard; getting out might be."

Wallace kept drumming on the table. "I'll call Apo myself and have a chat. If even a few of them made it past our team, they can still hit Singapore."

"Yes, sir. One last thing, some good news for a change— our team rescued two New Zealanders, journalists, from the jungle outside Aht."

Wallace grinned slightly and nodded. Good news never made the paper, but at least it offered them *something* at a time when he had just learned about two of their own not making it home.

They finished their briefing and headed off to their offices. Dex looked at Darren. "He's going to send Apo in to talk to Ali in Ali's office? That's a suicide mission. I don't like it, Darren. How the hell is Apo supposed to get anything out of the minister without getting grabbed?"

Darren shrugged. "It's Apo. He'll come up with something. Besides, Bruce and Ryan deserve some payback."

"Payback, yeah. Another dead agent—no."

Darren patted Dex's shoulder as he walked away to his own office. "Let's just wait and see . . ."

CHAPTER 57

Labi Forest

The eight ISIS fighters that had survived the ambush were almost back to Kampong Aht when Mohammed ordered them to turn around. While they were prepared for martyrdom in a dramatic attack on Singapore, being lost in the jungle was nothing short of terrifying. All eight of the men had grown up in Syria and Iraq—desert locations, not jungle. Their time at Kampong Aht had been physically miserable, with humidity, animal sounds, and mosquitos that were relentless. After Mohammed's threat to kill them if they returned, they were embarrassed and dejected. Their leader was right, of course—they might lead those same commandos to their base camp. They had panicked and fled, and now felt humiliated. They had turned back around after being reprimanded, and headed north again. They'd gotten one kilometer when their outboard motor ran out of gas.

The eight of them managed to pull the boat to the side of the river, into the mud and tall cogon grass which sliced their skin. Once they had gotten out of the boat, they looked at each other, unsure of what to do. Ahmet, their commander, tried to show some leadership.

"We can't return to base, it's too risky. We need to hide this boat and continue back north along the river. If the ship is still there at the port when we get there, we can join the others."

220

"It will take *days* to get there on foot in this jungle!" complained one of the men.

"Perhaps you'd like to ignore Mohammed's orders and return to camp by yourself? Go on! *Go*! We're heading north to complete our mission, God willing." Ahmet began walking without looking back.

Behind him, the men exchanged glances and then quickly fell into single-file line. The man who had complained took the last position in the line of march, sulking. It was already so hot they were drenched, and they had very little water and no food. The weight of their exploding vests added to their hot misery.

Invisible.

It was how the Penan people had trained their young men to be from the time they were old enough to play in the jungle. The group of Penan warriors had seen Kampong Aht and knew the fate of their friend Zyy. They tracked the eight men who marched along so noisily in the forest.

The group of warriors wore only loincloths and carried blowguns, primitive stone knives, and bows and arrows. They watched their enemies walk with heavier clothes and guns that weighed them down, and waited patiently. With each step in the heavy mud, the bearded men grew wearier and complained more. The distance between the men grew longer as they fought to keep up with each other in the sauna that was the thick jungle air.

After three hours of walking, the last man in the column stopped and doubled over, his hands on his knees as he caught his breath. When he stood back up, he thought he was stung by a wasp. The pain in his neck was immediate, followed by two more stings in the back of his legs. He stumbled forward, trying to call out to his comrades, but no sound would come out of his paralyzed vocal chords. After three more steps, his legs stopped working and he just stood in the trail confused and unable to will his legs forward. As he tried to make his lungs breathe, a small man ran up behind him and grabbed him by the hair, yanking his head back. With a quick slice from a stone knife, the man's throat opened and blood poured out down his chest. Four more men appeared for a second and carried him off the trail silently.

It was like he was never there.

By the time they had repeated the process for the fifth time, the remaining three men realized something was wrong. They had become stretched out along the trail because of fatigue, and were simply too tired and thirsty to chat as they walked, but now, as they called out to their friends, they knew something was wrong.

"Maybe they got lost," said one of the men.

"More likely, they're cowards! They returned to Kampong Aht against orders. Hamdi will gut them like sheep," sneered Ahmet.

The other two called out to their friends again. They started to feel panicked.

"Ahmet, it's just us! Only us three! Where did they all go?"

Ahmet hid his fear. "I told you, they're cowards. We continue north!"

Ahmet started walking again. The two men behind him stood an extra second, feeling terror build inside them. They turned to catch up to Ahmet, and felt themselves attacked by a swarm of wasps. As they tried to understand what was happening, arrows buzzed louder through the air than the small darts had, and found their targets with deadly accuracy. The men spent their last moment on earth gurgling and choking to death on their own poisoned blood.

Ahmet heard something strange. He turned around just in time to see his two men flailing on the ground. He squinted in disbelief. Arrows? Were those *arrows* sticking out of his men? His face showed his horror, and he turned around to run north, as far and as fast as his legs would take him. He found himself looking into the faces of five small brown men holding up long bamboo tubes.

Phhhht Phhhht Phhhht Phhhht Phhhht

The tiny darts hit him all over his exposed chest where he had opened his vest, and he dropped to his knees as his chest tightened and breathing became difficult. He pulled the darts off that had hit him between his open vest and watched the strange men draw arrows into short bows. Breathing was difficult, he began praying. He reached for his cord. He would die a martyr and take these men with him—but his arms refused to move. He coughed, white foam coming up out of his poisoned lungs. He barely felt the arrows that killed him.

The Penan tribesmen had never killed humans before. They normally only killed what they would eat. These intruders weren't food for their kampong. No. These would feed the wild pigs.

CHAPTER 58

USS *Ronald Reagan*

The team had arranged for the transport of Ryan O'Connor and Bruce Wang back to the United States through Dover, Delaware, where they would be treated as fallen heroes and returned to their families. Ray Jensen was in the ship's sickbay undergoing surgery, but his injury wasn't career ending.

After seeing off the plane carrying the bodies of Bruce and Ray, the rest of the team left the flight deck and showered and changed into clean clothes. They ate in silence and went to a small ready room provided by the ship's commander, who had treated them like VIPs.

Apo called into Langley and was patched through to Wallace Holstrum, who was fast asleep, twelve hours behind the team. He spoke to the director about Brunei's minister of the interior and guaranteed he would *personally* have a conversation with the man. Apo asked that the director speak to the ship's commander about giving them carte blanche to do whatever needed to be done. It would be Wallace's next conversation.

⊕

The minister of the interior, Abdul Ali, was a very busy man and didn't have time for Interglobe Oil. But after the third call and the mention of billions of dollars' worth of oil, and a request for the minister to come out to the *Sunrise* oil platform immediately for a very special briefing, he finally agreed to it. Perhaps if he could tell the sultan about a new oil field worth billions, it would lessen any fallout from the problems with the arrangement with ISIS.

That was supposed to have been a simple deal. Instead, two reporters from New Zealand had told the entire world they had seen ISIS terrorists and an ISIS flag flying in a camp in Brunei. Their reports had gone viral, and the sultan was getting calls from around the world asking for more information. To make matters worse, only one of the boats had made it to the port for transportation to Singapore. The report Abdul had gotten from his men at the port was that the rest of them had been ambushed, but by whom, it was unclear. All he knew was that he had arranged for enough trucks for sixty men to bring them from the river to the port to board a ship for Singapore, and instead, eight men showed up in one truck.

When he had tried to call Mohammed's sat phone, he got no answer. It was infuriating. Mohammed had told Ali that he was moving camp—okay, fine. But answer the damn phone and explain what the hell was going on! Abdul Ali was pacing around his office, praying the sultan wouldn't call on him before he had a chance to visit the oil platform and get some great news to deliver. The ISIS story would blow over. Having a new oil field worth billions would make him a hero. He just needed to be able to deliver the news personally to the sultan.

Abdul Ali would take two of his men and fly out by royal helicopter to the oil platform *Sunrise*.

The team was supplied with matching orange jumpsuits and hard hats by the *Reagan*. All insignias were sanitized from the uniforms, and they could easily pass as a crew of oilmen on the rig. Most oilmen didn't have their weapons and training, however.

The same Sea Hawk helicopter that had brought them in and out of Brunei would be flying them back to the *Sunrise*. The pilot watched the team cross the flight deck of the *Reagan* and climb into his bird. He was well aware that the size of their team was smaller than the first time he had seen them, and he snapped a sharp salute.

They flew off the flattop and headed northwest back to the oil platform—a place none of them thought they'd ever see again. They touched down on the helipad and hopped out with weapons hot, unsure whether anyone else had boarded their rig. The Sea Hawk lifted back off and roared over the mirrorlike ocean back to the carrier. The team split up and searched the entire ship until they were satisfied they were alone, and then got back down to business.

Apo and Carl would be doing the talking. The rest of the men would be stationed around looking busy. They had no idea how many men the minister would be bringing with him, but they'd be ready for whatever happened.

Hodges had his sniper rifle slung over his shoulder and was ready to start his long climb up into the tower of the rig. He spoke to Moose before heading up into the metal tower.

"Skipper, what about the pilot? Rules of engagement?"

"Pilot's just some poor shmuck taking orders. Probably the same deal with the rest of these guys other than the minister. We'll hold them as long as we need to, but I'd rather not kill them. Don't shoot unless they threaten anyone."

Hodges said "Aye, aye" and headed off to climb the tower. Moose looked out at the beautiful ocean and blue sky and hoped it wouldn't be another firefight. Ripper caught his expression.

"What's the matter, skipper?"

"Nothing. Getting old, I guess. Make sure everyone's good to go. Bird should be here soon enough." Moose pulled the walkie-talkie off of his belt. "Attention on deck. Stay frosty but do not engage unless fired upon. Apo and Carl, you all set?"

"Roger that, skipper," said Apo. "We'll be up here in the conference room acting like hotshots."

"Okay, I'll bring the shitbird up personally. Out."

Now it was time to wait.

⊕

The interior minister had been extremely fortunate. While the broadcasts from the two New Zealanders had hit international airwaves, all of the calls to the sultan had been sitting with secretaries unable to reach their leader. The sultan was too busy.

As was his habit, the sultan had flown in a dozen women from around the world for one of his "parties." While activities such as drinking alcohol, having sex while not married, and listening to nonreligious music were banned in Brunei, that didn't apply to the sultan. He had a lavish apartment set up for himself and a few high-ranking friends and family members for the sole purpose of "entertaining guests." These guests were paid as much as ten thousand dollars each for their "contributions" to the party. Basically, the world's finest call girls spent a weekend at a drunken orgy.

Because the sultan had been drunk for three days straight and was busy trying to have sex with as many strangers as possible, he was completely unaware of what had transpired with his ISIS guests. No one dared interrupt his party with something so trivial as a news story that might not even be true. The story would never appear on Bruneian television, of course, which was run by the state, but it did make it online for the few in the country who would dare to view such a story. Even so, speaking against the sultan was punishable by death, and no citizen would ever risk speaking about the rumors in public.

With the sultan busy, Abdul Ali was free from having to face him with the current catastrophe, and the minister hoped it would sort itself out. In the meantime, he and his two assistants got into their royal helicopter and headed out to sea to the new oil platform.

As they flew out to the *Sunrise*, the minister could see their artificial island under construction in the distance. The island was needed, of course, to counter the aggression of the Chinese, who thought that the entire South China Sea belonged to them. Even the Vietnamese were building islands nearby. Having ISIS attack Singapore was only the beginning. Mainland China would be next.

The pilot came over the radio. "Two Chinese fighter jets just made contact with me. They are on patrol and made me identify myself."

"What did you say?" asked the minister, angrily.

"I . . . I . . . I identified our aircraft, Minister! They can shoot us out of the sky!"

The minister cursed. "This is international air space and international water. Ignore them if they contact you again."

"Yes, sir. The platform is just ahead." The pilot wiped sweat off of his face. He was afraid of the interior minister, but more afraid of two Chinese fighter jets that had him radar locked.

He landed without incident and walked back into the passenger area. "Shall I return to Lapangan Terbang, or wait for you here?"

"Wait here," said the minister, still annoyed at the pilot, like somehow it was his fault the Chinese had bullied them. The two assistants followed him down the steps.

CHAPTER 59

Oil Platform *Sunrise*

"Bird inbound," reported Hodges from up in the tower.

The team moved to their assigned positions and waited. The royal helicopter was beautiful. Unlike their Sky Hawk, which was a beast, the royal helicopter was a sleek, elegant luxury helicopter. It set down on the oil platform gracefully and cut engines, the white rotors eventually coming to a stop. The pilot opened the rear passenger door and lowered the staircase. A tall, slim man in a dark suit walked down the stairs, followed by two other men, also in Western attire.

They stood and waited to be formally greeted, already looking annoyed. Moose walked over and smiled. He extended his giant hand and said, "Welcome to the *Sunrise*, the boss is upstairs."

The minister looked at his beefy paw and didn't extend his own hand. "And where is upstairs?" he asked in English.

Moose faked a smile and said, "Follow me." He walked straight to the elevator and the four of them got in. Moose pressed the button for the top floor and smiled again at the minister, who held his frown.

"Have a nice flight?" asked Moose, maintaining his giant goofy smile, knowing he was annoying the shit out of the man in front of him wearing the three-thousand-dollar suit.

The minister gave him the fakest smile of all time. "Of course."

229

The door opened and the four of them walked down the metal hallway to a conference room, where a table and chairs should have been waiting for them. Instead, there was only one chair in the center of the room. The large conference table had been hastily shoved to the back of the small room. The minister's face showed his disapproval of the surroundings, and he began to voice his objections.

It didn't matter. When Carl stepped out from behind them with a sawed-off shotgun and placed it under the minister's chin, the room became very silent.

Apo gave a chin-chuck to Moose, who took each of the two assistants by the arm, squeezing hard enough to cause them to wince. Ripper appeared from the hallway with Jon right behind him.

"Gentlemen, you'd be smart to follow me and you won't get hurt," said Ripper, turning back around to walk to another room.

"What is the meaning of this?" exclaimed one of the men, in heavily accented English.

"Your boss is a fucking terrorist. He can explain it to you later. For now, he's going to have a chat with our friend. Trust me, you don't want to be part of that. Now move," snarled Moose as he shoved them forward. The group walked down the hall to another room.

Inside the conference room, Carl held the shotgun under the minister's chin and Apo closed the door. He then walked over to the lone chair and pushed it toward Abdul Ali.

"Have a seat," he said coldly.

The minister's eyes were wide with fear. "Do you have any idea what you are doing? I report directly to His Majesty the Sultan!"

"No shit. He's got some explaining to do, too. But we'll start with you. *Sit down, asshole!*" Carl's voice at the end of the shotgun was enough to make the man drop into the chair with a plop.

Apo walked around in front of the minister. "You want to just tell us what the fuck you're doing with ISIS, or would you prefer I beat it out of you?"

"*We*," said Carl.

Apo glanced over at him quizzically.

"*We* will beat the shit out of him, not just you."

Apo smiled. "My friend's correct. *We* will beat the shit out of you."

The minister sneered at Apo. "You aren't a Canadian oil company. Who are you?"

"Your worst fuckin' nightmare. I'm only going to ask you this one time nicely. What's the mission your little group of terrorists are working on?"

"I have no idea what—"

Before he could finish his sentence, Apo punched him square in the face, breaking his nose and sending him to the floor. Carl stepped over and yanked him back into the chair, slapping his face repeatedly on both sides to shake him up.

"That's as nice as he's gonna ask, motherfucker," growled Carl. "And he's the nice one. If you piss me off, you'll wish you hadn't been born."

Abdul Ali was not a warrior. He wasn't a hard man. He began crying and raised his hands. "Please, please . . ."

"Please *what*?" asked Apo.

"I'll tell you, please don't hurt me."

Carl pulled a knife out of his belt and unfolded it. "I can shave with this, it's so damn sharp," he said quietly. "I can also remove your ears and fingers with it. So don't waste any more of our time. When he asks you a question, you answer it right the first time, or I'm going to start with your right hand."

"Why is ISIS in Brunei?" asked Apo.

"They had made an arrangement with the sultan. We would allow them to operate their camp in exchange for a guarantee they wouldn't attack Brunei." The minister spoke softly, his eyes downcast in humiliation.

"Well that's the stupidest thing I ever heard," said Apo. "Like ISIS honors a contract or something? You realize these animals are burning people alive, right? Beheading people. Torture. Slavery. You name it. But you think if they say they won't attack you, then you're all set? You insult my intelligence." He smacked the man open-handed on his ear, almost knocking him off his chair again. Abdul's ear was ringing and he began crying from the pain.

"There's more," he stammered.

"No shit. Get to it," said Apo.

"The Chinese have been extremely aggressive."

"You're wasting my time."

"No, wait. Listen. These ISIS soldiers . . ."

"*Terrorists*!" snapped Carl.

"Yes, yes, the terrorists, they said they would attack China. They'd start organizing China's Muslim population. Internal problems in China might slow their aggression in the South China Sea."

Apo leaned back and folded his arms across his chest. "Now we're getting somewhere. So were they going to attack China?"

Carl played with his knife.

"Singapore. An economic disaster first. China after."

Apo and Carl looked at each other. Bruce had told them Singapore, and now Abdul had confirmed it.

"Okay, Abdul. Tell us about Singapore. Everything. And you better hurry before my friend here gets bored and starts cutting off fingers."

Abdul leaned to the side and spit out a gob of blood. "There's a ship in Kuala Belait. It probably left by now."

"And . . . ?" asked Carl, leaning forward with his knife.

"They are traveling to Singapore by ship to attack the financial markets."

"What's the name of the ship?" asked Apo.

Abdul hesitated. Carl punched him in the face so fast Abdul never saw it coming. He flipped off the chair and landed on the floor, where Apo jumped down and grabbed him by his throat, giving it a quick squeeze. Abdul started coughing and pleading.

"The name!" shouted Apo into the man's bleeding face.

"*Ragam*," whispered the minister, defeated. "It's a small freighter. The *Ragam*, out of Kuala Belait. There, that's everything. Now let me go."

"Not quite. How many men are on the ship?" asked Apo, still straddling the man.

"Only eight of the men made it to the ship. The ship's crew, maybe another five or six. It's a small freighter."

Apo stood up and told Abdul to sit back in the chair. He looked over at Carl, then back at Abdul. "Who was running the camp?"

Abdul was about to say he didn't know, then thought better of it. After a brief pause, he said, "I only spoke with two men. Mohammed and Hamdi. That's all I know."

Apo nodded. "Very good. We met both of them. Good friends of yours?"

"They aren't friends of mine. I did what I was told by His Excellency."

"I think I heard something like this once before. Nineteen forty-five, maybe? *'I was only following orders.'* It was bullshit then, too," said Carl.

"One does not question the sultan," said the minister, his eyes down at the floor. His life was ruined.

Apo picked up a walkie-talkie from the table. "Moose. Small freighter in Kuala Belait called the *Ragam*. Eight tangos plus the crew. May have already left."

Apo walked over to the minister. "Serious question for you, Abdul."

Abdul looked up at him, sniffling at the blood from his nose.

"You want to live or die?"

"I've told you everything I know!"

"And I believe you. Now answer me. You want to live or die?"

"I want to live," he said so quietly they could hardly hear him.

"Okay then. We're going to let you live. You call your pilot with your phone and tell him to leave. Tell him to pick you and your friends up tomorrow at thirteen hundred hours. That gives us a day and a half to finish up and leave, and then you can go home. But here's the thing. And it's important that you understand. If you try and give him a distress code, or attempt to leave early, or fuck with me in any way, whatsoever, we will kill every single one of you. You understand?"

Abdul stared at him. The concept of surviving this encounter had seemed remote indeed. "That's it? I just have the helicopter come back tomorrow?"

"Thirteen hundred hours. That's it."

Abdul nodded. "My phone is in my jacket pocket."

Apo leaned in and reached inside the man's jacket, taking out his phone. "I speak Chinese, Malay, and Arabic. If you fuck with me, you're dead, right here, right now."

"I understand," said Abdul. He dialed the pilot's cell phone and explained they'd be staying over. The pilot was to go back to the airport and return the next afternoon at one. The pilot was surprised, but did as he was instructed.

⊕

Up in the tower, Hodges noticed the helicopter's rotors beginning to turn. He got on the radio. "Moose, it's E! Bird's starting up!"

Moose called over to Apo on the walkie-talkie and Apo told him it was okay. The helicopter banked off for Brunei.

CHAPTER 60

Moose called in to Langley and updated the director. Director Holstrum then coordinated with PACCOM to arrange mission support through the *Reagan* and whatever else was needed, including special instructions for Carl. Pacific Command went to work immediately and within two hours, they formulated a plan and had drones in the air over Kuala Belait looking for a freighter call the *Ragam*.

The team took their three prisoners and made them strip down to their underwear. Moose crushed all of their phones, then brought them to a room that had nothing more than a table and chairs.

"Okay, ladies. Make yourselves at home until tomorrow. If you make me come back up here, for any reason, I will kill you all. Do you understand?"

They nodded.

"No, see, it doesn't work that way. I want to *hear* you. Do you understand?" Moose barked.

They all said yes.

"Do you understand that I will kill you if you attempt to leave this room?"

They all said yes.

"Allowing you to live is very generous of us. Do not make me regret it. Your helicopter will come get you tomorrow, and you can forget this ever happened."

Moose looked at Abdul. "Well, except you. I'm not sure the sultan's gonna let *you* forget this happened. Let me know how that works out for you," he said with a wink.

235

Moose slammed the door behind him and shoved a chair under the doorknob. They could break out of it if they tried hard enough, but it really wouldn't matter. Even if they got out of the room, all communication equipment had been disabled and they were stuck until their helicopter arrived. There was no way off the rig, and swimming ten miles wasn't a good option. Besides, they were terrified and would most likely just sit and wait for help.

The team reassembled on the helipad and waited for their ride. The same Sea Hawk landed with the same pilot. Once they all loaded up and had their headphones on, the pilot came over the intercom.

"Welcome back. We'd like to thank you for flying US Navy. Use your valuable air miles for free travel and rewards . . ."

"Everybody's a comedian," said McCoy.

After a minute passed, Jon spoke into his headset. "You know, when I was laying on the bottom of the ocean at six hundred feet in the dark, wondering if I was going to die, all your bad jokes kept me going. Just wanted to say thanks for that."

His friends smiled. Moose chimed in. "Don't go getting all mushy on us, Jon. If you become a big pussy they'll make you fly helicopters."

"Very nice," said the pilot. "Want to get out here?"

"We only tease the ones we love," replied Moose. "And yeah, thank you to *you*, too. I think this is our third round-trip with you. Might be a new record."

"You're welcome," replied the pilot. "But just so you know, your baggage was three pounds over. There's going to be an extra charge."

McCoy pushed Moose's big arm. "His *baggage*? How about his fat ass? When Moose hauls ass, he's gotta make three trips!"

The men leaned back against the walls of the Sea Hawk and let the vibration lull them into a semi-sleep. They'd had a long week. A blink later, they were landing back on the deck of the USS *Ronald Reagan.*

"Wake up, ladies. Please return your tray tables to their upright and locked positions," said their pilot.

The team hopped down out of the helicopter and were greeted by a commander. The man was speaking loudly over the rotors and aircraft engines on the flight deck. The flight deck of a United States aircraft carrier was a dangerous, loud, and exciting place.

"Welcome back to the *Reagan.* Pat Coburn, commander, special operations. I guess it's about time we met in person. Just off the horn with PACCOM. You've been a busy bunch. Follow me to the briefing room and I'll give you your new orders. This is priority."

The team hustled after Commander Coburn, running up a few flights of metal stairs and down several hallways to a small conference room. The ship was immense. The men placed their weapons and duffle bags on the side of the room and sat down around a large table. A petty officer was at a computer waiting on the commander.

"Gentlemen, this is Petty Officer Christine Hart. She's my S-2. Okay, Christine, hit it," said Commander Coburn.

The intelligence officer started typing and images taken from drones appeared on the white screen at the end of the table. A small freighter with the name *Ragam* painted on the bow and stern was out to sea with several men visible in the rear of the ship. The camera images zoomed in and showed each of the men. All eight standing together in the open area at the stern of the freighter were Middle Eastern, bearded men who looked to be between the ages of twenty and thirty. Every single one of them was smoking. They were also wearing vests with bulky pockets protruding from the fronts. Only two crewmen were visible, who looked to be Asian, most likely local seamen from Brunei.

"Don't they know smoking is bad for them?" asked McCoy.

"So is being to blown to shit," replied Jon.

"Reminds me of those new dolls that came out last Christmas," said McCoy. "Talking dolls from all over the world, each with a saying in their own language. No one knows what the Pakistani dolls say, though everyone's afraid to pull the string."

"This product has zero reviews," said Jon.

"You finished now?" asked Moose, trying not to smile.

Ripper stared at the name and squinted. "For a second, I thought that boat said 'Reagan' on the stern. Is *Ragam* Bruneian for Reagan?" he asked sarcastically.

The commander avoided eye contact, fighting his own smile. "The *Ragam* is registered to Brunei. Her current position is about quarter way to Singapore, just past the Sembuni Reefs. There's a small series of islands further west, and then open ocean between them and Singapore. Any action taken has to happen between Pulau and Singapore in international water. Based on her speed, you have about six hours to decide how you want to take this down, assuming they want to enter the port in Singapore at night. It'll be dark in another hour. PACCOM has also instructed me to give you the option of declining, and simply alerting the Singapore authorities. They have a decent navy and can probably handle this themselves."

"We lost two friends on this mission. Their asses belong to us," said Moose quietly.

Commander Coburn nodded. "I was told that would be your reaction. I was actually the one who asked about just letting Singapore deal with it. We've been busy playing cat-and-mouse with the Chinese, but I understand your personal reasons for wanting to see this through. I've been fully briefed on your mission. Excellent work all around, gentlemen. I should also inform you that the two nuclear warheads have been made safe and disposed of."

"We don't have much time to put together an operation," said Moose.

"Correct. And we can't simply fire upon a civilian vessel. This whole part of the world is a tinderbox waiting for something to happen which could start a major war. American aggression on a civilian vessel will have China making excuses for expanding even further south. And I don't have to remind everyone that your targets are wearing explosive vests."

"One KIA and one wounded because of those things," replied Moose.

"So. Any ideas on how you want to approach this? We can put you in the water or onto the ship. We changed our heading to close some distance. You're less than thirty minutes out by air."

"You drop us into the drink with a high-speed raft. We board the rust bucket, kill the hajis, and let the crew go home."

"We have everything you need. If you hit them in a couple of hours, it'll be dark. You'd have an advantage."

Moose nodded. "On the water, in the dark, against exploding targets. It's sort of perfect."

His men smiled.

A different breed.

"This operation is code named Lionfish," said Commander Coburn.

"Invasive species?" asked Jon, who happened to know a lot about fish.

"Actually, the name 'Singapore' translates as 'Lion City' from Sanskrit. But I like your reasoning just as well. These men are invasive species all over the world, and just like the Lionfish eating the reefs, this ideology has to be exterminated with extreme prejudice."

The men nodded in silent agreement. Joke time was over, for the time being. ISIS and its like-minded organizations were responsible for hundreds of thousands of deaths. The death toll would grow to millions if the threat was not eradicated.

Commander Coburn continued, "Gentlemen, if not for the innocent crew, we'd have the *John Warner* put a fish into this tub, and the whole world could assume they sank. That's not how we operate, however. Instead, you get to risk your asses killing these animals without harming the *maybe* innocent crew."

"It's okay," said Moose. "This is what we train for. Well, most of us. Apo and Carl, you get to sit this one out."

They both began to object immediately. Moose raised a beefy hand.

"I run military ops. We're trained for this exact type of operation. Not that you can't handle it, I know you both can do almost anything—no disrespect, but this is what SEALs train for."

Hodges faked a dramatic cough.

"And one Marine who is brain-damaged enough to almost be considered a water-born amphibian killer. Besides, we'll need his sharpshooting skills. That's it, guys. No discussion, sorry. Five-man team fits in one Zodiac combat craft. Commander, I assume you have them on board?"

"Roger that. F470 ready to go. We'll bring it out by Sea Hawk and drop it in."

Apo and Carl were pissed to miss the operation, but they understood. They were highly trained killers and spies, with many talents the others didn't possess, but dropping out of helicopters in wetsuits, in the dark, into a black ocean to board a rubber raft, climb an enemy vessel in silence, and take out eight hostiles wearing exploding vests wasn't exactly their specialty.

"What can we do to help?" asked Apo quietly.

"*You* can monitor the drones with Petty Officer Hart and talk to us when we're on board that ship. You'll be overwatch. Carl, you fly out supersonic tonight."

Carl made a face. "What are you talking about?"

"Flash message from home. The *big* boss—Holstrum, himself. Wants you there *yesterday*. Commander Coburn offered a ride at Mach 1.8 with midair refueling. F/A-18

Super Hornet—you'll be in DC faster than we'll be at this rust bucket. Holstrum will brief you when you hit the ground at Langley. Whatever it is, it's important enough to get you a ride in a billion-dollar fighter—I'm extremely jealous. You're dismissed to get your ride. I suggest a serious crap before you get in that cockpit."

Moose pointed to a small crane on the rear of the freighter. "Hodges, you think you can get up there?"

"Of course."

"You'll be first man up. You get into position with Christine and Apo supplying extra pairs of eyes to help you start finding targets. When we're all on board we start at the stern and work forward. Silencers or close quarters, no noise. If we do this right, the crew wakes up eight passengers shy and doesn't know we were there. Everyone good?"

The room gave "Aye, aye's" in unison. Carl shook hands with his friends and wished them all luck, then ran off to find his first ride in a Super Hornet.

Game on.

CHAPTER 61

Ragam

The eight foreigners sat together on the deck in an open area amidships. They hated being below decks in an old rusty freighter that rolled heavily in the open ocean. They were simple, ignorant men who hadn't ever traveled before starting their jihad. To be on a ship in the rolling ocean at night was terrifying.

Malik was in charge of the group. It had been his bravery during the ambush that got the men out alive, as he gunned the outboard engine and swerved around the sinking boats in his way. The gunfire had been overwhelming, and it was only his cool-headed steering that saved his boat. They had hoped that some of the other boats might eventually catch up to theirs, but accepted the reality that they were the only ones who made it. It was God's will. They would make the final journey alone, and then bring death to the infidels in Singapore.

Malik read from the paper Mohammed had given him before the mission. "Singapore is the third largest financial market in the world, after London and New York. We have already shown our strength in New York, and London will be soon, but Singapore will change everything in Southeast Asia. They believe they are beyond our reach, but we will shut down their entire city and destroy global markets. Their streets will run red with the blood of the infidels, and the panic will last for months."

242

He looked up and was happy to see his men looked more excited than scared. He continued reading. "You will arrive in a port that places you at Keppel Terminal Road. Do not be confused by these names. It is a very short trip to your targets. A brother will be waiting for you in a yellow van at the dock, and he will take you to the Singapore Exchange, ten minutes away, on Shenton Road. Memorize this name. You will find places to hide until the morning rush has begun and the markets are open. Once the business day has started and the infidels are busy you will strike. Singapore Exchange, Monetary Authority, Conference Hall, Telok Ayer Market. You will be martyrs and greeted in Paradise as heroes for your eternal reward, God willing. Allah be praised."

Malik finished reading the note and folded it back up. He thoughtfully placed it back inside his vest and spoke to his men, making eye contact with each of them. "When we get off this boat, we will all arm the vests." He opened his vest and showed them the arming switch, which they all had been trained to use. "Once it lights red, you are ready for the great jihad." He began pointing to his men and calling off locations from the paper he had just read, assigning them their spots. Four of them would hit the Singapore Exchange together. The first would take out the security. Once the guards were dead, the others could run inside and get to the trading floor where they would wipe out the traders, computers, and business executives who filled the building. Malik would be one of those to get inside the trading floor. It would be a glorious end.

The men concluded their meeting with evening prayer, and decided to eat some dinner before shaving and preparing for martyrdom. Each of them were lost in their own thoughts, ranging from the pride their families would have, to their reward of virgins in Paradise. It was too exciting to contemplate real sleep. They would lay on the open deck and breathe fresh ocean air, and try to ignore the rolling of the deck as they headed west toward their destinies.

CHAPTER 62

Big Bear, California

Stephen Burstein had picked a tiny mountain community in California in which to chill out and hide for a while. Big Bear was less than a hundred miles away from LA, but it was a different world. The mountains were gorgeous, overlooking Big Bear Lake. If there was heaven on earth, Stephen had accidently found it. Well, not "accidently"—he had used Google Earth to find someplace "pretty" and far away.

He rented a condo, which was expensive, but ski season was approaching, and the skiers and snowboarders would descend on the mountains soon enough. Though he didn't need to work, he did want to keep busy. He took a job at a ski resort doing their online marketing. It gave him access to the web and decent computers so he could snoop around and not be on his own personal laptop. He had smashed his old computer with a hammer and literally destroyed every piece of the motherboard before he left Virginia. He purchased a new laptop with cash, upgraded it himself, and then split to California where he felt safer. Who would find him across the country in the mountains? Who would even bother looking for him?

Carl Stone was tired and grumpy. That was a dangerous combination for anyone who might come across him. He'd

244

been awake for way too many hours in a row. After arriving in California, he rented an SUV at the tiny Big Bear airport and drove off to find his subject. Wallace had apologized for making Carl do such a menial task, especially after being pulled from halfway around the world, but there were very few people on the planet he trusted to do this job. Holstrum had wanted to ask Chris Cascaes, but Chris was emphatic that he and Julia were staying retired. They jumped back in to help out their old friend Wallace, but that was *it*. They were just going to enjoy each other's company in the quiet normalcy of civilian life and stay retired.

When Holstrum gave Carl his assignment, Carl didn't complain or ask too many questions. He'd experienced an amazing trip halfway around the world in a fighter jet, flying at speeds most folks would never understand. He'd even slept a few hours in the cramped seat, although it wasn't nearly enough. Holstrum had told him that they'd traced the source of the files placed on his computer. The source was a college kid named Stephen Burstein who had actually submitted a request to intern at the NSA. He might have gotten it, too, if he hadn't taken a job with Jeff Dennis. Of course, the NSA didn't pay interns half a million dollars, either.

The kid had deposited the money into his checking account, which meant he wasn't trying to hide it. Perhaps the kid thought the job was legit. A young college kid—who knows? Carl was to find him and bring him back to Langley for questioning without physically harming him.

It was easy enough to find the kid. For all of his computer smarts, he wasn't exactly a super spy. Although he paid cash for the airline ticket, he still had to use his real name and show ID to get on the plane. The NSA and CIA had already flagged the kid after breaking his code into the director's personal computer. Even though the kid had destroyed his old computer, his old IP address had dozens of purchases made online over the years with his name on it. They traced the kid's movements from Virginia to Big Bear quickly, then used facial recognition software to search for him around the small town. Even a small town like Big Bear has cameras at places like convenience stores, gas stations, and the like. The NSA merely "borrowed" them for a moment.

Stephen sat outside on a huge boulder that provided a stunning view of the lake. He sat with his laptop open, taking pictures from his camera and then editing them on his laptop. It was gorgeous, with the autumn colors painting postcards for him. His iPhone also told Carl exactly where he was.

Carl walked out with his own camera. His camera showed Stephen's location on the satellite map, but the instant he saw the kid, he cleared the screen and acted like he was also taking pictures.

"Oh, hey, sorry. Didn't mean to intrude. I always come up here. First time I've ever seen anyone else up here," said Carl.

Stephen was startled at first, not expecting to see anyone else, but the man's mellow demeanor was enough to help him relax. He brushed his long blond hair out of his face.

"It's cool. You come up here a lot, too, huh? What an amazing spot," said Stephen.

"Yeah, all the time." He walked over and extended his hand. "Carl," he said, using his real name for the first time in months. He was too tired and unintimidated to give a shit.

The kid shook his head and stammered for a second. He fumbled his words.

"Forget your own name? Must be some good pot," said Carl with a knowing wink.

"No, no, I don't smoke," said the kid. "I just, I . . ."

"Forgot your name?"

"No," he said. Then a nervous laugh. "Stephen. But I gotta get going anyway. Enjoy the view." He closed his laptop quickly and started getting up. When Carl grabbed him by his triceps and squeezed, the kid let out a howl and almost dropped his laptop.

"Stephen Burstein, the United States of America would very much like to talk to you. If you behave well, you get to keep your half-mil and have a nice life. If you act like an asshole, I will personally skin you alive and hang you from a tree as grizzly bait." He twisted and squeezed harder, forcing the kid's knees to buckle. "I make hurting people an exact science, kid. Are you gonna fuck with me or do we understand each other?"

"I'll tell you everything!" he blurted. "It wasn't my fault! I thought I was helping!"

"I believe you, kid. That's the only reason you're still alive. Now we're going to take a walk to my truck and then a quick flight to Virginia. There are some folks who want to talk to you there. Once you get this all off your chest, you'll feel better. Then you can forget anything happened, and keep your cash."

Stephen was shaken and scared, and this stranger seemed to know everything already. All he could manage was a "Yes, sir."

CHAPTER 63

The team had been provided with combat scuba gear, night vision, and silenced, customized automatic weapons. Their faces were painted black, and with their black wetsuits on, they simply disappeared in the darkness. Commander Coburn walked them to a UH-60 Ghost Hawk, a stealth helicopter that was used to avoid enemy radar as well as keep noise down. The stealth helicopter was a thing of futuristic beauty.

The doors slid open and Commander Coburn snapped a salute at the team. "Good luck, gentlemen. We're closing distance behind you and we'll have you out of the water three minutes after you make the call."

Moose returned a quick salute and piled in with his gear. A Zodiac combat raiding raft was inside, taking up most of the space. The men sat on the inflated gunwales of the raft with masks and snorkels around their necks and silenced weapons in their laps, complete with condoms over the muzzles to keep some water out.

It was a quarter moon, and the sky was black except for a few stars peeking out from the high ceiling of clouds. Fairly gentle seas and a warm breeze made for a lovely tropical night.

Ripper leaned toward Moose in the hum of the stealth helicopter. "We got lucky with the weather. Perfect night."

"Yeah. Nice night to be a meat-eater. You fuckers stay frosty! We ain't here to hold hands on the beach. The hajis on that boat are wearing fucking claymores! We hit them so hard and fast, they never know we were there, and everyone goes home at the end of the night! You tracking me?"

All of the men on the team returned an "Aye, aye, skipper!" except Hodges, who couldn't help growling a Marine Corps *"Oohh rahhh!"*

High overhead, a US Navy radar jammer was working with two fighter escorts, lest the Chinese start meddling with their mission. The USS *John Warner* lurked below the surface at mast depth less than five hundred yards from the *Ragam*, watching in silence and ready if needed.

The helicopter raced over the black ocean at 150 knots, making very little noise. The typical *whump* of rotor blades had been silenced through American ingenuity, a trick the rest of the world was trying to steal via hacking into American defense networks. When the helicopter was two miles from the stern of the *Ragam*, the pilot dropped lower and hovered. The team stood up, got out of the Zodiac, and muscled it to the door where it was shoved overboard. As soon as the boat was deployed, it was masks up, and the team took giant-stride entries, splashing into the black ocean. Within two minutes, all of them were up in the boat and their helicopter was gone like it had never been there.

Ripper turned on the silent electric motor and manned the tiller as the men got into position in the raft, losing their masks and replacing them with night vision. They quickly checked their throat mics and earbuds, and satisfied that everything was working, Ripper opened the throttle. The engine was silent, but not as powerful as a gasoline engine. They caught up to the boat after a ten-minute ride, which put them right at the stern.

Apo was sitting next to Christine, watching the men from cameras on a silent drone, high overhead. The night-vision cameras made their mission as easy to follow as if it had been daylight. He spoke into his mic as they watched the monitor and Christine operated the cameras on the drone, which was being flown from another part of the ship.

"Nest to Fisher One, we have you five by five. No movement on the deck, but it looks like six of the tangos are sleeping topside. One light on inside the bridge. All quiet. Over."

Moose whispered, "Roger Nest. Boarding. Out."

They attached a large suction cup to the steel hull of the freighter and secured a line from the ship to their raft, then tied it off. They were officially "attached" to their target. McCoy gently tossed a line with a rubber-coated grappling hook up to the rear rail. The rubber coating kept it silent as it caught the rail. He gave a good tug, then began a quick climb up the outside of the hull until he was aboard and had his weapon out in front of him, scanning in every direction.

"Clear," McCoy whispered. He removed the heavy ropes he carried over his shoulder and attached the two lines to the rail, then dropped them down to the raft. Hearing it was secure, Hodges followed, carrying his heavy sniper rifle across his back. It was fitted with a silencer, but on such a quiet night, it wouldn't be fooling anyone. It was a cannon, and sounded like one, even silenced. Within a few minutes, the entire team was aboard the ship, moving out to secure the stern.

Hodges began his climb up the crane, something he'd done several times on the oil platform. This was a much easier climb, being only a fraction of the height. Once he found his perch, he took the covers off his sniper scope and began scanning the ship as the team moved slowly forward.

"Overwatch in position," Hodges whispered. "Six tangoes amidships. Probably sleeping, but they have their vests on. Searching for the other two. Over." Hodges shook his head. *"Who the fuck sleeps in a claymore?"*

Moose waited a moment and radioed Hodges again. "Any sign of the other two?"

Hodges had scanned all over the ship, but could only see the six men who looked to be sleeping in the open part of the ship behind the bridge.

"Negative, skipper. Only six."

Moose nodded to himself. The only easy day was yesterday. Oh well. He looked at Jon and McCoy and pointed to a door, then pointed to himself and Ripper and pointed to the position of the sleeping men, drawing a finger across his throat. Jon and Pete moved silently to the door and disappeared into the ship to hunt for the other two terrorists while Moose and Ripper moved forward. There were only two possibilities—they would murder six men in their sleep with total silence, speed, and overkill, or one of the targets would detonate his vest and kill all of them.

Moose and Ripper rechecked their weapons—fully automatic MP5s with laser sights, silencers, and extended thirty-round magazines. It was critical that all six men were killed as close to instantly as possible. Even a wounded man could pull a detonation cord. They moved up in silence, Hodges whispering in their ears.

"I still got nothing. Just those six in front of you. Over."

Apo's voiced joined in. "Nest confirms six amidships. No sign of the other two. Over."

Moose and Ripper could see the men in front of them now, sleeping as best they could on the uncomfortable metal deck. They had thrown a few old blankets on the steel deck, but it still wasn't exactly the Hilton. Moose and Ripper moved closer still. They didn't want to just open fire and have bullet ricochets waking up the entire ship. Silence was damn crucial.

When they were close enough to almost touch the six men, Moose aimed his weapon, as did Ripper. Red dots danced on the foreheads of two of the men. They had trained together long enough not to have to tell each other who was responsible for whom. They would each take out the three closest to themselves. Head shots, fast and accurate.

One of the men moved in his sleep.

It didn't matter. Twelve quiet pops with a couple of dull thuds for the few rounds that went through the smashed skulls and hit the steel deck, but there were zero ricochets. They nodded to each other and double-checked the bodies.

"Six down. Overwatch, how do we look?" asked Moose.

"Totally clear. Zero movement. Over."

"Nothing yet, Fisher Two, out," reported Pete from below deck.

Moose and Ripper quickly picked up the six bodies and dropped them overboard. The splashes were lost to the sound of the waves against the bow and the dull background noise of the diesel engines. They ran back, picked up their shell casings, and used the blankets to quickly wipe up the deck, and then threw them overboard as well. Once all trace of having been there was gone, they moved forward, two large black shadows, silent as the moon.

CHAPTER 64

Pete McCoy and Jon Cohen walked slowly, making sure their black rubber booties wouldn't squeak. They had raised their night-vision goggles to the top of their heads, the ship's ancient fixtures providing ambient light. They had started at the stern and moved forward. Their goal was to avoid killing any of the sailors who worked on the ship, but those same men were "aiding and abetting" terrorists, and if it came down to it, they'd kill anyone they felt was a threat.

The small cargo ship followed the basic design of the ships they had trained on too many times to count. Starting at the ship's stern, they first came to the large freezer below deck, then the engine room, and finally, the crew quarters below the pilothouse. A ship the size of the *Ragam* typically would have eight crewmen: the captain and his assistant pilot for when he slept, two or three men for the engine room, and three or so deckhands to operate the crane and handle the freight.

McCoy and Cohen had passed the freezer room and were now up to the engine room. Two men were speaking Malay inside, casually chatting about who knows what—neither Jon nor Pete spoke any Malay. They moved on quickly. The next steel hallway was cramped and empty. They stood outside the crew quarters door and looked at each other as they prepared to enter the room.

"We have movement in the pilothouse," said Apo into everyone's ear.

Hodges looked through his scope. "Roger that. Looks like the captain is talking to someone. Wait one." It was fairly dark

253

in the pilothouse, and the two men were almost shadows. One of them leaned against the rear window as he looked forward. He was wearing an exploding vest.

"Tango in the pilothouse is wearing a vest. I have a clear shot," said Hodges.

"Hold. Anything below deck?" asked Moose.

"Outside crew quarters. About to enter," whispered Jon.

"Go," said Moose.

Jon and Pete opened the door slowly, in total silence. Pete crouched and entered with Jon behind him, weapons out. There was light snoring from the bunks. Three men were inside. The men were Asian, and wore only boxers. They backed out and closed the door.

"Three crew. Negative contact. Moving up," said Jon.

With six men dead and one in the pilothouse, one was still unaccounted for. It was nerve wracking. That is, until Apo's voice came back over their earpieces.

"I wish you guys could see this. You sailors would really appreciate it. Your missing haji is in front of the wheelhouse, still in his vest, puking his guts up. Seasick little fucker went forward for fresh air I guess. He's one sick puppy. Out."

Moose and Ripper smiled. Landlubbers.

Pete spoke into his mic. "We're below the forward hatch. I can get to him, but what about the wheelhouse?"

"Hodges, sit tight. Let Pete take the one up front. If the guy in the wheelhouse makes a move, he's yours. Otherwise we wait and try and take him silently. Pete, when your target is down, he goes overboard. Out."

Pete and Jon moved up to the bow quickly. There was a steel ladder that led to a hatch that would put them very close to their target, assuming he was still at the rail heaving his guts out. "Apo, you got eyes?" asked Jon.

"Affirmative. Target is facing the rail. Hatch is clear. Go."

Pete climbed the ladder quickly while Jon watched his six down the hallway for any sailors. At the top of the ladder,

Pete opened the hatch very slowly. He lifted it with his left hand, raising it just a few inches. He could see the man's back, rounded over as the man dry-heaved.

"Your last moments on earth were not all that great," thought Pete. He aimed the red dot on his spine, just at the base of his head, which he couldn't see because the man was busy puking, and fired a five-round burst. Pete didn't have to push the man overboard; he was polite enough to simply fall overboard.

"Target down." McCoy found his five spent shell casings and shoved them into his pocket.

Moose and Ripper moved closer to the pilothouse. Although Hodges could easily kill the man from the crane, Moose preferred to be gone without a trace. They sat outside and waited.

"Pete and Jon, back to the Zodiac. Hodges, watch our six."

CHAPTER 65

Langley

The jet landed at the private airstrip near a CIA training facility in Virginia. Carl escorted Stephen down the stairs of the jet, where Wallace Holstrum and Darren Davis stood waiting for him, along with two men in black BDUs carrying automatic weapons. They were mostly just there for show, as if Stephen wasn't terrified enough already. Two black SUVs with tinted windows sat next to the tarmac.

"Mr. Burstein, do you know who I am?" asked Director Holstrum.

Stephen tried very hard not to pee where he stood. "Sir, I am *so* sorry! I had no idea. I thought this was just a test of your security. I thought I was helping the CIA, not attacking you personally . . ."

"Mr. Burstein, you're coming with us. You're going to make a recorded video statement explaining how Mr. Dennis described the mission to you, and what, exactly, you did. Then you're going to spend some time with our techs showing *them* what you did. You're obviously very good at what you do. You might even get a job out of this, if that's what you want."

"That's what I thought I was doing *last* time," said Stephen, still looking terrified.

"When you finish making the recording, you're going to make a phone call for us, as well."

"To who?" asked Stephen. "Oh," he said quietly. Holstrum smiled.

⊕

Four hours later, a very tired Stephen Burstein called the number he was given by Director Holstrum. The phone call was being recorded, and was being listened to by FBI director Bill Gallo across town in his own office, but this was simply for Wallace's personal satisfaction. There were five people in the room around the phone, which was on speakerphone. Wallace, Darren, Dex, Cookie, and Stephen.

"Hello, Mr. Dennis?" asked Stephen.

Jeff thought he recognized the voice, but the number was private. "Who is this?" he asked, cautiously.

"Mr. Dennis, it's Steve. Stephen Burstein. I'm the one who did the computer hack for you—"

"Jesus Christ! Not on the phone. What the hell's wrong with you? You were paid. I specifically told you *not* to contact me again. How did you even *get* this number?"

"You told me I was helping the NSA and CIA. You told me I was being a *patriot* . . ."

"And you were! Now be smart and disappear. Don't ever call this number again."

Wallace put his hand on the kid's arm and spoke. "Mr. Dennis. This is Wallace Holstrum, director of the Central Intelligence Agency. Recognize the name?"

There was silence on the other end of the phone. Holstrum continued. "I'm looking forward to your interview with the FBI. When you hang up the phone, you can just open your front door. They should be there by now."

The line went dead.

CHAPTER 66

Ragam

Moose and Ripper remained crouched in the shadows behind the pilothouse. Pete McCoy and Jon Cohen were back at the stern, maintaining security. The Zodiac bounced around behind the freighter in the white foam.

"Looks like he's on the move, head's up," said Hodges from the crane.

Malik hadn't been able to sleep. While his men slumbered, he remained awake, smoking and pacing around the ship, feeling responsible for the success of the mission. God had chosen him to lead the glorious attack. Only *him*. He felt proud, but also nervous. He had killed time with the ship's captain, who was extremely distressed about having eight men wearing suicide vests on board his ship, but his instructions had come from men that you didn't question—ever. The captain did as he was told and took some extra money for his trouble. All he knew was that there would be men in Singapore who would take care of getting the strangers off to wherever it was they were headed. He would simply unload, reload, and return to port in Brunei.

Malik had smoked a pack of cigarettes, and needed some fresh air. He looked out the rear window of the pilothouse,

258

down to where his men had been sleeping. He was surprised that none of them were down there. Where had they all gone? Malik stepped out of the wheelhouse and hustled down the steps toward the open area amidships. He never saw Moose until the muzzle flashed, but by then, two bullets were exiting the back of his skull. He dropped lifelessly to the metal deck without ever having had the chance to pull the detonation cord on his vest. Ripper was on him in a second, picking the man up and heaving him over the side in an instant.

"Clear! Everyone to the Zodiac, now!" barked Moose.

Moose and Ripper sprinted to the rear of the ship while Hodges climbed down. It was the first time he ever went on a mission without firing a shot, and it felt strange. The five of them met at the stern rail and dropped over using the ropes, except Jon. Once everyone else was in the raft, he untied the ropes, looked around to double-check there was no sign of their ever having been there, and then he jumped off the rear of the boat into the water near the Zodiac. Moose and Ripper pulled him in, and off they went toward the *Reagan*.

"Fisher One to Nest, we are returning to base. Request immediate evac, over."

"Fisher One, this is Nest. Continue your heading. You'll be met on the water, out."

Ten minutes later, a small launch from the *Reagan* roared toward them and came to a stop as it slid next to them. They jumped off the Zodiac, which was then pulled inside the launch, and the larger boat with twin high-powered engines roared off back toward the carrier.

CHAPTER 67

Ragam

Pink and orange streaks of light reached out over the blue ocean from the horizon, stunning and majestic in their grand scale. Sea birds squawked from high atop the crane. The captain had been awake all night, and it was time for his break. His assistant would steer for a few hours, and then he'd return once they got closer to Singapore, where tugs would help them enter the port. He called down to the crew cabin and told his assistant to come take the wheel. The man jumped right to it.

The captain walked out of the pilothouse and scanned the ship. His assistant emerged from a side door, looking only half awake. They exchanged good mornings and went about their business. The younger pilot took his place behind the wheel and double-checked his instruments and heading. The captain walked the center of the ship.

There was no one around. No one. Anywhere. He walked to the open area amidships where the strangers had been sleeping, but it was empty. They must have gone below, he thought.

The captain walked down to the crew quarters but saw only his few crewmen. He walked back upstairs to the deck and walked all the way to the stern. No one. By now, he was feeling uneasy. He ran forward, still finding no sign of anyone. When he stuck his head inside the engine room, he yelled to his two men working. "Have you seen the passengers?" They both said no, but then again, they'd been inside all night working on a boiler that was acting up.

The captain ran back to the crew quarters and woke everyone up. No one had seen or heard anything. Five minute later, the captain was in the wheelhouse blasting the ship's horn, and within a moment, all hands were searching every inch of the ship.

Damnedest thing he'd ever seen.

Not too far away in the same ocean, the *Sunrise* oil platform stood like a quiet sentinel. The royal helicopter landed, but the pilot couldn't reach his minister by phone. He and his copilot cut the engine and walked the platform, but no one was to be found. It was so strange—an oil platform was usually a busy place.

He tried the phone several more times without any luck, and the two of them finally started searching room to room. When they saw the door wedged with a chair and heard the screaming and banging from inside, they sprinted down the hallway and kicked the chair away. The door flew open, and three men wearing only boxer shorts stood in an empty room. The interior minister's face was swollen and bruised, evidence of a good beating.

"Don't just stand there! Find our clothes!" screamed the minister.

EPILOGUE

The team stood on the flight deck of the *USS Ronald Reagan* next to Commander Coburn. A Grumman C-2 Greyhound would be flying the team to Bangkok, where a Learjet would be waiting for them. The Learjet would take them back to Guam, where they'd be catching a larger plane for the long trip back to Virginia.

"Well, you prevented a terrorist attack and salvaged two nukes. What do you do for an encore?" asked the commander.

"Whatever the boss tells us to do," said Moose with a smile.

An hour later, Moose, Ripper, Jon, Pete, Eric, and Apo were snoring in the back of the plane, heading for Thailand.

Deep in the Labi Forest, the animals and plants began to overtake what had once been a Penan village. A plank dropped into the brown water, once a walkway for the families that lived there. It floated downstream, bouncing off some skeletal remains, spinning as it headed north.

⊕

Jeff Dennis stood with his arms handcuffed behind him, wife number three looking out from the front door, horrified and humiliated. FBI agents were scattered across the lawn, their blue windbreakers with large yellow letters across the back telling all the neighbors that they were federal agents.

262

"I know my rights. I want my attorney," was all Jeff would say.

"Please watch your head," replied the agent as he pushed him into the backseat of a government SUV.

Stephen Burstein stood with his left hand on a Bible and his right hand raised in the air as he swore to preserve, protect, and defend the United States of America. The CIA had just hired another very good computer technician. The man didn't really need the money at the moment, but he felt that a few years of giving back might just clear his conscious, and get rid of that looking over his shoulder feeling.

Most political analysts were shocked when the secretary of state downplayed rumors that she was dropping out of the primary race the following year. She insisted that she had never officially stated her intent to run anyway. While she appreciated everyone's support, she was happy to remain as secretary of state. A month later, when she resigned from that position, speculation was that the president had asked her to step down amid rumors of her connection to Jeff Dennis, who was facing twenty years in federal prison on multiple charges.

The Smithsonian opened a new exhibit called "History Saved," which featured art from war-torn areas of the Middle East—priceless artifacts rescued from Syria and Iraq, including sculptures, pottery, and jewelry dating back to the ancient Roman and Greek empires. The entire collection had been an anonymous gift.

ABOUT THE AUTHOR

David M. Salkin is the author of thirteen thrillers in various genres, including military espionage, crime, horror, science-fiction, action-adventure and mystery. With a writing style reminiscent of the late, great Michael Crichton, Salkin's work keeps his readers turning pages into the late hours. His books have received Gold and Bronze medals in the Stars & Flags book awards, and David has appeared as a guest speaker all over the country.

David is an elected official in Freehold Township, NJ where he has served for twenty years in various roles including Mayor, Deputy Mayor, Township Committeeman and Police Commissioner.

When not working or writing, David prefers to be Scuba diving with his family. He is a Master Diver and "fish geek," as well as a pretty good chef and wine aficionado. Some of his famous recipes were perfected in the parking lot of Giants Stadium.

Visit DavidMSalkin.com for all the latest news on book releases and appearances.